Stone and Spark

by Sibella Giorello

Published by Running Girl Productions
Contact the author at sibella@sibellagiorello.com

ISBN-13: 978-0692568941
ISBN-10: 0692568948

Cover and Title Page design by Okay Creations
Edited by Lora Doncea, editsbylora.com

This book is dedicated to T'liia "T-Bird" Franklin.
Thank you for the lessons. Thank you for the laughter.

Don't turn away. Keep your gaze on the bandaged place. That's where the light enters you.

—Rumi

CHAPTER ONE

I'M AVOIDING EVERY floorboard that creaks, tiptoeing across my bedroom, standing at the armoire, counting to fifteen. Because ten is never long enough.

At sixteen, I pull out the antique drawer beneath the wardrobe's double doors and listen again.

The seconds tick like they're attached to time bombs. But when nothing detonates, I slip the hammer into my open backpack, then my notebook. Two pens, some Ziploc bags.

I do another count to fifteen, listening. Then I grab my flashlight, camera—

"Are you in there?"

I freeze. Her voice shrills like a fire alarm, piercing the thick wood of my bedroom door.

"I know you're in there."

Crap.

"Yes, ma'am," I answer. My heart feels like a clenched fist pounding on my ribcage. "I'm in here."

"What are you doing?"

I glance down. My backpack, which contains my rock kit, is covered with dirt. So are my jeans and my blue Converse All Stars.

"It's Friday. I'm getting ready for dinner" I say to the closed door, telling myself, *This is not a lie.*

"Three-oh-three!" Her voice pitches with suspicion, so sharp and pointed it pierces my room. "The clock in the kitchen says three-oh-three and I believe it, I believe it. Why are you going to dinner at three-oh-three?"

I glance at my watch. It's three ten. But splitting hairs with my mom is pure suicide. I take a deep breath. The air tastes of dust and antiques, the dirt on my clothes.

"Drew wanted help with her homework," I say, hoping she will go away.

Nope.

"Drew?" Her voice rings with disbelief. "Drew Levinson," she adds, as if clarifying, even though we both know there's only one Drew. "She wants help with her homework?"

"For English." I shove the backpack inside the drawer. I raise my voice so she won't hear me closing it. "We're memorizing a poem. By Christina Rossetti."

I wait, hands on the drawer, eyes closed. I'm hoping the Rossetti reference will send my mom down a rabbit trail. She likes Rossetti. The kinship of tortured souls.

When there's no response, my mind starts ransacking through possible responses, scrambling for those just-right words that never seem to arrive in time.

She says, "I saw Brevaire Teager today."

Oh, crap.

"Good," I say.

"So you know Brevaire?"

I close my eyes. "Tinsley, her daughter. She's in my class. Remember?"

"Of course I remember." She pauses, making sure I understand what she's saying. "Brevaire also said there's a dance tonight. At school. Tinsley's going with that Fielding boy. They're an item."

Waiting . . .

Waiting, waiting, waiting.

I can sense the next thing rolling toward me like a rumble of thunder right before lightning strikes. Carefully, I open the armoire doors. My school uniform lays on the floor, bunched into a ball, like some polyester meteorite hurled to earth.

"You didn't tell me there's a dance," she says. "Did you."

I scoop up the white blouse, plaid skirt, sliding off my shoes, shimmying out of my jeans and T-shirt.

"Raleigh always liked going to dances. She was always happy. The sweetest girl in the whole world."

My fingers shake as I button the white blouse. My mouth twists. If I could, I would shout at the door—Yes, I liked going to dances because it got me out of this house!

The door knob rattles.

"You locked the door?! Raleigh never locked her door!"

I lunge for the knob and whip open the door to see my mother. She is beautiful. But today the color in her hazel eyes is cloudy and she's holding a pen and notepad.

My eyes start to burn.

"Let me see your foot," she says. "Socks off."

She drops the notepad. It slaps the old wooden floor. I obediently yank my socks off and step on it.

"Not that foot." She narrows her eyes as though she's caught me. "The other foot."

I switch feet and she kneels down. With the pen, she traces around my heel, my instep, brushing over every toe. I hold my breath until she stands up.

"Raleigh would be going to the dance," she says.

"I'm busy."

She flips through the pages, studying each. "What fifteen-year-old is so busy she can't go to a school dance?"

Do not cry. I tell the burn in my eyes to leave. Do. Not. Cry.

"What have you done with her?" she demands.

My hands go numb.

"Look at your shirt!"

I glance down.

"It wasn't wrinkled when you came home—what have you done with Raleigh?"

"It's Friday." My voice sounds dead. "I'm meeting Drew. For dinner. Like always."

"You're not fooling us." She turns the notebook, holding up the page so I can see it, showing me my own foot which is somehow evidence that I'm not me. "We know you're not Raleigh."

We. Not the royal We.

The crazy We.

In my eyes, the burn is too hot, ready to break through. I force myself to stare at her tracing of my foot until it's only a blurry blue line on yellow paper, until I see nothing more than a sketch, nothing that matters, nothing that can hurt me.

"Mom, I—"

"How dare you call me that!" She backs away from me, eyes wild. "We're watching you. Whoever you are."

CHAPTER TWO

RUN.

Down the back stairs, through the kitchen door, across the slate patio. I fly for freedom. But just before the gate, I glance back. Once. Is she watching? I've changed back into jeans and a T-shirt, my socks and Converses. My backpack slung over my shoulder. Does this "prove" I'm not her real daughter?

But the curtains are drawn over every window.

Throwing open the gate, I haul down the alley. It runs behind our house, the old cobblestones bisecting mansions from carriage houses. Its far end spits me out on Monument Avenue where Friday afternoon traffic circles the statue of JEB Stuart. When I race past the Confederacy's calvary hero, his bronze face glares at me. Sword drawn, he urges me onward—onward!

I cover the mile to downtown in just under seven minutes. But my pace drops as I hit the city. At 3:32 p.m. on a Friday in October when the sun glows like an advertisement for the last good day of autumn, everyone wants out. Dodging the suits and skirts that swell the sidewalk, I scurry to the other side of the city.

At Williamsburg Road, I take an immediate left. Suddenly the sun disappears, sinking behind a thick stand of gum trees.

Slowing to a walk, panting, I feel my lungs burn. The pain feels good.

About a block down, I see a spot where the long grass has been trampled flat, fading to beige. I kneel down, unzipping my backpack. My hands are shaking. Some of it from dealing with my mom. Some from the hard run. But now the shaking will get worse.

I hold my rock hammer in my right hand and follow the trampled grass down into a ravine. Rising from the ground like green hands, kudzu vines climb the gum trees and grip abandoned buckets next to warped wooden pallets. I even see a brick chimney, laying on its side on the ground. No house in sight. The stench of urine bites at my nose.

But when I look up, I see it.

The curved gray stone is high enough to catch the last rays of sunshine. Below the arch, the signs warn:

DO NOT ENTER.

DANGER. NO TRESPASSING.

Long flat boards seal the entrance, the kudzu nibbling at the edge. I kick my way to it, wiping my sweating, shaking hands on my jeans. When I wedge the hammer's claw between the boards, one of them swings open like a teeter-totter.

I peer inside. The dark is so enormous, I actually feel my eyes dilating. I shrug my backpack forward and find my flashlight. When I flick it on, the beam flickers into the tunnel's black mouth.

I want to quit. Right here.

Just pat myself on the back, turn around, and run for the sun.

But the bitter taste of defeat is fresh in my mouth. I've already lost my mother. And I don't want to see the disappointment on Drew's face when I tell her that I chickened out.

Again.

I step into the tunnel. The board slams shut behind me. I jump.

The flashlight cuts the dark like a saber but there's not enough of it. And the shaking light is giving me vertigo. When I shine it up, toward the curved wall, I see water weeping from the ceiling, sliding down the quarried stones, sobbing on the ground.

I count my steps. By thirteen, I'm forced into a crouch because the dirt floor is climbing toward the ceiling. At twenty-two, I'm duck-walking. The soil smells dank, mildewed. At thirty-four, gasping for air, I crawl forward on my stomach, feeling my heart pound the sand beneath my chest.

And then I'm stuck.

The ceiling, only about six inches from my head, has grabbed my backpack. I rake the flashlight but find only darkness. When I reach up, touching the curved ceiling, the stone feels slimy, cold. I use the hammer to scratch up soil from the ground. But when I toss the dirt forward, it doesn't land.

So I start counting.

One -one-thousand. Two one-thousand. Three one-thousand. . . .

Still nothing. Down and down and down, the soil continues to fall, until finally I hear the faintest little plunk.

Six one-thousand.

I swallow, feeling nauseated. Not just from the dark, the sudden drop. I feel sick for the four men buried down there, locked inside a steam train for almost one hundred years. When the tunnel collapsed, the city sealed it. Nobody wanted to revive this route to the rest of the world, even though it was supposed to revive a city limping along after the Civil War. Nobody wanted to think about what happened.

And nobody bothered to check the geology either.

I reach back, manage to tug open my backpack, and rummage until I feel that thin slithery plastic of Ziploc bags. I yank them out. Then freeze.

The bags.

Did she count the bags—find some missing? Is that what triggered her paranoia? Or was it the gossips at the grocery store?

Or both.

That's the problem with my mom. She goes crazy over nothing. And everything.

Setting the flashlight on the gritty floor, I lift the hammer with both hands. In the glow, I can see the stones' quarry marks. They look like deep cat scratches. I wedge the hammer's claw into the cracks and rock the tool back and forth. I can hear the water dripping, a relentless *plop-plop-plop*. It sounds like footsteps. Suddenly dust rains from the ceiling, falling through the light. I squint to protect my eyes but keep rocking the hammer.

Then a snap.

A solid object drops through the light. It lands with a thud.

Reaching out, I pat the ground. The soil feels cold, dead. My fingers tingle. Rats. I imagine rats, darting from the dark to bite. Bats. Rabid, stirred awake by the sound of cracking rock. Something sharp pricks my palm. My hand flies back. I hold it to my chest, heart pounding, breath chugging off the stone right above me.

When I reach out again, tentatively, my fingers tap what feels like stone. I grab it, throw it into the baggie and take off.

Snatching the flashlight, wiggling backwards, I get free enough to spin around. Using my elbows for leverage, I combat-crawl as fast as possible, a soldier under enemy fire. When the soil suddenly drops, I'm up, duck-walking behind the light, praying this is the same way I came. But everything looks different. The ground, the weeping walls. I worry there's a turn I missed. Suddenly the ground drops again and I fall forward, dropping the flashlight. The beam rolls across the soil. I lunge for it but in the sudden dark, I see pinpricks of light. Up ahead. The boards. Sunlight, leaking through.

I snatch the light off the ground and run. Fall, run again.

When I reach the entrance, my fingers shake across the planks. I yank on them until one swings open. I leap out.

Sunlight spears my eyes. Blinking, I run forward, but my feet get tangled in the vines. I trip, plunging into the ravine, falling into shadow. I grab the kudzu, holding on to stop my descent, then scramble back up the hill. I find the trail, sprint down the trampled grass. When I hit road, my feet suddenly hurt. Dirt, in my shoes. All that gritty soil from the tunnel is now rubbing across my toes. It feels like I'm wearing sandpaper socks.

But I don't stop.

The tall buildings are still purging people, choking Main Street with adults toting briefcases, firing orders into cell phones, clicking down the concrete in heels. I run past them, covered in dirt, every stride sending up a fresh bolt of pain. My shoes pinch like they're too small.

But something else is driving me. A feeling. It rises in my chest like a bubble, helium-light, freed from all the gravity around me. I feel almost giddy—I have a secret. And I'm bursting to tell it to the one person in the whole world who will understand.

I run faster, knowing she's waiting for me.

CHAPTER THREE

BUT NO SPARKLY purple bicycle is parked outside the small brick building in Scott's Addition. Keeping pace, I glance over my shoulder. The potholed road is empty. Trucks wait at the plumbing supply warehouse. Workers smoke outside the Sauer's spice factory. And two men skulk into a black door that advertises a "gentleman's club" which, obviously, isn't.

But no purple bike.

I kick into my highest gear and tear down the last thirty yards, slapping the iron handrail and immediately doubling over, gasping for air. My backpack slides off my shoulders, hits the dirty pavement, and I'm too tired to even pick it up.

Finally, when I can stand, I see no purple bike.

I won.

I limp up the steps and push open the glass door. It triggers a cowbell. Everyone inside turns to look—six men, sitting on swivel stools at a counter, and a huge guy standing at the grill that's as black as his skin. Titus Williams. The big man in Big Man's Burgers.

"I won!" I announce.

But nobody says a word.

"Hello—I finally won!"

"We got it," Titus says. "What flavor?"

I stare at him for a long moment. "Chocolate."

The guys at the counter have weathered faces, like broken-in baseball mitts. They've all swiveled back to the television. It's the playoffs for the World Series.

"Extra chocolate!" I call out.

Titus waves his spatula.

The guy named Journey points at the TV. "They oughta hang that pitcher by his thumbs."

"You'd have to go first," says Shortie, sitting next to him.

"Me? I caught pop-ups."

"I caught 'em!"

The bickering continues. I walk over to the red vinyl booth, specifically reserved for me and Drew. We've been coming here since April, and this is the first time I've ever beat Drew to our Friday dinners. And first one here gets the free milkshake from Titus. It's also a big deal because my chances of ever winning this contest were slim to none. My best friend is my favorite person in the entire world. But she has some seriously compulsive habits, and one of them is punctuality. Like, extreme punctuality.

Scooting into the booth, I position myself so I can see Drew's face when she comes through the door and realizes I beat her. As an added bonus, I open my backpack and take out the rock I stole from the tunnel. I set it on the table. Drew said I'd never have the guts to go in there, being afraid of the dark.

But today is a banner day.

And I refuse to let anything ruin it. Even the pain in my feet. Even the crappy music on the jukebox, that croony stuff from the 1950s.

I pick up the rock. It's pale gray, almost blue, marbled with dark gray veins. I rub my thumb over it, feeling the grains.

Titus plunks the shake on the table. It's still in the tall

silver container from the mixer, frosted on the outside.

"What's with the rock?" he asks.

"Nothing."

"So it's special."

"What? No. It's . . . it's just a rock."

He hands me the straw. I peel back the paper sleeve. According to Virginia law, trespassing on railroad tracks is a Class 3 misdemeanor—I know these things. I've also stolen property. So the punishment's even worse.

"What'd you do," Titus asks, "steal it?"

I give him my best are-you-insane expression. "It's a rock."

"Have it your way." He walks back to the grill, only when he passes the jukebox, he slaps its side.

The do-wop song dies.

"Thank God," says Journey. "That song was driving me nuts."

As the next tune warbles out, a collective groan rises from the counter.

"Can we send that jukebox to the Smithsonian?" asks Winder. "The thing's pure history."

I glance at the door. My mouth's watering, begging me to sip the shake. But it's rude to start without the other person. Drew never does. Closing my eyes, I say a silent grace. For one thing, it's a miracle I got here first. Plus I made it into the tunnel and back out. Alive.

When I open my eyes, the milkshake is still begging.

I glance at the clock above the entrance. An old Richmond Dairy farm clock. It says 5:05. One sip. I decide one sip isn't rude.

Titus's shakes are so thick that when you sip through the straw, the roof of your mouth feels like it's going to collapse. But then the taste hits and all is forgiven. Cold, creamy, sweet.

That hint of salt. Chocolate sending every taste bud into the Snoopy dance. I close my eyes again, relishing the flavor. My throat wants to hum.

"You want me to start the burgers?"

I look up. Titus is back at the table, wiping his enormous black hands on the apron that, once upon a time, was white.

I glance at the clock. Then lift my wrist, checking my watch because the clock has got to be wrong.

"She's late," I say.

"Yeah. No kidding."

"Drew's never late."

"So you want me to wait for Miss Never Late or start the burgers?"

"I don't know."

I really don't. This situation has never happened before. My mouth is watering, my stomach is growling, and Drew's not here.

She's always first.

"You want to live a little?" Titus asks.

"What?"

"Try something new," he says. "Until Miss Never Late shows up."

Every Friday, we've ordered the exact same meal. Cheeseburgers, fries, shakes. But I decide today is special. So special that I'm going to break tradition.

"What do you suggest?" I ask.

"My onion rings."

"Okay. Sounds good."

But Titus doesn't leave. He stares at me with his large brown eyes. He's got this way of looking at you that makes you really nervous.

"I said I'll try them. What's wrong?"

"Tell me you don't want mayonnaise."

"I said I'd live a little, not a lot."

"You're going to ruin my onion rings."

"I can't help it."

He shakes his head. "Girl, you're not wired right."

This time, when he walks away, he doesn't slap the juke-box. He pounds Journey on the back.

"Hey!" Journey says. "Can't I sing along?"

"Sure, if you want to starve."

The guys laugh. Somebody howls like a dog, imitating Journey's singing voice. But Titus never cracks a smile. He's like that. I've never seen him show anything resembling joy. Not even that first day when Drew and I first met him.

April 9. I will never forget it because it was Opening Day for the Richmond Braves. We sat together in the stands, Drew was scribbling statistics in her notebook. I was bored.

"You smell that?" I asked.

She didn't even look up from her notebook. "Concession stand."

"No—better. Way better."

I had to wait until the stupid game was finally over—Richmond Braves winning—and then Drew pedaled us from the baseball stadium on the purple Schwinn. I was balanced on the handle bars, my feet resting on the front wheel bolts. We rode through the industrial section behind the stadium, called Scott's Addition, both of us sniffing the air, growing more and more desperate to track the delicious scent. By the time we found the small brick building with the white sign BIG MAN'S BURGERS, I was drooling.

And that was only the beginning.

Drew walked through the door, tripping that cow bell, and screamed.

"Titus Williams!"

The giant black man behind the grill stared at her. Like we

just landed from Mars.

"June 2001," Drew continued. "Bottom of the sixth, you hit two triples and a double against the Orioles."

She kept rattling off the guy's statistics, going all the way back to when he played for the Richmond Braves, the farm team we'd just watched at the city stadium.

Titus didn't smile. But you could tell he was impressed. So impressed our meal was on the house. When we came back the next Friday—after a late afternoon game, the Braves lost—a CLOSED sign hung on the door.

But there were some people inside.

So Drew—being Drew—barged right in.

Not only were there no women and kids in the place, there were almost no white people.

"Eighty-eight percent black," Drew corrected me later. "Eleven percent white."

"Eighty-eight and eleven are ninety-nine," I pointed out. "You're off by one-percent."

"No" she said. "I'm Jewish."

"That's not white?"

"Mediterranean."

That was Drew. Precise. Particular. A total pain in the tuchus.

And the most awesome best friend anywhere.

But now I'm sick of staring at the door. I take out my geology journal and draw the tunnel's weeping walls. I make a note to myself about checking the city's water tables, and rub my thumb over the rock sample one more time, wondering if there's too much limestone or marble. Calcium carbonate, which would erode in acidic water.

I glance at the door again, the clock says 5:15.

My shake is melting when Titus brings the onion rings.

"What's wrong?" he asks.

"She's late."

"You keep saying."

"Drew. We're talking about Drew. The human clock."

"Yeah, so be grateful. You got walked to first."

"Is this baseball lingo? Because I don't speak baseball."

"That's part of your problem. Along with your palate."

"My what?"

"Ability to taste things." He plunks down the mayonnaise. "Go ahead, desecrate my onion rings. But I can't watch."

As he leaves, I dip one ring in the mayo. This is how I eat my French fries, too. But I'm not prepared for this first bite. When the golden breading crunches open, it releases a glorious steam scented with sweet Vidalia onions. I close my eyes.

"He ain't worth the spit on his ball!"

"You should know!"

The insults zing back and forth. I chew, savoring the contrast between the breading's crunch and onion's tenderness. And the mayo, tying both together.

"The ump needs glasses!"

"More like a telescope!"

Drew told me all these guys played minor league baseball with Titus. He's the only one who made it to the majors, playing two seasons for the Atlanta Braves before a knee injury sidelined him.

I eat another onion ring.

But the clock says it's almost 5:30, and suddenly the food isn't tasting that great.

I pack up my tunnel rock and notebook, carrying the basket of onion rings and empty milkshake to the counter.

Titus turns from the grill. "Something wrong?"

"Can I get our burgers to go?"

He gazes at me a long time, those eyes like pools of dark

water. But finally he whips open the steamer oven and takes out two buns. On the grill, the cheddar has melted over our burgers like golden lava. He wraps up everything in butcher paper, including the rings, then puts it all in a white bag.

"You're not going to wait for her?" he asks.

"She's not coming."

"You're sure?"

"Drew's never late."

He hands me the bag. "Never say never."

"Unless it's Drew," I say. "Then, never means never."

CHAPTER FOUR

I RUN HOME, cradling the bag of cheeseburgers and fries. My legs feel heavy as lead, but worse is the rock hammer. It pokes my spine like an insistent finger, reminding me of something that happened this morning. Something that bothered me.

Drew and I were standing at our lockers.

"I've got a surprise for you tonight," I said. "Prepare to be amazed."

But she didn't look prepared to be amazed. She looked a hundred miles away. "You know Newton's third law of motion, don't you?"

"Newton had three?"

"Raleigh, seriously." She closed her locker, spinning the dial lock just-so. "Newton's third law of motion states that for every action there is an equal and opposite reaction."

"Okay. So?"

"So. I have a surprise for you, too."

Here's the problem with having a highly-competitive best friend. I could trespass in an abandoned train tunnel and come out with rock samples—and she would still have to top it.

Now, as I run down Monument Avenue past the statue of Robert E. Lee, the idea hits me—Drew is pouting.

She knew my surprise was better. So she didn't show up.

The fries are starting to smell cold. I slow to a walk and head down the alley behind our house.

Quietly I unlock the carriage house and slide back the panel doors. Once upon a time the carriage house kept literal carriages—horses and buggies. Now it's our garage. My dad's car is parked beside my mom's. When I touch the hood, the metal feels hot. I wonder if she's telling him now, showing him the "evidence" that I'm not their "real" daughter.

I sneak past the cars, including my sister's old VW Bug that my dad wouldn't let her take to college. Helen left for Yale in August—early admission, art scholarship, the whole big nine yards. My sister is a superstar and when she left, my mom went into a tailspin. But I'm pretty happy with Helen gone. For one thing, she can't keep me from riding her bike. Which she would if she was here. Helen's like that.

I leave my backpack, toss the food bag in the front basket and wheel the bike into the alley. In six months, I'll be sixteen. Nobody's even mentioned driving lessons. And I don't bring it up because my dad's so stressed. My sister, however, whined for years, until he broke down and bought her exactly what she wanted—an old VW Bug. The hippie mobile. Right now it's hidden under a tarp, and as I wheel the bike past it, I feel the temptation to spit on it.

I bike down Monument to The Boulevard then pick up Grove Avenue. Heading west into a sinking sun, I keep scanning the road for a skinny girl with wild brown hair riding a purple Schwinn. Drew's so compulsive she never changes routes. So if she's heading to Big Man's Burgers, I will see her.

But I don't.

Right past Libbie Avenue, I turn into St. Catherine's School. Episcopal, not Catholic. But nobody can tell by our uniforms. I circle the buildings then stop at the bike rack behind the gym, where Drew always parks her bike.

It's not here.

Instead, a white panel truck is parked within inches of the bike rack. The truck's bumper has a sticker that asks, "How's my driving?"

Lousy.

"Yeah, yeah, yeah," says a guy walking out of the gym. His blue coveralls swim around his body. "Don't say it."

"Say what?"

"I already got the lecture. Once was plenty."

He throws open the back doors, barely missing the bike rack.

"Was there a purple bike here?" I point to the rack he's almost destroyed.

"Huh?" He glances over his shoulder. "No, no bike."

"You're sure?"

"Look, you girls want us out of here before the dance starts. So quit bugging me."

He yanks some white PVC pipes from the truck, carries them to the gym, throwing open the door. The wail of an electric guitar flies out. The band, I figure. Rehearing for tonight's dance. I bike away as fast as possible.

When I coast down Westhampton to Drew's house, I see her mom's Volvo in the driveway. It's packed with those long rectangular boxes that hold foil and Saran Wrap. Drew's mom is head of public relations for the cooking division of Reynolds Aluminum. Which is pretty ironic since Jayne Levinson doesn't even know how to boil water. I know, because Drew and I used to meet here every Friday night for cheeseburgers—frozen White Castle burgers nuked in the microwave.

After eating at Titus's place, there's no going back to that.

I lean my bike against an oak in the backyard and kick through the fallen leaves. The back door is always open and leads into the sunroom, which gets no sun because the trees are so thick.

I stick my head inside. "Drew?" I whisper.

The only reply is a hiss.

Sir Isaac Newton. Their satanic Siamese cat.

But her mom also calls out, "Drewery?"

Drew's full name, which means there was trouble.

"Drewery, is that you?"

"No, ma'am," I call back. "It's Raleigh."

I'm trying to sound polite, but on the list of People I Never Want To Talk To, Especially On Friday night, number one is Jayne Levinson.

"Raleigh?"

"Just looking for Drew. Is she here?"

I turn, glancing around the yard. It's smothered with leaves, enough that I can't see the burn marks in the grass. Drew likes to experiment with explosive propulsion, something the neighbors don't exactly appreciate. But the only thing out there is the wind, lifting the fallen leaves.

When I turn around again, Jayne Levinson is standing at the edge of the sunroom.

"How's life, Raleigh?"

The light from the kitchen outlines her petite shape, her expensive clothing. The glass of red wine in her hand.

"I'm fine, thank you, so Drew isn't here?"

"No."

"She wasn't at the restaurant either."

"What restaurant?"

"Big Man's Burgers." The name doesn't register. So I try another. "Titus's place?"

She laughs. She throws her head back and laughs like that's the funniest joke on the planet. I glance at the cat. Curled on the rattan couch, he kneads his claws into the cushions with lethargic cruelty.

"That's not a restaurant, Raleigh. It's a hole-in-the-wall."

Whatever.

"She's never late."

"It must be the slum factor—are your lives too privileged?"

"Excuse me?"

"I'm trying to figure out why you girls insist on going to that dump."

I smile. Politely. Then hate myself. I've vowed never to smile like this—this fake phony gross smile that people offer my mother all the time. Yet here it is, the awful pleasantness frozen on my face. And I'm pretty sure this fake smile is one of those things that, once you learn how to do it, you can never unlearn it. Like riding a bike.

"So you haven't seen her?" I ask.

Jayne sips her wine. "I suppose it's too much to hope you two are going to the dance."

The fake smile comes back. See? Already a habit.

"That's what I thought." She takes another sip. "On the other hand, it's probably safer this way."

A substantial part of me does not want to know what she means. But I have to ask, since it might help me figure out where Drew is.

"What's safer?"

"Your antisocial lives. This way, neither of you will get knocked up."

This is Jayne Levinson on a Friday night—any idea slipping into her mind will immediately launch out her mouth. During the week, Jayne recites scripted words for Reynolds Aluminum. She's even on TV from time to time, reciting scripted words about thing like turkey-baking bags. But on Friday evenings she pops the cork and out comes Weekend

Jayne. She's a big part of why we moved Friday dinner to Titus's place.

"Her bike isn't at school, either."

"That so?" She takes another sip of wine. More like a gulp.

"Did she say anything about changing plans for tonight?"

"No. But you can park your butt on the sofa until she shows up. Until then, I'm sure you can read."

The way she says the word, reading sounds obscene.

She walks back into the kitchen, her frothy silk skirt rippling behind her, and I wonder which is worse—my mom, trapped in her dark remote world, or Jayne, who speaks public fakery all week, then comes home and can't keep one thought to herself, no matter how hurtful.

Right now it seems like a tie.

I cautiously lower myself on one side of the wicker love seat. Isaac Newton sits at the other end, his blue eyes glowing like marbles hoping to find a slingshot. I keep two cushions between us and reach for the books. They rise like stalagmites from the floor. Jayne refuses to put bookcases in here, saying they would look "tacky." Which makes no sense because it's not like three-foot towers of books looks any less "tacky."

To be honest, Drew likes to read stuff that makes my eyes glaze over. Baseball, for instance. And, as if baseball wasn't boring enough, she combs through books about potential energies and String Theory and stuff that's totally abstract science. One reason I prefer geology is that you can smell, touch, and even taste minerals. It's real.

I open the book. But there's a distinctive *glug-glug* coming from the kitchen. I look up. Bottle #1 must be almost gone. Drew had to explain it to me, back when we ate dinner here. The ice dilutes the alcohol, so Jayne can drink longer before passing out.

I stare at the page in my lap. Drew's highlighted a quote

from Richard P. Feynman. He's her absolute hero, a famous physicist who worked on the Atomic Bomb, among other things. The line reads "Science is the belief in the ignorance of experts."

When a high whistle sails out of the kitchen, Jayne curses.

I glance at my watch. 6:18 p.m.

Drew knows how much Jayne hates the cuckoo clock, so she programs it for surprise attacks. I hear the bird's little door slam, followed by another curse.

Keeping one eye on Isaac Newton, I pick up the phone on the side table and dial the number I've seen a hundred times on that big white sign. The numbers spell BigMans.

When Titus answers, I say, "It's Raleigh."

"Oh."

He sounds surprised. And why not? I've never called before.

"Is she there?"

"No."

"She never showed up?"

"You said she wouldn't."

I did. But everything's out of whack. I'm second-guessing myself that Drew might be pouting because I made it into the tunnel. And it's possible—even likely—that she and Jayne are fighting. But not being on time would really *really* bug her. I can't see Drew holding out this long.

"I'm at her house. She's not here."

There's a long pause. I don't know what I expect Titus to say. But Isaac Newton snags the pillow with lethargic cruelty and there's more *glug-glugging* from the kitchen as Jayne pours another glass, and still Titus says nothing.

"Okay." I wait. Still nothing. "Thanks."

I hang up. Outside the sky is sapphire-blue swimming toward amethyst-purple.

My curfew is 7:00 p.m. Ridiculous for somebody six months from her sixteenth birthday. But I don't argue. Partly because of my crazy-paranoid mother. But partly because I feel bad. My dad doesn't know that we switched from Drew's house to Titus's place. I hate lying to him.

Ice splashes into Jayne's glass. Isaac Newton gives me a big yawn, like he's oxygenating for a good kill. I stand up and replace Richard P. Feynman on the stalagmite of books.

Like all good Southern girls, I know it's rude to leave someone's house without first saying good bye. And rude is bad. On this side of the Mason-Dixon line, being rude is equivalent to breaking one of the Ten Commandments.

But it's Friday night. And ice is clinking.

So I slip out the door, and ride away.

CHAPTER FIVE

WHEN I GET home, night has fallen and the autumn air is so crisp it feels brittle. Like the darkness is actually paper-thin glass that could shatter any second.

I pry open the carriage house doors, hang the bike on its hook, and pick up my backpack, still sitting on the floor where I left it. In the alley, I lift the lid on our trash can and toss in the bag of food. The white paper is covered with translucent grease spots. They look old, as if Titus bagged our dinner days ago instead of a couple hours ago. As some final precaution, I stuff the bag deep into the can, just in case my mom finds it and starts asking questions. Or my dad, who even doesn't know Drew and I eat dinner at Titus's place now.

The fact that I have no good answers for either of them makes me pray I won't have to see them. But when I walk into the kitchen, it's empty, and suddenly I feel lonely. Like, I literally have nobody to talk to.

"Hello?" I call out.

Nothing.

Something's baking in the oven. I open the oven door and see a casserole that looks suspiciously green, like too much spinach. But I'm more troubled by what I see on the stovetop.

A gray powder rings the burners. I pinch it, rubbing it between my fingers. Ash. Paper. She's burning her notes, again. It's one of the weirder things my mom does. She will spend hours writing things in paranoid gibberish. The pages look like some word version of Sudoku. And then the voices in her head tell her to burn them.

I wipe my hands on my jeans and check the answering machine by the fridge. There are three messages. And although Drew knows not to say anything about being at Titus's, I turn down the volume anyway, just in case.

The first message is Bessie Marchant. A woman from our church, Mrs. Marchant seems like a nice person, but I've noticed everything she says is like a string of Southern euphemisms. The message goes on about how she's hoping to see Nadine in church on Sunday, how much all the ladies miss her, etc. etc. But to me it sounds like, "We all know you're bat-guano crazy, Nadine, but we still want to help because we're supposed to as Christians." I give Bessie points for even calling.

The second message is from my dad, phoning home during a court recess. He just wanted to say he loves her. My heart literally aches hearing the tenderness in his voice, especially when he came home to note-burning on the stove.

I hold my breath for the last message, praying it's Drew.

"Hi, I'm calling for Raleigh."

It's not Drew. It's a guy.

"This is DeMott." He pauses. "DeMott Fielding. From church?"

Like we wouldn't know who DeMott is, after seeing him every week for the last ten years.

"I, uh, just wanted to remind Raleigh about the dance. Tonight. At St. Catherine's. Hope to see her there. Okay." Another pause. "Good bye."

I stare down at the machine, which has replaced the red three with a big zero. And I keep staring, like some idiot who is totally in denial of reality, that there must be a fourth message, from Drew, telling me why she didn't show up and where she really is. After a long moment, it hits me how I might be doing this because I don't even want to think about why DeMott Fielding is calling me about that stupid dance. Everybody not living in an abandoned train tunnel knows the guy's got a girlfriend, and that same girlfriend is organizing that same dance. What the—?

"Somebody switched her, David."

I freeze. They are in his office.

"Nadine, honey." His voice sounds pleading. "Raleigh's never given us a moment's trouble."

"She's not Raleigh. I checked her feet."

I start to go numb, not feeling my fingers. But the footsteps stop. Seconds later I hear the pocket doors slide closed. His office. They must have turned into his office.

I tiptoe down the hall. My dad's office used to be the smoking parlor, back when this huge house was a gathering place for Richmond society. I lean into the mahogany, balancing carefully so I don't touch it and give myself away.

"—and she put a lock on her door," my mom is saying. "Raleigh would never lock her door."

Before she left for Yale, Helen gifted me the lock from her door. My sister and I aren't friends, but we are soldiers in the same trench. We look out for each other.

"Why does she suddenly need to lock her door?"

The pause that follows makes sweat prickle on my back.

"You're right," he says. "It's not Raleigh."

"You already knew this?!"

"Nadine, I want to tell you the truth. But are you ready to hear it?"

"Tell me!"

"Our perfect daughter is gone. She's been kidnapped."

My mother gasps.

"Puberty," he says. "Puberty abducted Raleigh. We now have a teenager."

"David, I am not joking."

"Neither am I. Let's kick her out of the house."

"Stop joking."

"Think about how much money we'd save—in food alone? Raleigh eats for six people."

"David, listen to me. She's up to something."

I hear the softening in her voice. Once again, my dad's managing to chide away some of the paranoia. But as I back away from the door, moving down the hall, my eyes burn.

This is not the end of it.

Not by a long shot.

I STEP OUTSIDE and creep down the stone steps into the cellar.

Our house has sixteen rooms—not including the apartment over the carriage house—and they're all big and formal and kinda cool in a historical way. But the one room I hate is down here in the cellar. The laundry room.

For eight decades, the Harmons sent their clothes out to be "laundered." But around 1980, my dad's parents took a stab at modernity—they installed a washer and dryer.

The maids never complained about the laundry room being under house, accessible only by going outside. But now the maids are gone because when the woman of the house is full of paranoid delusions, maids create more problems than they take away. I started doing all my own laundry when my mom started this "You're not my daughter" thing. She only said it a couple of times to Helen. For one thing, Helen's always been her favorite. But for another, Helen always replied, "Promise me I'm not your daughter."

I lunge for the string connected to the light bulb then wait on the stairs. In case anything scurries into the dark corners. Then I run to the washer, kick off my All Stars and throw them into the machine with my clothes. I shake the soil from my socks into the floor drain, constantly glancing over my shoulder. Man, I hate the dark.

Shivering in my undies, I find a pair of my sweats and an old sweatshirt in the dryer—washed yesterday after I ran downtown to find the entrance to the tunnel, so there would be no more excuses for not going inside. As I pour the soap in, I can hear my parents' footsteps on the floor above me. They're in the kitchen. I hold the washer's knob, wondering whether to start it now or wait. If she hears the machine now, she'll think I snuck down here. Which I did. It might be the definition of crazy—I lead a secret life because my mom thinks I'm leading a second life, thus proving I'm apparently not me.

Crazy.

And sometimes I wonder if I'm going to go crazy too.

My hand is still on the knob when something squeaks behind me. I jump, spinning around, expecting rats.

But it's my dad.

He's opened the cellar door and is coming down the stairs. He's so tall he takes each step sideways, shoulders hunched because of the low ceiling.

He looks at me standing in sweats and says, "What happened?"

"Drew didn't show up for dinner."

"I meant your mother—what upset her this time?"

I turn around, yank the machine's knob and glare at the tub, relishing the whooshing loudness of the water.

"Raleigh?"

The sound of splashing water echoes on the stone walls.

He comes around the side, trying to look at my face. "Your

mother's upset."

"What am I—my mother's keeper?"

"Why are you so angry?"

"Because it's always about her."

"No," he says. "And yes."

I flick the washer's lid, letting it slam down on the machine.

"Alright," he says. "I get it. What happened with Drew?"

"She's didn't show up."

"For Burgers & Brains?"

"For dinner," I correct him. My dad is the only person still using our silly nickname. Back in seventh grade, when Drew and I started meeting on Friday nights, we decided to call it Burgers & Brains because we ate burgers and tried to outsmart each other. We like the fact that it creeped out her mom, Jayne, too.

"She didn't show up for dinner . . . at her own house?" He looks puzzled.

"No, she wasn't at—" I catch myself. My dad, the judge, can sniff out lies in any testimony. "—at school, her bike wasn't at school either, and Jayne said she hasn't seen her since breakfast."

"You mean, Mrs. Levinson."

"Dad, she makes me call her Jayne."

"Not in this house she doesn't."

"Okay, whatever. The point is, Drew's never late, and she didn't tell me she wasn't coming for dinner."

He nods. But he keeps glancing up the stairs. He's left the cellar door open, framing the dark sky above our patio. I can feel the evening wind swirling down the stairs. It makes a hollow sound, like someone blowing over a bottle opening.

"Hello," I say irritated. "Earth to Dad?"

"I'm listening."

31

"She's never done this before."

"Drew's a wonderful friend, Raleigh. But . . ." He tilts his head back and forth.

"But what?"

"She's run away before."

I turn around with a huffing sigh. "That was a long time ago."

"Really?" He lifts an eyebrow. My dad has this way of being skeptical without making you feel like a total moron. He just plants some doubt and lets you pluck the leaves from it.

"She didn't run away," I blurt out.

"You're sure?"

The washing machine water goes into the agitation cycle, filling the silence with swishing water. But it's not loud enough to drown out the accusation hanging in the air.

"Here's a better question," he says, smiling. "When does Drew turn sixteen?"

"January. First." Yes, the girl totally obsessed with numbers was born in the first month on the first day at 1:11 a.m. Like God knew what she'd be like before she even appeared.

"January," he says. "That's three months away. Then she can petition family court and ask to live with her dad. I can't see any judge denying her request, given that she's brilliant and capable."

"You're positive?"

"Ninety-nine point four percent." His eyes twinkle. Even down here in the dim light, the blue in his eyes is as luminous as stained glass. "Drew will want to calculate the percentage herself, I'm sure."

I don't say anything. The very same quality that makes my dad a judge everyone admires is the same thing that annoys me. He's too rational sometimes. Like he doesn't get why people are emotional about things. Which always makes me wonder if he's grasping the seriousness of any situation. My mom's insanity or Drew's absence—and yet I can't exactly explain this to him right now because he doesn't even know we're eating at Big Man's Burgers. He'd never let me go into that neighborhood.

He raises the eyebrow again. "Do you need me to say I'm one hundred percent certain?"

"No, forget it." I start folding my dry clothes. "But if she was going to run away, she would've told me."

"People keep secrets," he says. "You ought to know that better than most."

I stop, mid-fold. "What?"

"Pardon," he corrects me.

"Pardon?"

"Your mother thinks you're hiding something."

Before I can stop the heat, it rises up my throat. When I feel the blush heading to my face, I bend down, pretending to sort through yesterday's de-criminalized clothes. I am taking forever to do this, but he still doesn't leave.

"Are you?"

"What."

"Raleigh, we're Virginians. We say 'pardon.' "

"Okay, pardon, no, I'm not hiding anything, are we done?"

"You're not hiding anything?"

I glance up. He's the judge and my dad and it's all in his stare—truth and mercy and love. The silence grows tighter, like the walls are marching toward us. I don't see how guilty people walk into his courtroom and don't fling themselves on the floor screaming, "I did it!"

But I do know how—they lie.

"Right now I'm just really worried about my friend, and the last thing I need is the third degree, Your Honor."

He draws a deep breath, then nods. "Did I ever tell you

33

what Chesterton said?"

"I don't care what—"

"Chesterton said an optimist looks at the situation and sees it's serious but not hopeless. The Christian looks at the same situation and says it's hopeless but not serious."

I stare at him. Now I'm ticked off. "I have no idea what you're talking about. But that Chesterton guy's wrong. The situation is serious. She didn't show up, didn't call, didn't stay at school, and now it's dark out and her drunken mother—"

"Whose mother is drunk?"

We both spin toward the door. My mom stands in the opening.

"Oh, hello, honey." My dad walks toward her, opening his arms like we've been waiting for her the whole time. "Raleigh's feeling frustrated. She can't find her math teacher."

The patio lights half her face. The expression I see there is not comforting.

"What does her math teacher have to do with someone's drunken mother?" she asks.

Now we've stepped in it.

"Well, to be perfectly honest," he says, "Raleigh doesn't know the math teacher's mother that well. But the teacher is burdened by having to take care of her."

"The mother? Who drinks?"

"Yes, you see how complicated it is? We didn't want to bore you, honey." He smiles. "It's one of those times when life gets written up as an algebraic equation. All those unknown Xs and Ys."

She is looking at me so fiercely that I have to bend down to the basket again. I pick up a T-shirt and begin folding it with such extreme care it's like I'm moving in slow motion. But I am trying to appear normal. And this is what people do in laundry rooms, right? They fold laundry. This is what

Raleigh would do.

I glance at my dad. Somehow he always manages to tell her the truth. Drew really is my math teacher. Without her, I'd never have an A in Algebra II. And I don't really know Jayne. And Drew does feel the burden of taking care of her mother, especially on hangover weekends. I start to relax, my dad's got it covered.

"What happened to your feet?" she asks.

The question comes so fast, it's like some horrible dislocation. I suddenly look down at my feet, and even to me, they look wrong. Like they really do belong to somebody else. The skin on my toes is raw, a bright pink. The big toe is bleeding on top. The same feet she measured this afternoon.

I grab two socks from the basket and start pulling them on. "I went running. That's all."

"Well, kiddo," my dad says, "looks like you could use some new running shoes. How about we go shopping this weekend?"

I nod, like that's an excellent idea. But he's already heading for the door, like he knows she's got another question and my response won't hold up. I watch him go up the stairs, moving toward her, and something inside leaves me. It leaves me here, in the dark.

"Is dinner about ready?" He takes her hand. "I'm starving."

She's still staring down at me. I look away and continue folding the clothes that don't need folding. That familiar sensation returns to my throat. Like something's lodged in my windpipe.

"Raleigh," he says.

I look up.

"Try to get some sleep tonight," he says.

He waits for me to say something.

But there's no talking when my throat gets like this. Lifting the T-shirt in my hands, I bring it down fast, snapping it like a matador's cape.

He gives me a sad smile and says, "I promise. Everything will look better in the morning.

CHAPTER SIX

B UT SLEEP NEVER comes.

Normally, I would chalk it up to my insomnia—if anything about insomnia can be called normal. But this night breaks my usual pattern. One bad night of not sleeping always leads to a night when I finally crash.

But tonight, exhaustion's not working for me.

My mind refuses to stop picking at the puzzle.

From checking in at their house, it's obvious Drew and Jayne had another of their epic fights. Jayne practically sneered at the mention of Drew, who had booby-trapped the cuckoo clock. But was Drew mad enough to bike to her dad's house? Nothing ticks off Jayne more than Drew choosing her dad, Rusty, over her.

Except . . . Rusty's apartment is twenty miles north of town, and Drew despises exercise. If I even mention jogging, she'll say, "I'm waiting for you to realize running is a total waste of friction."

I toss and turn for several hours. Should I call Rusty, or not? A starving artist, he works through the nights. But Drew once said he hardly ever answers his phone. In that way, he's like the two of us, hating the phone. Which might explain why Drew would bike all the way out there, to talk to him.

But twenty miles?

Drew complains about a flight of stairs.

I flip on my side, listening to the wind outside. It's been kicking up since I got home and now the magnolia branches are scraping across the brick walls, a sound I could record and sell to haunted houses. My next flip over puts me face-to-face with the digital clock. It reads 11:11. Like I needed another reminder about Drew's compulsion for perfect order, her need to dictate how everything will go.

And suddenly those odd words come back to me: *I already got the lecture*.

That guy, outside the gym. The plumber, his white truck parked inches from the bike rack.

He said, "I already got the lecture."

If Drew's purple Schwinn was locked to the bike rack, that truck would've come *thisclose* to crushing her prized possession.

I sit up in bed.

Who will not hesitate to lecture any teacher who gets one fact wrong?

Who would berate a plumber about the destructive force of a truck colliding with a bike?

Drew.

She would grab her bike and take off for . . . where?

Not home. Not when she's fighting with Jayne. And not Rusty if she has to bike twenty miles.

So why didn't she come to dinner? I start to wonder if my dad has a good point. If Drew wanted to make Jayne sweat, really twist the knife, she could pretend to run away. Again. And she didn't tell me about her plan because I'm part of it. My search for Drew is supposed to scare Jayne. And Drew won't call my house because of my mom.

I throw back the covers.

The Physics lab. Drew stayed after school most days,

working on projects and tutoring numbskulls. What if she wheeled her bike into the lab? Hiding out late during the dance until Jayne got so distressed she lost her drunken mind.

The cold floor stings my raw toes. I suck air through my teeth, slipping out of my pajamas and back into my sweats. When I pick up my shoes, tiptoeing down the servant's stairwell, I can hear the wind, whistling over every stair that squeaks.

CHAPTER SEVEN

THIRTY MINUTES BEFORE midnight, my neighborhood looks like somebody pulled a plug and drained all the color. Black pavement. Black sky with white stars. One long string of street lights, like pearls pulling me down the road. The only thing resembling color are the leaves, blowing from the trees.

I run. My feet ache.

Between the gusts of wind, I hear my breath and the *slap-slap-slap* of my All Stars. It hurts too much to bend my toes. Of course, the bike would've worked better. But my mom's insomnia is often worse than my own, and my parents' bedroom window looks out over the back patio and alley.

By the time I get to St. Cat's, sweating and panting, the dance is still going strong. Cars fill the parking lot outside the gym, including a half dozen limos. Slowing to a walk, I keep my eyes on the two people who guard the gym's double doors.

Our headmaster, Mr. Ellis.

And his assistant Mrs. Parsons, otherwise known as Parsnip.

Ellis speaks first. Naturally.

"Miss Harmon," he says. "Very nice to see you. But the dance has a dress code."

Parsnip giggles.

"Yes, sir." I wipe the sleeve of my sweatshirt across my

forehead, mopping the sweat and the shame Ellis has thrown my way. "I'm not here for the dance."

Parsnip's pinched face, by some miracle of genetics, can pinch even further. "You're simply out running around town—at this hour?"

Like Ellis, Parsnip dangles this kind of shame all the time. You're supposed to reflexively feel so bad about yourself you'll do anything they say. But it doesn't usually work on me—I feel too bad about myself already.

"I need to get something inside the school," I explain.

"Absolutely not," Parsnip says.

"You know the rules, Miss Harmon," Ellis chimes in.

"It'll only take a minute."

"Did you not hear us?" Parsnip says.

I consider explaining the whole situation. But that's the nuclear option. After Drew ran away in sixth grade, she sparked a potentially fatal amount of electricity between herself and Ellis. Our headmaster likes to remind us how St. Catherine's prides itself on being the best and oldest girl's school in Richmond. So great that Lady Astor went here, way back when.

"Can't you make one exception?" I ask. "It's an emergency."

But Parsnip has shifted her squint toward the parking lot. "Who would dare drive up this late?"

A white stretch limo has pulled to the curb. The driver jumps out, hustling to the back door and holds it open.

"I might have guessed," Ellis says.

MacKenna Fielding stumbles out. She grabs the door, waiting for her date. When he lurches out, she grabs his arm. She giggles. The two of them shamble toward us. MacKenna's crimson gown shimmers like fresh blood.

"Miss Fielding," Ellis intones. "Arriving rather late, aren't we?"

"Engine trouble," MacKenna says.

Only "engine" sounds like "injun."

Parsnip moves from the door, leaning down toward MacKenna. Our assistant headmaster is conveniently shaped like the vegetable we've named her after.

She sniffs the air. "Miss Fielding, really."

"Yes." Ellis glares at her. "Perhaps we need to have a talk with your father."

I really don't want to see this. And somehow I feel like I'm making this worse. Ellis likes an audience, especially when using someone as an example. So I look away, and that's when I see it.

The bike rack.

And a purple bike locked to it.

"It's here!"

The words burst from my mouth. Suddenly they're all looking at me, MacKenna's eyes shiny as glass, Parsnip's expression saying she gnaws three times a daily on lemons and loves it.

"Miss Harmon," she says, "would you mind?"

"I have to get into the school!"

Ellis looks at Parsnip, "Have we not made ourselves clear?"

"But I lost something," I say. This statement is true. So of course I push it even farther. "And I won't be able to get my homework done without it."

That stops them. For a moment.

"What, pray tell," Parsnip says, "did you lose?"

"My math." I really wish I'd inherited my dad's talent for coming up with the right words at the right time. "I lost my math assignment."

"Really!" Parsnip snorts. "Your carelessness doesn't absolve you from consequences."

Ellis looks at MacKenna. "Now, Miss Fielding . . . "

I glance at the bike. Sitting under the parking lot lights, the purple paint glitters like a freshly cracked geode. I can hear them lecturing MacKenna. It could go on forever. Time for the nuclear option.

"But Drew's inside."

Parsnip laughs. At least, I think it's a laugh. It sounds more like Isaac Newton the cat coughing up a fur ball.

I point at the bike.

"Wonders never cease," Parsnip says, recovering. "Miss Levinson rides her bike to a formal dance."

"However," Ellis says, "I don't recall seeing her enter. Do you?"

MacKenna's date glances at her. His eyes are bloodshot, but he manages to wink at her.

"I can state unequivocally," Parsnip says, "Miss Levinson did not darken this entrance tonight."

"Doubtful she would even attend the dance," Ellis asks.

"Right," I say. "Because she's in the school."

The two of them turn to refocus on the bike. MacKenna's date maneuvers her behind their turned backs.

"She's probably in the Physics lab," I say.

"Impossible." Ellis is still staring at the bike. But he shakes his head. "No students are allowed inside the school after hours."

"I'll go remind her," I say.

"Absolutely not," Ellis says.

"Out of the question!" Parsnip says.

"We will take care of this matter after the dance," he says.

"And take care of it we will," Parsnip echoes.

MacKenna's date grabs the door handle. She covers her mouth, stifling a giggle. I watch them, almost marveling at how they simply bypassed these people, like authority didn't matter. And here I am, begging for permission.

"Miss Levinson needs further instruction," Ellis says. "She's under the mistaken impression that she's in charge."

"Indeed," Parsnip says. "Lessons need to be learned."

MacKenna's date flings open the door. A blast of music rushes out. I see that red dress bleeding into the gym, their laughter trailing.

"Why I never!" Parsnip says.

Me, neither.

I run for the door, slipping inside just before it closes on Parsnip's voice.

"Miss Harmon—come back here!"

CHAPTER EIGHT

I HANG A fast right inside the gym and sprint past the couples.

Couples dancing, holding hands. Couples getting their picture taken. And couples gaping as I run past.

Somebody calls out something, but I can't hear because the band is so loud. I hustle to the far end of the gym, where our P.E. teacher, Mr. Galluci, stands by the snack table. He's cradling a giant bowl of Doritos in one arm.

"Harmon!" he yells over the music. "What's with the outfit?"

I yell back, "I need to get something!" I point to the doors behind him that lead into the main building.

"Can't let you!"

"Please?"

He leans in close, so he doesn't have to yell. "By order from the queen vegetable." He frowns. "Or is she a tuber?"

Parsnip.

"But Mr. Galluci, I can't finish my homework without it." This is true. Until I find Drew, I can't possibly think about homework. "I have to get in there."

But he's not listening to me. Lifting his head, he gazes over the dance floor. The band's lead singer is whispering into the microphone, moving to a slow love song, and every single couple is pulled toward the gym's dark middle. They look like metal shards sucked toward a magnet. Mr. Galluci sets down the bowl of Doritos and falls in with the rest of the chaperones who are circling the lovefest.

Call me an opportunist, but I pounce. Shoving the door open, I hear Mr. Galluci say, "Hey!"

But I'm already running down the hall when the door slams behind me. By the first corner I'm flinging my arms wide, sliding around the turn like one of Drew's beloved baseball players rounding second on a tight play. The floor is the usual Friday mess of castoff litter. Flyers for basketball tryouts, lunch menus, hyped-up reminders for everyone to have a super time at tonight's dance. I can see one light shining up ahead. English. The Lit classroom. Drew hates English. But she'll do anything to keep her GPA a pristine 4.0. That whole "perfect number thing" obsesses her.

I pick up speed on the straightaway and slide across the door, grabbing the doorframe for a stop.

"You are out!" I cry.

Mr. Sandbag looks up from his desk. "What is the meaning of this?"

I want to ask the same thing, but it's his classroom.

"Sorry. I was looking for Drew." And, in case he doesn't remember his most difficult student, I add, "Drew Levinson?"

"A rather impulsive inquiry."

"Assonance," I sigh. You have to work with this guy. "Have you seen her?"

"The more refined query is: 'Does the road wind uphill all the way?' "

Oh, God. Not now.

I glance around the room. Chairs are twisted away from their desks. White paper sprouts from the trash can, testifying to how much frustration we feel with Mr. Sandberg, a.k.a.

Sandbag.

"Well, does it?" Sandbag demands.

" 'Yes,' " I reply, quoting the Rossetti poem we're supposed to memorize. It's called "Uphill" and right now that's how everything feels. " 'to the very end.' "

"With feeling, Miss Harmon. Try to recite with feeling."

If you pull out a dictionary and look up the word tedious, you'll probably find a framed photo of Sandbag. In addition to wearing his glasses on the tip of his nose, he's one of those teachers who sees everything as a "teachable moment." If you bump into him on the street—God help you—his thin lips will peel back and he'll drop some drippy line. Right there, you've got to tell him whether he's using assonance or alliteration or symbolism, and if you don't, he'll call you out later in front of class.

"Drew—have you seen her, anywhere?"

He gazes at me over the glasses. "And the next line begins . . . ?"

" 'Will the day's journey take the whole long day?' "

" 'From morn to night my friend.' "

"Her bike's outside."

"Miss Levinson, I presume?"

Who does he think I'm talking about, Christina Rosetti?

"She did make an appearance this afternoon."

"What time?"

He reached down, snaps open his briefcase. On the floor by his feet is a small black suitcase. "If memory serves, she was speaking with Miss Teager. Probably attempting to press the parameters of geometry into a cerebellum struggling with its synapses."

He gazes over the glasses.

"Alliteration," I reply.

"Ah, but you neglected to note imagery, which could well

appear on next week's parts-of-speech test."

"What time did you see Drew?"

"At what time?"

He has to correct everything. Like I said, tedious.

"Yes, sir. At what time?"

"Two thirty." He stands, but almost simultaneously sweeps his leg toward the suitcase, pushing it under his desk. "Or perhaps it was closer to three," he adds. "The real question is, 'But is there for the night a resting place?' "

Quoting the poem again.

I want to strangle him. And that's no metaphor.

"Miss Harmon, the next line?"

I don't know it, because I haven't memorized that far. "Something about a roof. Where was she, when you saw her?"

" 'A roof for when the slow dark hours begin.' " He gives the suitcase another push, sending it deep under the desk. " 'May not the darkness hide—' "

That's it.

His words trail behind me like some neglected ghost and don't fade away until I reach our lockers. They're side by side, and when I lift Drew's combination lock, I see that little white arrow. It points directly at zero.

She's compulsive about that, too.

I spin the dial and click through her five-digit combination. Maybe she's setting up some scavenger hunt. Leaving me clues. Like suddenly having her bike outside. I pop open the tinny metal door and see her textbooks, standing like soldiers in alphabetical order. On the back wall, a photo shows the Milky Way, expanding into crystallized eternity; on my right, inside the door, Richard P. Feynman grins.

I dig behind the books, lift Feynman's photo.

Nothing.

I slam the locker shut, spinning the combination dial, but

refusing to replace that white arrow at zero. I walk down the hall and kick all the paper across the floor. I've known Drew for three years, and it started at these lockers. We had just moved up to St. Cat's Upper School, the hallowed ground worshipped by the Lower School. Drew was the weird girl who had already explained to our math teacher that space travel was only mathematically possible if the universe was rotating instead of expanding.

One day she looked over at my open locker and asked, "What is that?"

It was a photo of a geode, taken right after my dad gave me a rock hammer for my twelfth birthday. In the photo, the quartz crystals radiated like frozen sparks.

"It's a geode," I said.

"Oh." She stared a moment longer. "I assume the crystals have perfect atomic form because they're growing in a relatively unconfined space."

"Uh. Yeah. That's right."

Holy. Cow.

We slammed our lockers, walked to the cafeteria and spent the next thirty minutes talking about earthquakes, pyroclastic ash—even synclines. And that day, I felt something lift from my shoulders, some invisible weight I never realized was there until it was gone. By the next Friday I was eating dinner at her house, watching Jayne down an entire bottle of wine in one hour while Rusty went upstairs. Drew nuked our frozen cheeseburgers and fries, and when I asked for mayonnaise for the fries, she said, "That's entirely gross, but I can live with it." Ever since, we've lived with each other's idiosyncrasies— even celebrating them. For me, it felt like I'd finally found the place where I belonged.

The lights are out in the Physics lab. I slide my hand along the wall, flicking on the switch.

Unlike Sandbag's classroom, here the chairs are all aligned behind their desks. The whiteboard gleams clean. Probably Mr. Straithern, our Math and Physics teacher. He is just about as compulsive as Drew.

Her purple jean jacket hangs on a chair at the back of the room. I walk over, see her notebook with one stiletto-sharp Ticonderoga poking from the pages like a bookmark.

"Drew?"

The wall clock ticks to 12:15.

So, Miss Compulsive was working in Mr. Compulsive's classroom. Every table wiped clean, the chairs just-so, no scraps of paper on the floor. But the purple in her jacket looks as vivid to me as bruises, due to an experiment she came up with when I was playing with acids and alkalis to grow geology crystals. Chemistry was a passing phase—literally— for Drew, but she liked it enough to try soaking her jean jacket in various relative percentages of alum, vinegar, and grape juice. The result looked metamorphic, like the denim boiled inside the earth's molten layer before it was coughed up by some tectonic disaster. But she loves this jacket. And she would only leave it if she was coming back.

Like the pencil in her notebook, holding her place.

"Drew, are you hiding in here?"

I feel stupid waiting for a response.

I flip open her notebook. Yes, I'm violating her privacy, but too bad. This has gone on long enough.

Under the heading, "Burgers & Brains," I see her calculations from two weeks ago when she wanted to test the hypothesis—which will freeze faster, boiling water or cold water? It sounded like a stupid question to me—of course cold water would freeze faster. But she did the experiment at Titus's—and took bets. Everyone picked cold water. Except Titus. Turns out, boiling water freezes faster than cold water.

Drew won $18. She told me there's no rational theory that explains why water behaves like that. But her notes hypothesize "evaporation affecting mass measurements."

"Hey!"

My voice echoes back.

The clock ticks.

So I flip through more pages, feeling a little bad when I see how she's spared me some baseball stuff. Wooden bats versus aluminum. Something called the "Center of Percussion." Or COP. My eyes are already glazing over, but she's drawn stickman diagrams to show how the bat behaves with the COP. If the batter grips too far away from the center of percussion, he might feel the bat pushing against his finger, "possibly with enough force to lose control of the bat," she notes. "But, crucially, when the bat connects with a pitch precisely at the COP, the batter will experience zero force in his hands. This is key to understanding the mechanics of powerful hitting."

How can someone so interesting be obsessed with something so boring?

I flip all the way back to the front cover. She's handwritten that Feynman quote, the same one she highlighted in that book stacked in the sunroom.

"Science is the belief in the ignorance of experts."

I replace her pencil. Give the room one more glance and see a shadow falling between the closet's double doors. The neat freak Mr. Straithern only allows one student to use his supplies. That rat.

She must've heard me coming down the hall and jumped into the closet.

That skinny rat.

And now, I feel the need for revenge. Tiptoeing over, holding my breath, I yank open the door.

"Gotcha!"

Dull black magnets. Iron levers. Dowel rods swinging in the breeze I've just created.

"Drew." My throat feels hoarse. "This is so not funny."

But the only reply is the clock, ticking away the silence.

✧   ✧   ✧

WHEN I STEP into the hall, there's an unmistakable sound. Like a horse whinnying.

"Oh, Herb, stop!"

Parsnip.

I am immobile with shock. Herb is Sandbag's first name.

"Will you please be patient!" she whinnies.

I sneak down the hall in the opposite direction, skirting the litter, until I reach the girls' bathroom. It's as dark as the Physics lab. When I flick on the light, I see three of the four stall doors are closed.

"If you're hiding in here, I'm going to kill you."

No response.

I have to crawl under the doors because you can't really see under them. And because Drew never gives up. But what I find are toilets clogged with stuff that triggers my gag reflex. I'm coming out of the third stall when the bathroom door opens. I have a moment of hope versus panic—is it Drew, or Parsnip?

Neither.

The janitor gapes at me. "What in blue blazes?!"

"Hi."

"What're you doing?"

"Nothing."

"Nothing?" He keeps the door propped open, one hand on the rolling cart that holds his cleaning supplies. "You're not supposed to be in here."

"I know, I was . . ."

But I don't know what to say.

"Who let you in?" he demands.

"I don't know."

"You don't know?"

I don't want to get Mr. Galluci in trouble. But I can't keep eye contact. I have nothing but lies and this is John, the janitor. Not Ellis or Parsnip, but a guy who's been nice to me and Drew. To everyone. And to make me feel even more guilty, every time I look away from him, I catch my guilty reflection in the mirror. Somebody's left a giant lipstick kiss, and it sits right above my head, like a bad joke about kissing my decency goodbye.

"I was looking for something," I manage to say.

"In the bathroom?"

His voice has some kind of northern accent, New York or New Jersey or someplace where they say exactly what's on their mind in a tone of voice that says you're an idiot. He's still holding the door open, expecting me to leave. But then something dawns on him.

"Oh. Okay. I got it. Come out when you're done."

He starts to leave.

"Wait!" I call out.

He turns around. He's bald and the skin on his scalp is all wrinkled up with baffled questions.

"I mean, hang on a second. You know Drew, right?" I make a motion with my hand, indicating her wild brown hair. "Drew Levinson?"

"If you two burned up something, I'm—"

I shake my head. Last spring Drew and I simulated the volcanic explosion of Mt. St. Helen's. We made sure to wait until school was out for Friday, but our model left some nasty scorch marks outside the gym. John saw us. He chewed us out pretty good, but he also let us go.

"No, nothing like that. I just can't find her. And her bike is outside."

"You girls." He rolls his eyes. "Working here is like being in a soap opera." He pronounces "here" like *hee-yah.*

But it's what I hear behind him, in the hallway, that startles me. Paper rustles off the floor. I dart back into the stall, pulling my feet up on the seat.

"John."

"How ya doing Miz Parsons."

"Have you perchance seen a student wandering the halls?"

"Here?" *Hee-yah?*

"Of course here."

"Tonight?"

"Of course tonight!"

"Seems kinda late, is all."

"I know perfectly well what time it is. We have a student—Raleigh Harmon—who ran into the building without permission. We haven't seen her come out. All the doors are locked, I presume?"

"Locked up tight."

"And you've seen no one?"

"Mr. Sandberg. If you hurry he might still be in his classroom."

"And what is that supposed to mean?"

"Nothing, I guess."

"Mr. Sandberg has every right to be in his classroom at whatever hour he chooses."

"Course he does."

"He's an educator."

"Yes'm."

There's a moment of tense silence. I count to twenty-five. Then fifty. Then I hear the spritz-spritz of a spray bottle.

When I poke my head out, John is squirting down the mirror, soaking that stupid lipsticked kiss.

"Thank you," I whisper.

"Yeah, yeah." He scrubs at the greasy lips, smearing them on the glass. "Now get outta here, would ya? Before I lose my job."

CHAPTER NINE

WHEN I STEP into the still-dark gym, Mr. Galluci is waiting.

"Harmon," he says, pointing a finger which is stained bright orange with Doritos powder. "Just for taking off like that, you're running double miles on Monday. Hear me?"

Like that's a punishment. Running, even with aching toes, is my favorite thing.

"Yes, sir." I proceed to apologize, sincerely, because Mr. Galluci, like our janitor, is one of the few people around here who won't rat on us. Sandbag, not so much. He probably told Parsnip he saw me.

But I'm midway through my apology when the band downshifts to a sultry pulse.

Mr. Galluci's head snaps toward the dance floor.

"This is the last song," the singer murmurs into the mic, "so grab your honey and get real close."

"Oh, great," Galluci mutters.

He joins the chaperones, nosing their way to the dance floor while the couples, like minnows avoiding sharks, gather under the disco ball that's twisting spheres of prismatic silver light around the gym.

I navigate to the far wall, stepping around the pushed-up bleachers. Even from over here, even in the dark, I can see them.

Couples.

Couples everywhere. So close they merge into one. I push away the pang in my heart, needling me. I remind myself that these couples have no idea. Love isn't a corsage and a limo ride and a shiny dress. It's not even a love song. In fact, if these couples knew the truth, they might avoid the whole thing altogether. I mean, look at my dad. He's vowed to love my mother and what does he get in return? Pain. Suffering. Grief.

And yet, if I know all that, why does it feel like an invisible hand is squeezing my heart?

But when I step outside, the feeling evaporates.

"Where is Miss Parson?" Mr. Ellis says.

"I don't know."

"She went inside to retrieve you."

"Really? I didn't see her." This statement is true. I heard her, while locked in the stall.

"Ah, there you are!" he calls out, as Parsnip barges from the gym.

The woman always looks one degree from boiling over, but her temperature rises as she informs Ellis that Mr. Sandbag "caught" me "running through the halls."

"Neither you nor Miss Levinson have permission to sneak into this school after hours," Parsnip says. "There will be consequences."

Before she can count those out to me, the doors burst open again. The couples start pouring out.

"Form a line!" Ellis shouts. "All rides must be accounted for!"

I walk away, feeling a deep stab of resentment. But the chattering crowd seems to fade when I reach the bike rack. Drew's purple Schwinn is here. Now. I stare at it, trying to figure things out. Maybe she moved the bike after the plumbing truck left? But that still doesn't explain why she didn't come to dinner. I touch the metal frame, glancing around, hoping to see her step from the darkness, a huge smile on her face. The frame feels cold under my fingers. When I look down at the lock, the black cable snakes through the front spokes.

Once.

I lean down.

The lock circles the wheel and the bike rack. But only once.

I stand up. My heart is pounding again. Drew maintains more compulsive habits than I can count, and one of them is twisting that cable through her bike spokes twice. She always makes a figure eight—the sign of infinity.

And another habit—the combination's numbers.

I lift the black bar, reading the five numbers: 5-8-3-9-2.

My heart is rioting.

Never. She would never lock her bike like this. Like that white arrow on her locker must point at zero, Drew always sets this combination back to 0-0-0-0-0.

Always.

I stare at it, feeling like I must be going crazy.

"Raleigh?"

I glance up. My heart kicks again. But this time for a totally different reason. I shake the hair from my eyes, look away.

"I thought that was you," he says.

Unlike all these other rent-a-tux guys, DeMott Fielding's tuxedo looks like every seam was stitched to fit his body. And it's a very nice body. My heart does another flip.

"Why were you running through the gym?" he asks.

I keep telling myself he's not my type. But if that's really true, how come I always find myself looking for him in church? And how come right now I'm trying to find some really cool reason to explain why, dressed in baggy sweats, I bolted through the dance?

As usual, no great words come in time.

"What's wrong?" he asks.

"Nothing."

"You don't look like nothing's wrong. No offense."

I glance down at the bike. It sits there, waiting like some Exhibit A to prove I'm really not a total dork.

"I'm looking for my friend." I even pat the bike frame. As if this proves something. "This is her bike."

He nods. But it's vague, some gesture of politeness. Which makes me feel like an even bigger dork.

I don't want to sound crazy, since everyone knows my mother is completely nuts. But I really don't have a lot of options right now. Tell him the truth, the whole truth, and nothing but the truth? Yeah. I snuck out of my house, ran all the way here, in the dark, and searched the classrooms—and the girls' bathroom—because I can't find my friend.

That doesn't just sound weird—it sounds like I'm gay. Not that I care what he thinks, of course.

"Raleigh." He tilts his head to the side. "I can see something's bothering you. What is it?"

I glance over his shoulder. Ellis is thirty yards away. Parsnip stands across from him, big feet spread like a drill instructor. When I glance back at DeMott, his eyes seem as blue and calm as a clear summer sky.

"I can't find her."

"Who—your friend?"

"Drew, her name's Drew." The rest of it tumbles out, not even in the right order, and I data-dump all over him—her stuff in Physics lab, her mom, dinner-every-Friday, and this bike, Exhibit A. "It was not here when I came by earlier."

I sound crazy.

"I swear it wasn't here," I add quickly. "There was a plumbing truck. Right here. And it backed up to the bike rack and—"

"I believe you."

"—her lock. See how—"

"Raleigh. I believe you."

"You do?"

"Yes. Something's not right."

But I can only stare at the ground. At his black shoes, so polished that the overhead light make the tips appear white. *Something's not right*. His words both make me feel better . . . and worse.

"I'll help you look for her," he says.

Every single thought inside my head starts to collide with its opposite.

First I think—Wow, that would be great. Then—No, terrible. And then—Maybe it would work.

And all that hesitation steals my one chance to invite De-Mott Fielding into my life. Because here comes Satan herself . . .

Tinsley Teager.

Her long platinum hair curls perfectly from her flawless face. She seems to float over the pavement, her lemon yellow gown frothy and feminine.

"I've been looking for you," she says, batting her green eyes at DeMott.

"Raleigh can't find her friend."

"Shame. One more picture, pretty please? The photographer promised he'd wait."

"I was going to help Raleigh."

Tinsley's neck looks rigid. "Help her . . . how?"

"I told you, she can't find her friend."

"Are we talking about Drew Levinson? Wait. What am I

saying?" She giggles at me. "You don't have any other friends."

"Tins, that's not—"

"Missing." Tinsley's smile grows large and white, a veritable glacier of perfect orthodontics. "DeMott, you should know something about Drew Levinson. First of all, she enjoys being the center of attention."

"That's a lie!" I say.

Tinsley turns to him, not faltering for one icy second. "She just called me a liar."

"Raleigh's upset, that's all. I think we should—"

"You're right, DeMott." Her smile grows bigger. "Of course, Raleigh's upset, bless her heart."

Those three words, coming from Tinsley Teager, is like being stabbed in the back and then asked to admire the knife's handle.

"DeMott," she says. "Did Raleigh happen to mention that Drew's run away before?"

He looks at me, questioning.

"That was a long time ago," I say.

"Actually, no," she says. "The whole school turned itself upside down and inside out trying to find that girl. Do you know where she was? Hiding. Hoping to get more attention. Bless her heart."

DeMott is frowning, taking in this new information. I wonder if he thinks I'm a liar.

"Yo, Fielding!"

He turns. In the parking lot, a guy leans from a limo's back window. His red bow tie is askew.

"You and Tins coming?" the guy yells. "Drinks are melting!"

Tinsley gasps. She is our student body president—or, as Drew says, "student busybody president." She spins around, checking to see whether Parsnip and Ellis heard. But they're dealing with Harper Conneally whose black shrug is way too small for her enormous new chest. In fact, a blanket might be too small, but that doesn't stop Parsnip from pinching the shoulders of the little shrug and tugging it down, as if this will change the fact that Harper, who last year was flat as an ironing board, realized she will no longer be ignored by all the guys if she gets a pair of boobs. This summer, she did. As Parsnip makes some futile wardrobe adjustments, Ellis is acting like some termite inspector, staring up at the gym's roof.

Once again, I pounce on opportunity. "Tinsley, did Drew happen to say anything during tutoring?"

"Tutoring?" DeMott looks surprised. "Tins, you're tutoring this girl. That's great."

She takes his arm, patting if flirtatiously. But her smile looks cryogenically frozen. "DeMott, honey. Would you do me just the biggest grandest most wonderful favor in the whole wide world?"

"Of course."

"Please go tell Stuart Morgan to be quiet?" She bats her eyes. "I really can't have him broadcasting across the parking lot. And I'll be right there after you."

"But I have to help Raleigh."

"No, that's okay," I say.

"You sure?" he asks.

No, I'm not sure. I'm not sure of anything tonight, except that having DeMott Fielding wearing his tuxedo while he searches for Drew with Tinsley hounding us in her lemony gown is not the help I need.

"I'm fine," I say. "But thanks. I appreciate the offer."

His blue-eyed gaze lingers on me. One second, two, three. Then he nods, as if some thought has come to him. He turns to leave.

But Tinsley sinks her claws in deeper. Lifting her face to him, she puckers her glossed lips and says, "Kiss, kiss."

I could hurl right here, except for the fact that DeMott only pecks her forehead.

She blinks, stunned.

And then we both watch him walk away. DeMott's one of those guys who looks so comfortable when he walks, like he expects life to move at his speed, not the other way around. I feel so much better just looking at him. And I can't really say why.

But from the corner of my eye I see a yellow flash, right before Tinsley spits out the words.

"Just what the hell do you think you're doing?"

CHAPTER TEN

"I ASKED YOU a question," Tinsley says.

Now that DeMott's out of range, Tinsley's reverting to her true self. It's like seeing Barbie morph into a pit bull. I shift my gaze to DeMott's back, a much-improved view.

Tinsley reaches out, squeezing my arm. "Answer me!"

I shake out of her grip. "I'm looking for Drew."

She laughs, coldly. "Do I look stupid to you?"

"Actually—"

"You know what's wrong with you?" she says, cutting me off. "You've got issues."

"I've got issues?"

"Raleigh, face the facts. Your real dad dumped you, your mom's crazy, and your only friend has run away. Again. And now look at you, bless your heart, wearing sweats to the dance. You're having a public meltdown."

Something runs down my spine, colder than the night wind. Colder than Tinsley's glacial smile. It's true that my birth dad took off. I was four. My mom had to get a job, Helen and I went into cheap daycare, and we rode city busses because we couldn't afford a car. But my clearest memory from those hard years is standing next to my mother in the grocery story. She was picking out collard greens—cheap green food—for our dinner. A song played overhead and she was singing to it. A man stopped to stare at her. He was very, very handsome and I felt ashamed of my mother, singing in public, picking over that stiff green food we hated eating. But the man didn't leave. He kept watching her, looking at her like he knew her. More than that—he looked at her like he'd known her his whole life. Eight months later, that man, David Harmon, married my mom and we moved into his big house on Monument Avenue and never rode the city bus again. David Harmon is my real dad.

And yet still the cold feeling sinks all the way into my bone marrow. I don't like Tinsley. But right now I need her help. So I strap on that fake smile I swore never to use and which is already becoming a habit.

"I'll make you a deal, Tinsley. You tell me what Drew said during your tutoring session today, and I won't tell DeMott you're the one who's getting tutored."

Her beady eyes narrow. She might be dumber than sandstone and shallow as a dry creek bed, but she's also the snakiest of snakes. So our stare down continues and I don't blink. I notice her skin, how it's perfect. No freckles. Not one zit. Not even a blemish. I decide evil has to look this good or else we'd immediately recognize it.

She breaks eye contact first. "Drew didn't really say anything."

"Tinsley—"

She lifts one skinny arm, waving to the couples hurrying across the parking lot to the waiting limos. "See y'all real soon!" she chirps.

I want to grab her bony shoulders, shake her, force her to talk. But my dad, the judge, says lawyers often make the mistake of "leading the witness" with questions that make him doubt their testimony. I want the truth. So I wait.

"Lookin' good!" she calls out.

"Tinsley." My teeth are gritted. "Tell. Me."

"Before I say anything," she turns to me, her white smile like frost, "you have to make a promise."

"What."

"Promise-hope-I-die-stick-a-needle-in-my—"

"What!"

She looks offended. "Don't be rude."

"Cut to the chase."

"Promise you'll stay away from him."

I frown. "Who?"

"Who else would I be talking about? DeMott!"

"You must be kidding."

Her green eyes widen. "I most certainly am not kidding. He's interested in you, for some ungodly reason. It should automatically disqualify him, but . . ." She gives a skinny shrug.

"But he's so rich."

"Oh, please." She rolls her eyes and laughs. It sounds like crackling ice. "Rich guys are a dime a dozen."

I wait, just in case she actually realizes her ironic pun. But the wit sails right over her pretty head.

"Oh, I get it." I nod. "It's the Fielding name you want. All that land, the mansion—"

"In any event," she cuts me off. Because I'm right. The Fieldings own 3,000 acres of prime real estate along the James River. It's been in their family since England owned Virginia, since the King gave charters to colonists. Something like sixteen generations have lived in the estate's mansion.

"So we have a deal?" she asks. "You stay away from De-Mott, which means you can never tell him I'm being tutored."

"Okay, fine, whatever, just tell me what Drew said."

Tinsley leans in close, like we're suddenly co-conspirators. Her perfume smells sweet but simple, like hothouse flowers.

"Drew cancelled."

I pull back to get fresh air. "Why did she cancel?"

"You think I care? I was thrilled not to have to listen to her babbling about the 'wonders of math,' especially when I needed to get ready for Homecoming." She runs another cold glance over me, stopping at my Converses. "Not that you would understand."

She's right—I would never understand a lot of other things. Like, why the world keeps putting people like Tinsley at the top.

"So Drew didn't tell you why she cancelled?"

"No."

"You're lying."

"I beg your pardon!"

"Tinsley, she's obsessed with cause-and-effect. So even if *you* didn't care why she was canceling, she'd give you a reason. She can't help it. So, what did she say?"

She rubs a skinny hand over a skinny arm. "It's freezing out here."

"Okay, look, if you can't—"

"I need to get DeMott's jacket."

I step in front of her. "Tell me what she said."

"Raleigh, here's a news flash." She smiles. "Nobody cares about y'all. So even if Drew did say something, I didn't pay attention because nobody's paying attention to you two weirdos. Understand?"

"Tinnnsleeeeee."

We both turn.

Norwood Godwin is heading our way.

Most of us Southern girls have family names for our first names—Tinsley, MacKenna, and probably Raleigh, although my mom's never given me a clear answer—but of all of us, Norwood got the short end of a stick with a name that sounds like a euphemism for dork. It doesn't help that she's a husky girl—not fat, just big—who should go out for softball or shot put, but instead squeezes herself into clothing made for girls like Tinsley, girls as bony as coat hangers.

Tonight, Norwood has crowbarred her substantial figure into a bright orange satin gown held up by floss-thin spaghetti straps. The sight of her makes the words fly off my tongue.

"That dress!"

"Isn't it gorgeous," Tinsley says. "I picked it out myself."

"And she's still your friend?"

She turns to me. "Orange is very au courant right now. Not that you have any great fashion sense."

This is also true.

But I know enough not to dress like a shellacked pumpkin.

"Tins," Norwood says, "what're you doing way over here?"

"You'll never believe it. Drew Levinson ran away."

"Again?"

"Not 'again.' " My voice rises with frustration. "That was a long time ago."

"Sixth grade." Norwood looks at Tinsley. "Does that count as a long time ago?"

"No. But Raleigh's in denial. Bless her heart."

"Hey," Norwood says. "Let's tell Mr. Ellis to start the phone tree again." The phone tree is for emergencies. Snow days. School cancellations. "Worked great last time. Everyone got to see how weird Drew really is."

Tinsley sighs. "I'm sure she's going to pop up somewhere tomorrow, expecting us to care."

"You need to come on. They're waiting for us in the limo."

"DeMott, you mean." Tinsley fixes her green eyes on me. "DeMott is waiting for me in the limo."

They start to walk away, but before they've gone three paces, Tinsley turns her head, calling over her emaciated shoulder. "Don't forget your promise, Raleigh."

I stand by the bike rack, watching the human pumpkin and a skinny slice of lemon meringue walk over to Ellis and Parsnip. Both Tinsley and Norwood have that practiced fake smile. I wait to see if they say anything about Drew, but after practically bowing to authority, they dash to the waiting white limo. Parsnip and Ellis don't even look over at me.

The limo's back door opens. Laughter and cheers leak out.

I don't like those two. I really don't. But that ache is back, grabbing my heart again, the feeling that hit me inside the gym.

Tinsley's wrong—I'm not in denial. I know exactly what I'm feeling.

Jealousy.

I'm jealous of two really awful people.

Because at least they have each other.

I RUN THROUGH the darkened West End, occasionally seeing a blue flicker in a window. Somebody up late, watching television. The idea only makes me feel more alone.

River Road, also empty, pulls my legs down the hill, gravity doing all the work because my legs are too tired. I jog across the Huguenot Bridge, over the James River, then cut directly underneath where I can hear water washing over the rocks, splashing its way to downtown. And my breathing. I can hear my breathing—I am breathing hard.

Once I asked her, "Where did you go?"

The end of seventh grade. We'd been friends for almost a year, the whole time I was dying to know what happened that night she ran away. There was plenty of speculation around school—Drew took drugs, Drew had sex with random guys. I heard it all.

But nobody knew. For sure.

"Where did you go?"

The question came suddenly, when we weren't even talking about That Night. But now, walking beside the river in the dark, searching for her, I realize that's one of the things about having a best friend—you don't have to explain. Anything. You find your best friend, and suddenly some secret code gets written into your cells. You know each other.

You just know.

"The river," she answered, immediately knowing what I was asking. "I went down to the river."

"What for?"

"Because water is required in order to drown oneself."

Back then, Jayne and Rusty were fighting like caged rats. They divorced soon after.

"Only you didn't drown yourself," I pointed out.

"Obviously," she said. "I realized that if I drowned myself, nobody would finish my experiments. Not even you."

That was Drew—totally rational, completely focused on cause and effect, even when contemplating suicide.

The gravel crunches under my shoes. And I can smell the river now, its deep, rich layered mud on the banks. I walk to the only light, shining over a small wooden boat launch. The water slides past like a channel of black ink.

"Drew!"

My palms are already sweaty from the run, but as I walk away from that single light, I feel a new spurt of perspiration. And panic. The dark feels as thick as molten tar. The gravel snaps like teeth.

"Drew Levinson!"

I know there's a narrow trail down here; I've run it plenty

of times in daylight. But as I creep forward in the dark, it seems to get farther away. I turn my head sideways, forcing my peripheral vision to work on the black curtain in front of me. Finally I find the wooden bridge that crosses the feeder creek, but halfway across, I stop. The water gurgles below me. But there's another sound. Something moving.

"Drew . . .?"

A groan fills the dark.

"Drew!" I pivot, trying to locate the sound. Coming from my right. I think. But a second groan rises on my left. I turn in a circle, feeling blood pounding inside my head, so hard I can't hear straight. Adrenaline. Running. Fear of the dark.

"Drew—it's me—Raleigh!"

Something flies out of the dark. I jump back, scream when it lands at my feet.

More. They come moaning and leaping, bellowing into the night—frogs springing up from the creek, sliming my face, kissing my arms.

My next scream cracks my voice.

I race down the trail, hands swinging in front of my face. Something squishes under my shoe. My throat gags. At the end of the bridge, I trip, get up, sprint until gravel crunches under my shoes.

I cannot stop.

CHAPTER ELEVEN

W HAT STOPS ME is Drew's back door, which I throw open—it's never locked—and burst inside.

"Drew," I pant. "Please. Be here."

There's not even a hiss from Isaac Newton.

The house feels dark, a different kind of dark than outside, more like what you get pulling a blanket over your head. Suffocating dark. When I step into the kitchen, two empty wine bottles stand by the sink. Above them, on the wall, the cuckoo clock swings its pendulum. But the *tap-tap-tap* coming from behind its little door means Jayne still has the little bird locked inside and he's trying to announce my arrival—1:30 a.m.

In the den, I find Jayne sprawled on the couch. An almost-empty wine glass waits on the coffee table. Her eyes are closed, but the television is on and some woman is demonstrating how to sauté garlic. And prawns. I look back at Jayne. She wears faded yellow pajamas that match the dying leaves outside.

I've never seen the woman so much as stir a can of soup, but for some reason she's obsessed with the cooking channels. You'd think it was because she works for Reynolds Aluminum, but I've seen the expression on her face when she watches these people. Like somebody who can't swim, stranded on the beach while everyone else splashes in the water.

"Jayne."

Her forehead is scrunched down, like she's arguing her way through a dream.

"Jayne!"

Nothing. Not even an eye twitch.

I walk upstairs. In Drew's bedroom everything looks exactly the same, which is to say—in order. Her books line three walls, each section grouped topically, then alphabetically by author. Baseball gets an entire wall; to the right, applied science. Then chemistry, general science—with a nod to geology for me—and then tons of physics books that include everything written by Richard P. Feynman. Above her twin bed, the famous physicist grins from a poster. He looks like he's watching the hanging mobile of sun-surrounded-by-planets.

Her closet door is ajar. When I open it further, Isaac Newton leaps out.

After the attack of frogs, I'm feeling fairly freaked out. There's enough adrenaline remaining in my system to yell, "Get lost, Newton!"

He arches his back, displaying his sharp little teeth.

"Not impressed," I tell him.

Drew's clothes hang in compulsive color-coded order. One empty hanger waits in front, where she hangs her St. Cat's uniform. Her shirts—nearly all purple and never pink—look like they're all here. Same with her jeans, which she hangs because she hangs everything, even summer shorts. Her laundry hamper is empty.

I check the other bedrooms, five total. So many that I've always wondered if Rusty and Jayne hoped for more kids, before they realized they couldn't stand each other. In the master bedroom, Jayne's king-sized bed is layered with satin pillows. The rest of the room looks surprisingly spare. Same with two bedrooms that are guest rooms. Everything looks stripped down. In the final room, cardboard boxes sit on the floor, their flaps open.

I walk back downstairs. The television tutorial continues.

"Make sure you don't overcook the peppers. Two, three minutes at most. Nothing's worse than overcooked peppers."

I stare at Jayne. There's something so pathetic about her that half my anger evaporates. She's curled on her side, knees tucked into her stomach like the dream's shifted to somebody coming to kick her. I lift a blanket off the back of the couch and lay it over her. She doesn't even twitch.

I carry her wine glass into the kitchen, dumping the half-inch of ice-diluted wine into the sink. It splashes like blood.

Newton yowls.

I look over. His Siamese-blue eyes lock on mine.

"Now what's your problem?"

He minces over to his bowl, letting out another yowl.

Inside the pantry, I find a can of choice liver niblets. After two years of Friday nights here, this kitchen feels more familiar than my own. I dump the meat-barf into his bowl and rinse the can in the sink—restraining my gag reflex—because one of Drew's rules is clean garbage. She doesn't care if it's an oxymoron. I'm about to turn off the tap, but when I look up, I catch my reflection in the window.

If I thought I looked bad in the girls' bathroom tonight, things have gotten worse. Shadows circle my eyes. My pony tail has drifted down to my shoulders, loose hair framing a face almost sheet-white. For as long as I can remember, night has always scared me—not just the dark, but the fact that there's going to be this long stretch of time when I'm all alone. Even when my mom and dad used to let me crawl into bed with them, once they went to sleep, I was alone again. Everyone else slumbers until dawn. But my mind only ramps up, the thoughts pinging through my head so fast I can't follow them. And then, as soon as I see that gray hint of light on the horizon, I suddenly feel like sleeping. Because I stop worrying. A little.

But this night is the longest of my entire life.

I walk back to the den. The cooking host says, "The food should look pretty on the plate, too."

Newton comes into the room after me, licking his whiskers. He jumps on the couch, walks up Jayne's legs and squats on her head. He stares at me, victorious, some sphinx guarding the temple of drunkenness.

I pick up the telephone on the end table and a notepad with Drew's precise penmanship explaining the speed dial crib sheet: Raleigh #1. Dad #2. And way down the list—after information hotlines for Harvard, Yale, and Massachusetts Institute of Technology—is Jayne, at work, #9.

I glance at my watch, trying to decide if eccentric artists stay up all night and whether Rusty will even pick up the phone. I hit the 2-button and listen to the rings. The cooking host starts making dessert.

I hang up, call again.

And again.

He picks up as the show is ending.

"What?!" he says.

"Is this Rusty?"

"Who's this?"

"Raleigh."

There's a pause.

I give him a clue, "Drew's friend."

"Oh. Right."

"Is she there?"

"Who?"

"Drew."

"Drew?"

"Your daughter?" It's rude to say, but it's a good thing these people only had one kid. "She didn't show up for dinner tonight. I've been looking for her. She still isn't home."

"What time is it?"

Restraining a sigh, I explain the whole night. Dinner. Bike. Physics lab. "I even went down to the river. You know, because last time . . ."

"Yeah, yeah," he says. "Where's her mother?"

I look over at Jayne. Sitting on her head, Newton whips his tail across her face.

"She's right here."

"Put her on the phone."

"I can't."

"Why not?"

"She's passed out."

"What a surprise," he says bitterly.

"Rusty, do you know where Drew is?"

"No."

"You don't sound worried."

"I'm not. She pulled this same stunt last summer, when she was here for a weekend. I told her she couldn't live with me, and she was gone the rest of the day. Next morning she finally showed up for breakfast."

"Did she tell you where she went?"

"No. She just needed to blow off some steam."

I sympathized. Right now I'd like to blow off both Rusty and Jayne.

"But her bike's at school," I tell him, again, since I'm not sure he's listening. "And her notebook and jean jacket are in the Physics lab at school."

"So?"

"So I think we should call the police."

"Oh, c'mon. Take it easy. She's just ticked at her mother. Thanks for calling."

He hangs up.

There's a new host cooking on the TV. She's telling me about her favorite breakfasts for cold autumn mornings. I barely hear the words. But in the kitchen, the cuckoo seems loud. It taps at its door. Twice.

Morning, morning.

Everyone is talking about the morning—my dad, Rusty, the cuckoo—like some automatic change will happen. The woman on TV starts putting together an egg casserole.

It's 2:00 a.m.

Which means morning is already here.

And Drew is not.

I call the police.

TWENTY MINUTES LATER, Officer KC Lande is standing on the front stoop. She is tiny and freckled and the widest part of her is the gun belt circling her waist. She listens as I explain why I called—listens to the whole story with a face that looks hard as stone.

"Where are her parents?" she asks.

I lead Officer Lande into the den, where Isaac Newton is still camping on Jayne's head.

"Ma'am?" she says to Jayne. "Hello, ma'am?"

Officer Lande looks over at me. Under her freckled skin, the cheekbones seem as prominent as rock formations.

"How much did she drink?" she asks.

"Couple bottles of wine. But that's every Friday night."

She reaches down, shaking Jayne's shoulder. Isaac Newton hisses but Officer Lande doesn't even pay attention to him. She shakes harder.

"Ma'am! It's the police!"

Jayne's face contorts. But it still takes several more prompts from Officer Lande until Jayne sits up, throwing Isaac Newton off balance. Her eyes open, sort of, trying to focus on the person in the blue uniform standing right in front of her.

"Ma'am, we received a phone call about your daughter," says Officer Lande.

"What she do now."

All one word—Wa-shee-dew-now.

"Have you been drinking?" Officer Lande asks.

"Jussalittle."

Sir Isaac Newton has left an electrostatic charge on Jayne's hair. The rising strands make her look even more messed up. She looks at me, frowning.

I explain that it's past 2:00 a.m. and Drew's still not home.

"Teenagers." Jayne rolls her head toward Officer Lande. "You got kids?"

"No, ma'am. When was the last time you saw your daughter?"

"Breck-fust."

I wonder if that's true. Jayne usually leaves for work at 5:30 every morning—so she can be the first person into the office—and Drew usually gets herself up, riding her bike to school. I try to signal Officer Lande, but she's watching Jayne.

"Ma'am, do you have any idea where your daughter might be?"

Jayne waves her hand, indicating my general area. "Ask her."

"Me?"

"Ma'am, she's the one who called us."

"Wants to make trouble."

"No I don't!"

Officer Lande gives me a long look. Then back to Jayne. "Ma'am, why would she want to make trouble?"

"Why?" Jayne starts to laugh. It only lasts a second. Then she looks confused. "What time's it?"

"Quarter after two," Officer Lande says. Then adds, "In the morning."

"Time for bed!"

Jayne shoves herself off the couch. Isaac Newton seems to know what's coming because he leaps all the way off the couch. Jayne stands, wavering like she's going to fall backwards, before Officer Lande grabs her elbow. Jayne yanks it away and manages to shuffle around the coffee table. Then shuffles over to where I'm standing. Her wine-drenched breath makes me blink.

"You can't stop me," she says.

"What?"

Her glassy eyes find Officer Lande again. "Experiment. They do this. Gonna hide. Call the cops. Try to stop the move."

"What move?" I ask.

"North."

"North?"

Officer Lande moves closer. "Ma'am, are you saying your daughter ran away because you're moving?"

"Zactly. Refuses to go."

I can feel Officer Lande watching me, expecting me to say something, but every word is bunched into my throat.

"You're moving—?" I manage, finally.

"Monday."

"But—" I can't find other words, even with my mouth hanging open.

"N'York." Jayne smooths her hair. "Promotion. Can't wait."

The boxes. Suddenly I remember those cardboard boxes in the empty bedroom. The bare appearance of Jayne's bedroom. She's packing up, heading out. Drew's refusing to go.

But why didn't she tell me Jayne planned to move? How could she keep that big a deal from me?

"Ma'am." Officer Lande is following Jayne from the room. "I'd like to get some clarification, if you don't mind."

But Jayne makes a direct path to the front door, opening it with a flourish. "Not interested. G'night."

Before we are barely outside, she slams the door.

CHAPTER TWELVE

O FFICER LANDE TOUCHES the radio clipped to her shoulder. She tells them where she is, that she's leaving the house. I stare out at the yard, blanketed with leaves, hoping Drew will step out of the dark.

"So that's it?" I say.

"Raleigh—it's Raleigh, correct?"

"Raleigh Harmon."

"Do you know it's against the law to file a false report with the police?"

"It's a Class 1 misdemeanor."

She stares at me. "How do you know that?"'

"I just do." I've spent so many hours sitting in my dad's courtroom—escaping the hell that is home—that I could practically work as a paralegal. But I'm not telling her that. Last thing I need is a cop calling my dad when I've snuck out of the house. "And since I know it's a Class 1 misdemeanor, I also know it can carry a heavy fine. Filing a false report to the police is probably, what, two thousand dollars? So if I know all that, why in the world would I file a false report?"

She opens her mouth but I continue.

"The answer is—I wouldn't. Drew Levinson is missing."

"You might also know that she's not officially missing until twenty-four hours have passed."

"She's a minor."

"And with minors," she says slowly, "the parents have to file the report. Unless we see signs of foul play, suspicious activity . . ."

"You just saw her mother—she's drunk."

Officer Lande hikes her shoulders. "She gets behind the wheel of a car, okay, I can do something. Otherwise, no. Where's her dad?"

"Forget it."

I scan the dark trees again. If Jayne's really planning to move to New York, Drew might've taken off. But why wouldn't she tell me? It's not sixth grade, when she had no friends. I'm closer to her than my own sister. And how come Rusty didn't mention the move?

"And why is her stuff still at school?" I say out loud.

"You got me," Officer Lande says. "If it helps, we get these calls almost every night. Kids take off, do stupid things. Most of the time it works out. Eventually."

"Drew doesn't do stupid things. Her mother does."

I shiver as another gust of wind kicks up the leaves. The night feels cold, damp. Rain is coming. Then what?

Officer Lande nods her head toward the police cruiser, parked in the driveway.

"Need a lift?"

THE SEAT IS hard plastic. The back curves inward at the base. When I sit down I realize what it's for—when a person's hands are cuffed behind their back.

"You do this often?" she asks.

I look up. A steel mesh cage separates the front and back seats. "Do what?"

"Sneak out at night?"

"Never."

"You mean, just this once?"

I can only see her eyes in the rearview mirror, so it's hard to judge her expression. Is she being serious? Mocking? Her eyes were gray inside Drew's house. But the pale light from the dashboard makes them look watery blue, like opals.

"I'm not lying about Drew, if that's what you're implying."

"I'm not implying anything. But if you're lying to me, you're a good liar."

"I'm a lousy liar. You can ask my—"

I stop.

I was going to say, *You can ask my mom*. But Officer Lande might think that's a really good idea. I can only imagine what would happen if a police officer pulls up to our house—at this hour—to ask my mom why I'm not in my room.

The whole idea scares the night-fear right out of me.

"So your parents don't know you're out here," she says, as if reading my thoughts.

I stare out the back window. The stark city still looks black-and-white. And everything inside of me feels gray. "No, they don't know."

When we reach Monument Avenue, I hear the familiar rumble of the cobblestones. Only now it sounds ominous, like a menacing drumroll. I sit forward as Officer Lande swings around the Robert E. Lee rotary, then show her how to cut behind our house into the alley.

"I take it you don't want your parents to know," she says. "Why's that, if your friend's in trouble?"

"My mom—she—" But I can't finish the sentence. What's the point? Nobody understands. Nobody except Drew. Finally, I say, "My mom worries a lot."

"What about your dad?"

"He worries when she worries. So my job is to make sure he doesn't worry."

"Sounds like a big job for a kid."

The cruiser's headlights rake the brick wall guarding our back patio. She stops at the carriage house then leans forward, taking in the buildings.

"I always wondered who lived in these grand old houses." She turns her head to look at me. "Now I know."

"Only we're not like any of the neighbors."

She laughs.

"Seriously."

"Even better." She smiles and reaches into a cup holder attached to her dashboard, taking out a small white card. She writes something on the back, bends it lengthwise, and pushes it through the cage. "Call me if you hear anything about your friend. Good or bad."

"What if I don't hear anything?"

"Then get her parents to call."

"You mean there's nothing I can do?"

"Not unless there's evidence of foul play." She turns serious. "And we don't want that. Let's just hope she goes home soon."

I thank her for the ride, the card, and—though I don't say it out loud—for not getting all righteous about telling my parents.

She nods.

I open the gate and sneak across the patio. The cruiser pulls away. I glance up. My parents' bedroom window is dark. My sister Helen's room above theirs is also dark, and then above it is the slate roof. The night sky is no longer clear. The wind has pushed in thick clouds, their bellies lit by the city lights. They have dark charcoal smears, the color of rain.

The French doors to the kitchen are still unlocked, like I left them. But now a heavy layer of condensation has formed on the glass panels, a problem Drew once explained to me. Our old wooden mullions aren't good at heat differential, transferring the cold outside between the warm inside. I'm careful touching the glass. Smear all that beaded up water, and my mother might freak out tomorrow morning.

My next hurdle is the staircase. Thirty-seven steps to the third floor—I've counted it, daily—and since the house is a hundred years old, every step wants to say something. But one good thing about my mother's paranoia, it's taught me how to creep around my own house. I stick to the outer edges of each step and reach the third floor with only one squeak. Next up is my bedroom door. It has iron hinges that squeal like pigs in damp weather. I spend forever opening the door an inch at a time, then another forever closing it.

But finally I'm in my room, leaning against the wood door, closing my eyes, wanting to cry from relief. Or maybe just loneliness. I want to call Drew and tell her about tonight, and she's the sad reason tonight even happened.

I can feel a really sickening sob waiting at the back of my throat. I press it back, keeping my eyes shut tight.

Suddenly there's a rustle of paper nearby.

I open my eyes. My desk. The paper. Wind flows through my open window. Touches my hair. Sends a chill down my spine.

When I left, my window was closed.

Drew!

I rush over, leaning over the sill, reaching out, nearly touch the magnolia tree that runs up the side of the house. But I know the limbs would never hold her, even as light as she is. I reach down, touching the ivy climbing over the brick. The vines grip the brick, secure, the leaves shining milky in the floodlights from across the street, glowing around Robert E. Lee. I brush my hand down the ivy again and again. But nothing's torn.

Then again, Drew only weighs ninety-eight pounds.

I turn around, checking out the room. My backpack still sits by my chair. The zipper isn't completely closed but when I reach inside, rooting around, nothing's gone. Even the soil samples from the tunnel are still there.

I check the armoire, see my school uniform once again balled up on the floor right where I threw it after my mother traced my foot. I check under the bed. I even tiptoe down the hall to the bathroom.

She's not here.

When I climb into bed, I start to wonder if maybe I did open that window and forgot. I'm so tired, it's possible. Still wearing the sweats I ran in, I lay still as stone until my eyes won't stay open. I feel myself slipping into sleep, that delicious exhausted sleep that even insomnia can't catch. I take a deep breath, letting it take away the sting in my toes, my raw toes. Then I pull in one last breath. Sleep is here, waiting for me. Dawn is coming, safe to fall asleep.

The bolt of panic makes me sit straight up. My heart slams into my ribs.

It's not just the open window.

Before I snuck out, I stuffed my pillows under my comforter in case my dad—or mom—happened to check on me.

I reach back, touching the pillows.

Somebody took them out.

CHAPTER THIRTEEN

I WAKE UP to the smell of cinnamon. Warm, sweet, delicious, the scent drifts under my door. My mouth waters.

Except I know better.

I want to yank the covers over my head and beg sleep to come back, but all of last night flashes in my mind.

Drew.

Maybe she's home now.

I jump out of bed, wincing at the pain in my toes and shivering. I left the window open, just in case she climbed up the side of my house, and the air is icy cold in my room. And wet. The rain has left a small puddle on the floor. I mop it up, change out of my sweats into pajamas, and pull clean socks over my wounded feet. When I walk down the back stairs to the kitchen, the ones made for the servants who no longer live here, I make sure to hit every squeaking step. I don't want anybody in the kitchen surprised.

My mother, however, doesn't turn around. She's at the stove, which I expected, given the deceptive cinnamon scent. But she's also wearing a bright pink apron—with ruffles on it. Generally, I hate pink. But right now I really hate this pink because it screams Suzy Homemaker Took Her Meds!

Now I know we're in trouble.

I glance at my dad. He's sitting at the table, reading the

morning newspaper.

"How'd you sleep?" he asks, lowering the paper.

"Fine."

My mom continues to keep her back to me. She's gazing into the oven's glass door. When these domestic moods hit her, she will watch casseroles bake and water boil. Even the meds can't change Paranoid Cooking 101.

I check the answering machine by fridge. It still shows a big red zero.

"Anyone call this morning?" I ask, hoping to sound casual.

My dad answers from behind the newspaper. "No."

My mother turns. "Was someone supposed to call?"

The paper lowers. We've both heard her tone but when I glance at my dad, I can see he's expecting me to say something. The next split second stretches to eternity as I scramble for the right reply. But this is what comes to me—"DeMott Fielding."

"DeMott Fielding?" she says. "From church?"

I glance at my dad. Relief washes over his face.

"Yes, DeMott." I feel my own relief. First, this is not a lie—DeMott did call yesterday, so theoretically he could call today. Second, my mother adores that guy. And third, she's looking at me like maybe I really am her daughter.

"That young man is the most handsome thing in Richmond," she says.

"You're making me jealous." my dad says.

"Now, David, you know I wouldn't trade you for all the pie in Georgia." She walks over to him—actually leaves her vigil over the casserole—to kiss him.

Maybe the meds are working.

Normal for my parents is an all-out flirt-fest. Hugs, kisses, teasing. It's embarrassing.

I turn around so I don't have to watch and open the fridge,

rummaging for my Coca Cola. It's way at the bottom in back, behind all the disgusting healthy food. I keep my head down long enough for them to finish their gooey flirting.

But when I stand up my dad says, "Raleigh?"

"What?"

He clears his throat.

"Pardon," I say.

"Your mother asked you a question."

"Sorry, what?" I turn to my mom.

"Raleigh," he sighs. "Pardon."

"Pardon. Ma'am?"

"Why would DeMott Fielding be calling you?"

"I don't know." I stand there, the cold can of Coke freezing my palm. My mind has gone blank.

And my dad knows it. He jumps in.

"Nadine, if I didn't know better, I'd think you were the one with a crush on that boy."

"I don't have a crush on him," I say.

They aren't listening. They're back to flirting.

"Now David, you know the facts. You're the love of my life. But Raleigh ought to marry that boy."

Okay, great. Maybe now she really does think I'm her "real" daughter. This whole conversation is way too much to process after four hours of sleep. Snapping open the Coke, I draw out the phffftt of carbonation, letting it express my feelings on this subject. My dad gives me a look over the top of the newspaper, the one that says I'm once again breaking the South's Eleventh commandment: Thou Shalt Not Be Rude.

But I've apparently earned enough goodwill bringing up DeMott that he doesn't correct me. I sit down across from him and stare at the newspaper's front page. It tells me everything else that went wrong in Richmond last night. Two shootings in Creighton Court. One armed car-jacking on East Main Street.

Robberies on Northside.

Not one word about a fourteen-year-old girl genius who disappeared, leaving her bike at school.

Because she's home now?

I want to run. Run all the way to the West End, run over the leaves in their driveway, run up the stairs to Drew's compulsively neat bedroom and find her snoozing in bed. But on a Saturday morning, when my mom's taking her meds and acting like Betty Crocker, no quick exits exist.

I gulp my Coke.

She turns on the exhaust fan over the stove and lays what appears to be bacon—but can't be—into a smoking pan. The sizzle smokes. She turns the fan on higher, louder. My dad had the powerful fan installed after she started burning those crazy notes.

When he lowers the paper, he speaks to me in a voice so low she can't hear. "I found the carriage house unlocked this morning."

"Sorry. I went bike riding."

"Where to?"

"Oh, you know, Drew's house."

"What time?"

"After school."

I hold his gaze. Holding, holding, holding until suddenly my mom is here, slipping plates of food in front of us.

"Let's eat!" she sings.

Barring the cannibals in New Guinea, my mother could be the worst cook on Earth. It's probably her most un-Southern trait, and my dad doesn't seem to care.

"Oh, sweetheart," he says, "you really outdid yourself."

He folds his paper and she settles into the chair beside him, still wearing that stupid frilly pink apron. My parents always sit *thisclose*. Even in restaurants, they'll push their chairs together.

I stare at the food, commanding myself to choke it down. When I look up, my mom is dabbing her eyes.

"What's wrong?" he asks, sounding worried.

She points, misty-eyed, at the empty chair beside me.

Helen's empty chair. My sister.

"It's simply not the same without her." My mom's voice quivers. "I miss her so much."

I pick up my fork, disgusted.

My dad kisses her cheek. "Let's dedicate this morning's grace to Helen."

"Like she cares," I mutter.

"Raleigh," my dad warns.

Helen is an atheist. One of those people so passionate about God not existing that atheism turns into a religion. She also declared herself a vegetarian—at age eleven. Given the cuisine in this house, it's almost understandable. But by sixteen, she joined a bunch of freakish political groups, including one my dad said was probably too Communist for Stalin. The list of stupid things my sister does is a mile long. But my mom never sees any fault with her.

Helen is just too smart.

Helen needs room to grow.

Helen's finding her way.

Personally, I'm glad she found her way to Yale. Let her be somebody else's pain in the butt.

"Raleigh, why don't you say grace for us?" My dad looks at me as if reading my mind.

I stare back at him.

But he's giving me a really weird look. Not just reminding me to love my sister but something more. Something that tells me, right there over a meal that will nauseate me, that he opened my window last night. He removed my pillows. He checked the carriage house. A sudden stabs of panic hits my chest. I glance over at my mom. Her head is bowed, waiting for grace, her black hair hanging over her face, touching the silly pink apron.

I look back at my dad. Another horrible pang hits my heart. My dad, he's holding us all together.

I close my eyes. "God, I don't ask you for much."

My dad clears his throat.

"Okay, I ask you for a lot of things." My throat feels raw, like I swallowed nails. Not enough sleep, too much screaming at the river. Drew. Oh, Drew. "Please keep her safe, God. And please let her know how much she's loved, even if the people around her aren't good at showing love. And please—please bring her home safely. Thank you. Amen."

Two "Amens" echo back.

When I open my eyes, the scrambled eggs stare up at me like a dare. They are suspiciously pale, probably made from that powdered egg mix that makes me crave potato chips. They're scrambled with other things too—diced onions? potatoes? I can't tell. The only thing I recognize are green peppers. Suddenly I hear that TV chef from last night, saying there's nothing worse than overcooked peppers.

The TV chef is wrong.

The worst thing is staring at this food, knowing you have to eat it. Because if you don't, your mom will feel wounded, then scared, then start asking if you didn't eat the food because you think it's poisoned. And when someone's paranoid-crazy, that question doesn't have any good answer. "No" means "yes."

I pick up my fork.

But my mother is crying, dabbing her eyes with her napkin.

"Nadine?" he asks.

She doesn't say anything. He glances at me. I shrug.

"Honey?"

Maybe her meds need adjusting. Maybe ramping right into Homemaker mode was too much, too fast.

I stab the eggs.

"That grace," she sobs.

"What Raleigh said?"

Oh, no.

She sniffs, wipes her eyes. "I knew it was only a matter of time."

He glances at me. I hold my breath.

"Only a matter of time until . . . ?" he asks.

"Until Raleigh would pray for Helen like that." She beams at me. "I'm so glad you're back, sweetheart!"

I take a bite of the eggs.

They turn to dust in my mouth.

CHAPTER FOURTEEN

MY MOM'S BALLAST-LIKE meals make running feel impossible so I unlock the carriage house and haul out the bike. The rain starts to fall hard as I'm riding past the headquarters for the Daughters of the Confederacy, slashing leaves from the trees, pummeling them on the pavement until it all turns into a dull amber confetti.

When I get to Drew's house, I leave my dripping jacket in the sunroom with Isaac Newton, who recoils, and find Jayne sitting in the kitchen. She clutches a large blue Reynolds coffee mug and stares into space.

Her eyes are as red as last night's wine.

"Is she here?" I ask.

She barely shakes her head.

There's an odd stillness to her, a blank expression that reminds me of something last week, when Drew came bounding down the hall to Lit class. That alone tipped me off, since Drew says purgatory does exist and it's English Literature with Sandbag, so I asked her, "What's going on?"

"We talked," Drew said.

"Who?"

"Me and Jayne!"

"Jayne and I," I corrected, sounding like my dad.

"The point is," she said, laughing, "Jayne wanted to talk. I mean, really talk. I thought I was in trouble but she was asking about my experiments. She said we might get a dog."

"Was she drunk?"

Drew didn't answer that question. "I kept thinking, Who are you and where have you been all my life?"

That whole day, Drew was giddy, floating with happiness I'd never seen in her before. Maybe because she finally had a normal mother.

But the next day, her cynical self was back. And then some.

"What happened now?" I asked.

"I told Jayne how much that talk meant to me."

"Okay."

"What do you think she said, after that? You get one guess."

"She said you can't name the dog Richard P. Feynman."

"Hardly. She said, 'When?' "

"When—what?"

"When did we have this talk."

"Oh."

"Raleigh, you don't get it." Drew's eyes stormed with emotion. "She doesn't even remember. Any of it. That whole great talk? It got washed away by wine."

And now I see why Drew was so distressed.

I stand there, watching Jayne as Isaac Newton saunters into the kitchen, jumps on the island and cat-walks down to her. But she doesn't seem to see him. Even when he yowls, her eyes look like the people with Alzheimer's, like they're made of glass. Suddenly, I wonder if Drew came home, would Jayne even know it?

I take the stairs by twos. When I push open Drew's door, Feynman grins from the poster.

The bed is still made. I open her closet, just in case. That empty hanger swings at me. On the floor, I see the empty space where she compulsively parks her Converse All Stars— purple All Stars, of course. But I know she brings those shoes to school, pulling them on as soon as the final bell rings, to match the purple jean jacket.

Which she left in the Physics lab.

I can hear footsteps on the stairs.

It's Jayne. She steadies herself, holding the handrail. God forgive me, I feel a really strong temptation to push her.

"Aren't you even worried?" I say.

"She'll come home when she gets hungry."

"She's probably already hungry—she's been gone since yesterday."

Jayne waves me off, walks down the hallway to her bedroom.

"Did you call Rusty?" I call to her back.

"You call him." She closes her door.

I go back into Drew's room, grab the purple Princess phone, and push #2 on the speed dial.

Rusty picks up on the first ring. "Drew, is that you?"

"No, it's Raleigh."

"You found her?"

"No."

"Well where the hell is she?!"

I pause, because, seriously, these people are about as mature as toddlers. "Jayne thinks she took off because of the move."

"What move?"

I pause. "You don't know?"

"No."

Oh, boy.

"Jayne got a promotion. She didn't tell you?"

He lets out a couple curses, then says, "Why am I the last

to know everything?"

Like he's the victim here.

And just for that, I say, "The police came by last night."

"What!"

Rusty, according to Drew, smokes pot around the clock. Literally. She told me he will actually wake himself up to light a joint, then go back to bed. So of course he's not thrilled about law enforcement.

"You called the police?" he demands.

"Yes."

"What for!"

"If she really ran away, she would tell me. And how do you explain all her stuff left at school, including her bike?"

"But how's calling the cops going to help?"

Sometimes I wonder if the Fifth Amendment was created because you can't answer stupid. I take the Fifth, and wait.

"Okay, so," he says, finally, "what'd the police say?"

"They can't do anything unless her parents file a report." I wait for that fact to sink in.

But turns out, I'm stupid for expecting him to get it.

"Oh, that's just great," he says. "Just great."

He hangs up.

Again.

I BIKE THROUGH the rain to St. Catherine's. Drew's purple Schwinn is still locked—incorrectly—to the bike rack. It sits under the eaves, dry despite all this rain, and somehow that only makes it look more lonely, like an orphan afraid to get wet.

I lock my bike next to hers then walk around all three buildings. I tug on each door handle, peek through the windows, and stare into every classroom. They're all empty, the desks back in orderly rows.

I ride down Granite Avenue, blink against the slanting rain, then coast to the end of the street, to the homely house with a wooden ramp tilted over its front steps. I leave my bike under the big maple and walk up the ramp. My All Stars slip on the wet leaves.

I knock on the front door, but nobody answers.

So I ring the doorbell.

Then I ring it again before pounding my fist.

When the door finally opens, the red-headed man sitting in a wheelchair says, "Anyone ever call you a pest?"

"Yes. You."

"This doesn't exactly change my mind."

Teddy Chastain is my geology teacher at St. Catherine's. Next to my dad, he's the adult I'm closest to. Teddy never takes anything seriously—sometimes it's like he doesn't even realize he's paralyzed.

But right now he sees something serious written on my face.

He frowns. "You okay?"

"No."

"Good."

"What?"

"You Southern girls. Y'all got a bad habit of lying about your feelings. Speak the truth. You can start with why you're pounding on my door on a Saturday morning."

"I can't find Drew."

"Took off again, did she?"

"Why is everyone assuming she ran away?"

"Because the girl's rough as pig leather," he says. "Brilliant. But rough."

"Drew did not run away. This time."

"You're sure?"

"Positive."

"How many times do I have to tell you—leave room for examiner error."

"Teddy, I found her notebook in the Physics lab. You know, the one with all her experiments? Drew would never leave her notes behind."

"Not unless she wanted to throw you off track."

"For what reason?"

"She likes to experiment. Maybe you're part of one right now."

"I'm not!"

"Okay." He hikes his shoulders. "Go call the cops."

"I already did." I explain what Officer Lande said about her parents, and about needing twenty-four hours before Drew can even be called officially missing. As I talk, Teddy keeps his hands on the wheels of his chair, rolling forward two inches, back two inches, forward and back, like a paralyzed person's version of pacing the floor. "The only way the police will look for her is if there are signs of foul play."

"Proof," he says. "You need proof."

"I have proof."

"What you have is circumstantial."

"But you said everything's circumstantial."

"Raleigh, I was talking about geology."

"You also said geology is the best metaphor for life."

"I take it back."

"You can't, it's on the record."

He hangs his head, as if exhausted, and sighs. "Man, I hate talking to a judge's daughter." He rolls back, opening the door all the way. "Alright, c'mon, get outta the rain."

My geology teacher's house smells like minerals, like rock dust is floating in the air, rising off all the stones scattered around his living room. Schists and limestones and granites, sands and feldspars and silts. But I smell something else—hot, earthy—which turns out to be in the kitchen, where a cast-iron pan smokes on the stove like it's going to explode.

Ignoring the fire hazard, Teddy rolls over to his refrigerator and tugs on a knotted rope, wrapped around the handle. He's never said how he wound up in a wheelchair—and swears he never will—but whatever injury snapped his spine also curled up his fingers. He can work his thumbs okay, but his fingers look like their sides were Superglued and stuck together.

"How much bacon can you eat?" he asks.

"None."

"You don't want bacon? Man, something is wrong."

I regret my choice as soon as he lays the thick slices in the smoking pan. The sizzle of grease forces Teddy to turn his head. He doesn't consider turning down the flame.

He yells over the spattering, "You think something bad happened?"

"Yes."

"Drew ain't no shrinkin' violet."

"I never said she was."

He paws paper towels off the roll secured to the lower cabinet. As always, I feel an urge to help. But the one time I tried, he seemed insulted.

"Let's say Drew didn't high-tail it out of town. What would be your first step?"

"Identify the problem."

"Which is . . .?"

"Drew is missing."

"Then?"

"Gather all the information."

"Then?"

"Form my hypothesis—Teddy, I know the scientific theory."

"You forgot the whole point of it."

"Test the hypothesis."

"Right." He looks over. The green in his eyes looks both wise and wicked. "Which part you expecting me to help you with?"

"Gathering the information."

Suddenly his mouth drops open, he looks down. "You see that?!"

I hurry over. "What's wrong?"

"I'm paralyzed!"

I glare at him. "Everything's a joke to you."

"Ain't it? You want me—a man in a wheelchair—to gather information? Raleigh, that's what I hire *you* for."

For the past two summers, I've been Teddy's research assistant, collecting those rock samples.

"But you know things," I tell him. "Things I don't."

"Why don't you ask your dad to help?"

He waits. I don't reply.

"What I thought," he says. "You ain't told him."

"I told him Drew's missing. Last night."

"But I'll bet you left out this whole part about rootin' around for information. What else you hiding from him?"

"The point is, if her parents weren't retarded, I wouldn't even have to do this."

He cuts the flame and tongs the brown-almost-burned strips onto the paper towels. As the grease spreads through the paper like a flood, my mouth waters.

"Raleigh, do you know who pays my salary at St. Catherine's? Parents."

"So?"

"Parents pay my salary. Drew's parents, for instance."

"I'm sorry. But I need help and my dad's got his hands full

dealing with my mom. Okay?"

Teddy rolls over to the sink, tosses the tongs into the stainless steel tub. Then looks at me. "Does it help, knowing you're part of a long Southern tradition?"

"The Harmons?"

"I don't give a flip about that landed-gentry stuff. I'm referring to your having a crazy mother. It's a Southern tradition."

"No, that doesn't help."

"Well, there's always bacon."

He offers me a slice.

I bite down, and my mom's horror-breakfast evaporates. This bacon tastes of smoke and maple and meat. I close my eyes, feeling a dance on my tongue, and when I open them, Teddy is smiling.

"All right," he says. "What d'ya need from me?"

I smile back, relieved.

But my heart is some weird mixture of glad and sad.

Glad, for Teddy's help.

Sad, for why I need it.

CHAPTER FIFTEEN

T EDDY'S VAN BELCHES black smoke all the way up Grove Avenue. I ride my bike behind it, grateful for the rain that washes the sooty clouds into the pavement.

When he pulls into St. Cat's parking lot, he bypasses his reserved space with its sign, "Science Teacher of the Year!" Teddy's won that award twice—once for Virginia, once for the entire United States. I'm pretty sure the awards are the only thing keeping Ellis from firing him. It's obvious they have a mutual dislike because whenever Ellis comes around Teddy's classroom, Teddy will slip into even deeper hillbilly talk, just to drive our grammatically-correct headmaster crazy.

I coast over to the van. The driver's side window is down, letting in the rain and letting out his cigar smoke.

He stares at the bike, tapping the cigar, sending the ash onto the ground.

"You need to look at her lock," I say.

He jams the cigar between his front teeth, raises the window and begins the long process of getting himself out of the van and into his wheelchair. The procedure never fails to provoke some new names for his chair.

Now I hear, ". . . conniving contraption from the clutches of Hades!" and wait for it to end—while fantasizing about using that example the next time Sandbag asks for alliteration.

I push my bike beside his chair as we roll over to the rack and stand under the eaves. My hair is dripping.

"See the lock?" I ask.

He yanks the now-wet cigar from his mouth. "Raleigh, I'm crippled, not deaf."

I shut up. For about five seconds.

"What—" I can't stand it, he's looking so intently at the bike. "What do you see?"

"Get my kit." He tosses me the van keys.

I climb through the vehicle's back end, coughing as the cigar stench coats the back of my throat, and clumsily dig through mounds of accumulated stuff. Hammer-shattered rocks. Rubber-encased glass jars of river silt. Science journals. Old empty film canisters. Boxes of who-knows-what. Finally I find the titanium briefcase buried in the corner, probably here since the summer.

I yank it out, set it on the ground under the eaves, wipe the rain from my face.

"You're going to take the soil from her back wheel," he says. "But not all of it."

"Why not all of it?"

"And take photos," he says, ignoring my question. Which means, again, *shut up*. "Photos of the whole bike, close-ups on the lock, and the wheels."

I dig through the rock kit for the tools. Over the last two summers, working as Teddy's hands and feet, I've gotten to know this kit like my own as I help him collect geology samples for articles he writes in those science journals. He puts my name in there, too, as "assistant."

I take the photos, which make Drew seem really gone, then wedge a soil knife—kind of like a butter knife—into the tire's nubby treads. Carefully, I slide the grains into an empty film canister. No one uses cameras with film anymore, so

Teddy's collecting these little plastic cans. They're made to keep light away from film, but they also keep soil totally uncontaminated.

I press down on the canister's plastic cap. "Now what?"

"Now," he says, "it's time for fun and games."

TEDDY'S WET RUBBER tires squeal on the school's polished floors. The sound echoes off the lockers and sends a chill down my spine. My school has never looked so empty, especially with all the litter gone from last night. Now a gray gloom seeps through rain-streaked windows.

Teddy turns into the Earth Science lab. "Fire up the scopes, would ya?"

I crawl under the long counter and flick on the power strip. When a teacher wins national awards, science foundations donate all kinds of state-of-the-art equipment. Like two polarizing light microscopes, made specifically for geology samples. They cost about ten grand each.

I crawl out.

"You know what's good about dirt?" he asks. "It won't lie to you."

"Drew didn't lie to me."

"You gotta admit it's possible."

"You told me possible is not the same as probable."

"Man, I hate it when you quote me to myself." He rolls away.

"Where are you going?"

"You can do it."

"But this isn't some experiment."

"Use your noggin." He slides into his messy desk. "You'll figure it out."

I've learned a lot of geology from Teddy, but I've also

learned that arguing with him is like trying to break glass by screaming.

I stomp over to the far wall, ripping off a sheet of butcher paper. Then I hold the paper up like a sail, letting the massive sheet thunder in the air as I walk back across the room.

Teddy starts whistling, some hick-sounding jig.

Laying the sterile paper on the counter, I deposit the soil from the canister and spread out the grains with a clean knife. I see taupe-colored sand, some bright pink pebbles, and some dark objects shaped like tiny icicles. I divide the tiny pile into quarters, placing one part in a glass beaker with just enough distilled water to make a slurry. After I swirl that mixture, I strain out the water and place the beaker under a heat lamp.

"Why can't you girls spell porphyry?" Teddy complains from his desk. He's grading papers.

I ignore him, practicing my petty version of the Golden Rule, and spread another dry quarter into a thin layer. I see some gray dust, so pale it almost disappears on the white paper. I decide not to focus on that right now, in case it dissolves in the water-washed sample. That would mean the substance isn't a mineral, but something soluble. Organic. Not geological.

I pick out the pink pebbles. They look like some kind of granite. Then I check on the weird icicles. They're long and narrow, tapered at both ends.

And the color of dried blood.

"Will you please come look at this?" I ask.

He doesn't even look up from the papers.

I pinch the dry sample and dust it over a glass slide, placing it under the microscope. The way polarized-light microscopes work is that they have a polarizer on either side of the dock, each positioned perpendicular to each other so that only the light passing through the specimen reaches the eyepiece. Regularly-spaced crystalline parts of a specimen will rotate the light that passes through. And some of that rotated light will pass through the second polarizing filter, turning the regularly spaced areas bright against a black background. Like stars in a night sky.

Staring through the eyepiece, I move the slide around, searching for those blood-red icicles. The magnification is so high that every grain looks like a mountain. I find the icicles. Magnified, the edges look jagged. Like icicles that are snapped off. I wonder if they could be wood—tiny bark shavings?

When I check the heat lamp, my rinsed sample is dry. I place some of it on a clean glass slide and slip it under the other microscope. Then I move back and forth between the two scopes, comparing the samples. The water-wash eroded a bit of the red icicles, rounding the edges. That leads me to believe these things are sedimentary—a sandstone or siltstone, created by other deposited sediments.

I look over at Teddy. He's still acting busy.

I remove the pink pebbles and turn them under the scope. Granite, definitely. The quartz grains are large, which means the rock formed slowly over time. Maybe some magma that cooled at the Earth's surface.

Problem is, granite is everywhere.

But the color. That's more intriguing. Pink granite is kind of rare.

"Can you please come look at this?" I call out. "I've got pink granite mixed with some kind of sedimentary rock and I just don't see how that's possible."

"I'll make you a deal," he says. "We'll trade places. I want you to read something."

"I really don't want to correct papers, Teddy."

"Just do it."

He wheels to the counter, and I grumble over to his desk.

The book he's left open is called *Evidence from the Earth*. I've read parts of it before, but Teddy's marked a new section. In 1904, German police found a woman murdered and left for dead in a bean field.

"This is not helping," I tell him.

He doesn't even lift his head from the microscope.

German police also discovered the woman's scarf was used to strangle her. Wonderful. Near her body, they found a dirty handkerchief containing nasal mucus.

"This is really gross!"

And yet, I can't stop reading.

Along with the snot, the handkerchief contained dirt and flecks of coal. When the police later found a suspect, they scraped his fingernails and his trousers and gave the sample to a scientist, a geologist named George Popp.

Using his microscope, George Popp identified the minerals. But using a geological map, he also pinpointed the location of those elements. Turns out, there was only one place—the bean field where the woman was murdered.

Police presented Popp's geologic evidence to the suspect, and he confessed. Case closed.

"Fascinating," I say, walking back to the microscope. "But I never said Drew was dead."

He keeps his head down. "You say something?"

"I should throw that book at you."

"You'd do that, wouldn't you?" He looks up. "I think I know what this is."

I wait. "So. What is it?"

He nods.

"What is it, Teddy."

"You'll figure it out."

"Stop! Stop doing this to me!"

"Raleigh, the only way you'll learn this is to do it by yourself."

"But this isn't some class exercise—Drew's missing."

"Which is why I drove to school on a Saturday when I could've been eating more bacon."

"Please, help me."

"I am." He leans back, sighing. "Just like when I ask for help, I don't expect anybody to walk for me."

He turns and wheels out the door.

CHAPTER SIXTEEN

AT THE CORNER of First and Franklin, the Richmond Public Library stands like a dried out wedding cake, regal and abandoned and waiting for somebody to appreciate it. I do, but not many other people seem to hang around this place. Except some homeless guys.

But I've hung around here so much, I'm now on a first-name basis with the Reference desk librarian, Nelson Heid.

"Hi, Mr. Heid."

He looks up from the book, laid open on the Reference desk, and takes in my wet sweatshirt, my wet jeans—dripping on the library's marble floor—and my wet hair. He says, "Nice to see you, Raleigh." A true Southern gentleman. "How may I help you?"

"I was wondering if you had a surface map that also shows Richmond's geology."

"The tunnel again?"

"No, actually. I'm looking at other side of town. Around the West End."

"Branching out?"

"You could say that."

"The archives might have something along those lines," he says. "When do you need this information?"

"Now."

Slowly, he lays a bookmark on the thick book's page and sighs. I've learned these sighs are nothing personal. The guy just hates to stop reading. And if it wasn't for me, he wouldn't have to. This particular branch of the library, stuck on the edge of downtown but not yet in any residential area, isn't the most happening place. I've seen two or three elderly people checking out those large-print books where the pages look like they're yelling at you, and there's always that one homeless guy camping in the club chairs, reading the newspaper like he's in his own living room. But otherwise it's usually just me roaming around the abandoned stacks. I've learned that if you pull out a random book and start reading, you will soon forget about whatever's bugging you. Like your mom is saying the mailman is a CIA spy. Like your mom is asking you if you've done something to the water in the faucet.

That's how I found out about that train tunnel with the dead men inside. I yanked out a book and started reading.

Mr. Heid closes his book like a parent gently tucking a sick kid in bed. I glance at the gold embossed title, *Definitive History of Plantation Homes of the James River*. I feel a huge yawn tickling my throat, but I'll bet that book's first entry is DeMott Fielding's plantation house.

"You're certain you need this information today?" Mr. Heid asks.

"Yes." Already impatient with his slow pace, I'm getting cold standing here in these wet clothes. "It's urgent, Mr. Heid."

"Urgent," he says, shuddering at the thought.

Dripping on the marble floors, I follow him through the stacks to the back of the room. He keys a service elevator, and we take it down two flights to the basement. This place smells like they mothballed the Confederacy.

Mr. Heid draws a deep appreciative breath.

"What precisely are you looking for?" he asks.

"Some place that has pink granite."

"Nevermore."

"No, I saw it. It's out there."

"You cannot be serious." He draws himself up, appalled. "I was quoting Poe."

Edgar Allen Poe, the famous writer, was born a Yankee but was later adopted by a Richmond family. Now he's a city icon and that final line from his poem "The Raven" is a particular favorite around Richmond, maybe because the Confederacy is "Nevermore."

"I'm sorry, what's the connection between Poe and pink granite?"

"His statue."

I shake my head.

"Over by the capitol? The base? Pink granite?" He acts like I should know this fact. And since I don't, he feels compelled to name all the other Poe statues around town. "—and the one by the Bell Tower, where he holds a tablet, in his left hand, or is it his right?"

"The pink granite," I say, returning him to my search. "Maybe it was mined locally?"

He gazes at me. He has hooded eyes, but I can see the expression. He's hurt by my interruption. "Perhaps you've heard, patience is a virtue."

"Not when something's urgent," I point out. "Then patience is probably a vice."

"Raleigh, urgent can only be used if Yankees are marching into Richmond to burn us to the ground."

But he strides over to the map cases. These are metal drawers about two inches deep and they hold amazing things: surveys from the 1600s, commissioned by the King of England; maps from the 1800s by America's first trained geologists; surveys from The Great Depression; and then soil sample records from during the wars, when people desperately needed commodities like coal and gold and even gravel.

Mr. Heid yanks opens several drawers. The dust plumes. But he closes each of them, still searching, until he says, "Ah. Yes." He turns to me, pulling out an ancient tome. "This should be what you need. But good luck reading it."

"I don't believe in luck."

"Fascinating." He smiles, looks at his watch. "And even with only twenty-one minutes to closing, I don't believe in urgent."

RICHMOND IS, OFFICIALLY speaking, sixty-two square miles. I know that number because Drew actually measured the squiggly city boundaries to calculate Area. That's her idea of fun. For a real hoot, she also calculated how many square feet existed for each of us 218,000 citizens. Theoretically, of course. But I don't remember that number because theoretical rarely interests me. It's why I like geology—it's real. And why I like maps. These places actually exist, and you can get to know them down to the rivers and rocks and hills. This map, done by the U.S. Geological Survey, details the fault line that runs through town. It's a tectonic break that turns the amiable James River into Class 3 white water. And I can see why Mr. Heid chose this drawer—there's a ton of granite exposed around the river, mostly mound-backed boulders. But the map confirms my suspicion . . . that stuff's not pink granite.

I open more drawers, blowing off the dust that tells me I'm the only person interested in this stuff. Each map shows Richmond bedrocked by granite composed of three minerals: quartz, feldspar, and mica, all mixed together in varying proportions and textures. But nothing's pink. I keep pawing through the maps—coughing and sneezing and shivering in my wet clothes—until I discover the geological survey map showing the section of the James River where I screamed at frogs last night.

Geology maps are not like road maps. They're more like human anatomy charts, the ones that show surface skin, then veins, muscles, ligaments, until you're down to the bones. These show rock formations, stones, minerals. Each piece has its own separate color.

The elevator doors open.

Mr. Heid stands inside.

"You have ten minutes," he says.

The doors close.

I run my finger over the topographic lines that show the cliffs above the river. I follow it down to where frogs jumped all over me. The mapmaker marked those soils in gold and green colors. On the right, I read the vertical chart that explains the sediments. Quartz sand and clay-silts. Green to symbolize ferrous-bearing—or, full of iron.

But no granite.

The elevator opens again.

"Five minutes."

Mr. Heid sounds cheerful, like he's determined to teach me about urgency.

I keep running my eyes over the map, begging it to speak. Once more, I run my finger over where St. Cat's would be. I rub and rub, almost stirring the page, and suddenly I see one tiny oval. It's purple. The size of a small spider. It doesn't match anything around it. Once again, I read the explanation on the map's right side.

"Petersburg Batholith," it says. "Typically a homogenous pluton but subdivides into four distinct units. Granite gneiss, foliated granite, megacrystic granite, porphorytic granite, and subidiomorphic granite."

Geology descriptions—like all the adjectives are beating up the nouns.

I know exactly what a batholith is. It's an area where hot magma bubbled up through the Earth's crust. Like cherries baking inside a pie. If it gets too hot, the cherries break through the crust. But when the liquid magma cools, it develops into crystals. Whatever the surface temperature is will determine what size the crystals are. Fast cooling—like, if the magma plunges into water—will create a stone that's as smooth and shiny as glass. Slower cooling temperatures give the chemistry time to do its atomic thing and create larger crystals—that's what's meant by the "megacrystic" granite.

But I don't see any mention of color.

Staring at the map, it's like I can feel the room closing in, like I'm in another kind of tunnel, underground with all this old information nobody cares about. I fix my eyes on the map's purple spot and suddenly it's like seeing an invisible hand reach through time and connect the dots. The cartographer chose green for those ferrous sands, because they often look green. So why not choose this color—my best friend's favorite color—for granite that happens to be pink?

When the elevator door opens, Mr. Heid is tapping his watch, sounding like the Raven crying, "Nevermore."

CHAPTER SEVENTEEN

I RIDE HOME over the wet streets, the air full of that slushy whisper of water spraying under wheels. Though the rain's finally stopped, I'm still soaked to the skin. My plan is to sneak up the servant stairs, change into dry clothes, and then go find the location of that Petersburg Batholith, so I can maybe figure out how it got into Drew's bike tires.

Maybe it will tell me where she rode her bike. Maybe even why.

But when I get to my house, Betty Crocker is still hard at work.

"My lands!" My mom exclaims, wearing the same pink apron though it's late afternoon. "How did you get so wet?"

"It's been raining."

"Yes, but—" She looks perplexed.

Uh oh.

I move for the stairs. They're right there, within sight.

"Why would a person stay out in the rain like that?" she asks.

A person.

"I didn't stay out in it, I was riding my bike."

"Whatever for?"

"I wanted to see Drew." Not a lie, I tell myself, still aiming for the stairs.

"But you saw Drew yesterday." She steps from the stove, coming closer. "Someone told me that."

Someone.

That other girl. The one who pretends to be Raleigh.

If I run up the stairs, it will only make things worse.

So I turn toward my mother and her pink apron. She is guarding the oven like a bank security officer in front of a vault. Yes, the meds are working, she's more cheerful. But the paranoia? It's here, I can feel it.

"Is dad around?" I ask, trying to sound casual.

She doesn't answer.

Our eyes lock and the shiver that goes through me has nothing to do with cold wet clothes.

"Mom?"

"David is in the den," she says.

Her voice isn't cheerful anymore.

I STAY HOME the rest of Saturday with my parents. It's agony. My dad, whose work consists of judging opposing sides, is forced to become the judge between me—the defendant, and my mom—the paranoid prosecutor. Calm and steady, my dad spends the rest of the afternoon orchestrating activities for all three of us. Scrabble, until she starts thinking our words mean something else. Monopoly, which goes so slowly her mind wanders into dark places that nobody would ever want to buy or rent. By dinner, he's switched to playing black-and-white movies on the DVD player. We eat a second casserole. They are coming out of the oven with sickening regularity.

I know what my dad's doing. He's trying to reclaim the family we once knew.

And I don't blame him.

But that family seems like a very long time ago.

Every hour, I excuse myself and call Drew's house. Then I call Rusty's apartment. By seven p.m., when I'm pointing out to Jayne that more than twenty-four hours have passed since anyone saw Drew, she acts like Rusty—hangs up on me.

I check my email all night long.

There is nothing from Drew.

SUNDAY MORNING, I hunker down in our family pew at St. John's Church. My hands are clasped so tightly my knuckles are turning white.

Reverend Burkhardt stands in the high pulpit, built before the Revolutionary War.

"We're all smart people," he says. "We're capable. We have good jobs, money. Nice houses, nice families. We're in charge of our lives."

Please, I pray. *Bring her home.*

Although far more than twenty-four hours have passed since anyone saw Drew, when I called Officer Lande late last night, she said the police still can't do anything. Not unless the parents want to file a report. Not unless there are signs of foul play.

She even called Jayne and Rusty. They're still saying Drew's playing games.

"But you have to wonder," Reverend Burkhardt says, "do we really know what's going on?"

He leans forward. The pulpit is shaped like a ship's prow, elevated over the sea of St. John's congregation. His deep voice slides along the concave plaster ceiling, landing with a thud in our pew.

"You can't see the whole story. So don't be fooled."

I glance at my dad, seated beside me. My mom's on his other side. His eyes shift toward me, just long enough for me to acknowledge his own concern. He holds my mom's hand, tight.

"God himself says the invisible is more important than the visible."

Just what we needed—a sermon pointing out the positives of paranoia.

Right there, my prayer changes.

Shift the topic. Or close his mouth.

"What do we all like to say when we don't understand something? We say, 'God works in mysterious ways.' "

I slide down in the pew. *Help me.*

"And that always sounds great. It makes us sound wise and benevolent. But then we turn right around and focus only on what's right in front of us, completely forgetting that there are things hidden from sight. Important things. Crucial things."

I slide so far down I can smell the lemon oil that's been buffed into the old southern pine pews.

"For instance, consider the empty tomb."

From this perspective, the man's eyes look black, smoldering in his hard face.

"The women were crying because Jesus wasn't there. But then Jesus himself told them He would be leaving. Did they listen? Or did they focus on what they could see?"

I slide my eyes to the right. My father is rubbing his thumb across the back of my mom's frail hand.

"He also promised to send somebody after Him who was even more powerful than God's own son. The Holy Spirit." His voice drops to a whisper. "And guess what? The Holy Spirit is invisible."

I raise my gaze to the ceiling and plead. He has to give this sermon now? When the meds are just kicking in, when my dad is pouring everything into making her well?

Although Reverend Burkhardt keeps talking about invisible worlds and things happening below the surface, his voice seems to fade. His words sound muffled, like they're coming through water. I stare at my dad's thumb brushing her skin, over and over and over again, like someone trying to release a magic genie trapped inside a bottle. And then, before I realize what's happening, people are standing. Everyone is singing. My dad's voice says there are new mercies morning by morning.

The service ends. And I can't get out of there fast enough.

"Dave." Wade Tounsend is ambling over. City councilman, king of networkers, he must want to plant some seeds. "Sounds like the Johnson case is keeping you busy."

The councilman never acknowledges my mother. Most people don't, even in church. Maybe especially in church.

She stares out with glassy eyes, some robotic rabbit.

My dad never lets go of her hand.

I move past them, heading outside. I can taste the men's cologne, smell the women's perfume, feel invisible walls of repentance. Someone mentions seeing frost on their mums this morning. Somebody talks Redskins football. I burst through the front doors.

The wind is gusting, sending dead leaves swirling over the brick entrance. I follow the leaves all the way to where they pile up against an iron gate surrounding the church cemetery. I lean on chilly rails, gulping down the fresh air. The sun pushes through the clouds and strikes the tombstones, throwing shadows on the sunken graves. Harmons are buried here, colonists from the 1700s who stacked foundation stones for this church. Their descendants are here, and the generations that followed, and the bad thought climbs into my mind before I can stop it. Someday, my dad's going to die. And my mom—

"Hi."

I spin around with a gasp. "Stop sneaking up on me!"

DeMott smiles. "Stop running away."

My heart is pounding too hard to think of a response, so I try to act calm. I look down, hoping to hide. His tux, naturally, is gone. But his creased chinos and peacoat look just as formal. On anybody else, the navy wool coat would look dorkus-majorkus. But somehow, the thing fits DeMott, like it's some ancestral hand-me-down from a Fielding who fought in the War of 1812.

"How's your friend?" he asks.

I look at his face. He's serious. "I don't know."

"You don't know?"

"I still can't find her."

He looks alarmed. "Did you call the police?"

"Twice." I explain all the official rules regarding missing persons, how the situation is moronic because her parents are morons. "They can't seem to get it through their thick heads that she didn't run away."

"Why can't you file a police report?" he asks.

I don't say anything for a long moment. Yesterday's adventure in family-togetherness ruined my plan. "I'm trying to," I finally say.

"I'm really sorry, Raleigh."

"Thanks, but I don't see why people insist on saying they're sorry for things that clearly aren't their fault."

"We can't be sorry with you?"

I turn around, gazing at the graves, not trusting myself to talk right now. Something too warm is waiting at the edge of my eyelids. And unfortunately, this bone yard is only making it feel worse. The old marble stones are blank, all the names and dates eroded from too much rain and snow and sun. It's like these people never really existed.

"And why do people pick marble for headstones?" I say. "It just deteriorates."

He steps forward, standing next to me, gazing into the cemetery. "Drew," he says. "That's her name, right?"

I squint, fixing my gaze on the white steeple. Its iron bell sits silent. "Yes. Drew."

"If there's anything I can do . . ."

I wait for the second part of his oh-so-polite statement, the things people also say when talking about my mother. If there's anything I can do, don't hesitate to call. But it's not something they really mean. Or else, they would just call.

"I mean," he says, as if reading my thoughts. "Anything you need."

I look at him. His eyes are so clear I can see the tiny gold flecks inside the blue. Like sparks in his eyes. He holds my gaze but doesn't say anything. We stand like that for a long time, what feels like forever, and then something leaves my shoulders, just rolls off, and I want to take a deep breath and hold this moment forever.

But Satan clops into it.

"You can't be serious," Tinsley says.

She's on her cell phone. No longer dressed like lemon meringue, she's sheathed her toothpick legs into tight winter-white jeans, topped with a white jacket and scarf. She resembles a polar bear, starved, with its claws out.

"I'll have to call you back." She cuts the phone and gives me an icy glare. "What's going on out here?"

DeMott answers. "Her friend Drew is still missing."

"What a clever girl," Tinsley says.

"Tins, it's really serious."

"Did you not hear one word that Reverend Burkhardt said?" she asks him. "It's clear as day that we can never see what's really going on right in front of our own faces."

I look at him. Is he trying not to laugh?

Tinsley keeps yapping about the point of the sermon, but I

shift my attention to the church's door. My dad is leading my mom down the steps. The blank expression on her face says she's orbiting Neptune. Worse, his expression seems distant, too.

"Raleigh?" asks DeMott. "Is there anything we—"

"I have to go."

But Tinsley steps in front of me. "Don't forget your promise."

Her smile. It tells me that sermon is right, that what I'm seeing isn't what's really here. Beautiful perfect Tinsley, she is a black hole of hate.

I smile back at her. "What promise are you talking about?"

Her smile sticks. She's used to playing mean. "You know, the promise you made Friday night."

"I don't remember." God, forgive me for the lie. "Why don't you remind me. What did I promise?"

Her lips stretch back so far it's like she's baring her teeth. "You promised to tell me if your poor mother suffers another breakdown, bless her heart."

The cold heavy feeling climbs back on my shoulders. "Oh, that promise." I nod. "I thought you meant the promise about not telling anyone that Drew's tutoring you because you're flunking math."

Something flickers in her mean eyes. But otherwise she doesn't move.

Stepping around her and DeMott, I walk toward my parents. They stand on the ancient sidewalk, holding hands, waiting in a narrow beam of sunlight.

CHAPTER EIGHTEEN

B UT I SHOULD'VE known it wouldn't end there.

"Yoo-hoo!"

My mother is calling up the front stairs, after a strained lunch, after my rushing upstairs to change out of church clothes. I had a plan.

But of course the plan is thwarted.

"Raleigh Ann? Are you there?"

Of course.

Instead of using the servant's stairs in back of the house, I was trying to sneak down the front, running out the main door onto Monument Avenue before anyone realizes I'm gone. But now, coming down the stairs, carrying my backpack, pulling on my St. Catherine's sweatshirt, I realize the best laid plans are going to be laid to rest.

She is running up the wide stairs toward me. Crying out, "No! Turn around!"

I freeze.

"Put on a skirt—a dress—something—anything else— hurry!" She pivots, calling downstairs. "Give her one moment, she'll be right down."

But in that one moment, the world tilts on its axis. I am here with my backpack full of geology equipment, my manic mother is flying up at me, and DeMott Fielding is standing at the bottom of our front stairs, smiling up at me.

She whispers. "Go put on something nice."

"Uh, this is nice." I stammer.

"You look like you're doing yard work!" She spins back to DeMott. "Make yourself at home in the parlor, DeMott, I'll get you something to eat."

"No!"

She startles.

"I mean," I try to think of another way to block his impending food poisoning. "He doesn't have time."

She pulls back. The expression in her eyes shifts. "How do you know?"

One moment. I have one moment before the world begins tilting again, all the way back to suspicion.

"I don't know that," I say, truthfully. "I'm just guessing."

Her eyes roam over my face, searching for signs, clues, signals that she was wrong to think I belong to her.

"She's right, Mrs. Harmon," DeMott calls out. "I just came by to see if I could help her—"

"Get to school," I cut him off.

"School?" She frowns, confused. "It's Sunday."

"I have a big project due tomorrow."

"Project." She lets the word hang there.

"Yes. A special project."

Her eyes darken.

"Monday comes up fast," DeMott says.

Both of us look at him. His handsome face is so open, so kind—so totally guileless—that once again the atmosphere shifts.

Before it can change back, I hustle down the stairs. My pack feels heavy with the rock hammer, camera, and notebook, but compared to the gravity behind me, it's featherlight. I rush for the big door with its leaded glass. DeMott, who has also changed into more casual clothes, is making his polite goodbyes.

"Thank you for the offer, Mrs. Harmon. I'll take you up on it next time."

I glance back, once.

She's still waiting on the landing, staring down at us, but all that happy glee about DeMott's appearance is gone. It's gone and I can see it, like one of those invisible-but-real things. She's going back in, the black caves calling her name.

"Do come again." Her voice is wooden. "Won't you?"

DeMott drives a pickup truck, a fact that boosts him ten points on a scale I never even knew existed. Every guy at St. Christopher's, our brother school, seems to drive a BMW or Benz or some other hot sports car daddy shelled out for.

This truck isn't even new. I give him another five points for that.

He holds the passenger door for me. I add three points— most Southern guys would hold the door.

I watch him cross around the front of the truck and hop inside.

"Thank you," I say.

He turns the key. "For what?"

"For picking up the signals."

"Oh." He nods, pushes in the clutch and shoves the stick shift in first. Manual transmission gets another two points. "You're welcome. And I like your mom."

I try to make a sound in my throat, to express my parental annoyance, but what gurgles out makes my face turn bright red. I sound like I've got the flu.

He laughs. "Raleigh, I'm serious. She's great."

"Yeah, right."

"I don't lie."

That statement shuts me up. We roll down Monument Avenue. He drives around JEB Stuart on his horse.

"In what way?" I ask.

"Pardon?"

No "what" for him.

"In what way is my mom great?"

"For one thing, she's genuine. Like your dad. I wish more people were like them."

I stare out at the window at the cobblestone road. This is true. My mother is genuine—mostly genuinely nuts—but even when she's well, she's herself, always. And my dad, I've never seen him be phony. Ever. That's probably what Drew most despises about Jayne—her mom doesn't ever drink alcohol in public, but hides in their house getting bombed.

"Thanks," I tell him. "I needed to hear that."

He shrugs, like there's no need to thank him. Which somehow only makes me want to thank him more. I steal glances at him. He's wearing jeans now and a Carhart jacket the color of toast. The hum of road fills the cab as he steers around Stonewall Jackson. It gets to me.

"Okay, look, I'm sorry," I blurt out. "I shouldn't have treated Tinsley like that."

"It was rude."

"I know, I'm apologizing."

"But you didn't say it to me. You said it to her."

I turn away, staring out the passenger window. The row houses display their autumn flags, a Richmond tradition. They wave in the breeze.

I speak to the window. "If you think I'm going to apologize to Tinsley Teager, you can let me out right here."

I don't hear anything for another block. Then he says, "How about I tell her you feel bad about it."

"Is that absolutely necessary?" I ask the window.

He laughs.

When I look over, his profile is so perfect, so proportional, that it's like each feature was designed mathematically. Straight nose. Strong, but not jutting, chin. Smooth forehead. His looks actually freak me out—he's too good looking. I find myself searching for flaws, anything that will make him seem more human. More like me.

He downshifts at the light on Libbie Avenue and coasts to a stop.

"Okay," he says, "if you really, really don't want me to, I won't say anything to Tinsley."

Now I feel worse. What kind of a creep takes back an apology? The whole idea that I could be like that makes me want to confess even more. So I do.

"You should also know I'm not headed to school right now."

He keeps his gaze on the red light. "Oh."

"Yes, and the project isn't for school either."

The light turns green, he shifts into first. Our silence is way too uncomfortable, but I have no words to add that will make it better. All I can think is—he just praised my parents for being genuine and true, and I just pulled a fast one on my mother. Who is crazy? Nice. Really nice.

"DeMott, you can let me out here. It's okay. I was going to get my bike—that's what I planned to do and—"

"Where are you going, if you're not going to school?"

"To look at a hole in the ground."

He keeps driving. "I better come with you."

"Why?"

He looks over, and smiles.

"In case you fall in," he says.

CHAPTER NINETEEN

O N BOTH SIDES of Teddy's house, his neighbors work in
their yards, raking leaves, sweeping driveways—and
stealing glances at me and DeMott sitting in his truck.

DeMott hasn't cut the engine yet. And he can't take his
eyes off the house. The window shutters hanging slanted on
busted hinges. Gutters choked with leaves and moss. The
wheelchair ramp smothered with even more leaves.

"This is the hole in the ground?" he asks.

"No." I climb out of the truck and stomp as noisily as
possible up the wooden ramp, announcing my arrival to Teddy
and getting even more stares from the neighbors.

I knock on the door. Six times.

When it opens, I don't wait for "hello."

"Petersburg Batholith."

He nods, rubs an odd hand over his red whiskers. "Afternoon to you, too."

"You could've just told me."

"What's the fun in that?"

"Fun? Drew's missing. Why can't anyone get that through
their heads!"

"Because she brought this on herself."

"Once. She ran away once. And that was—"

"Also, it doesn't help that she makes the other girls feel so dumb. And half the teachers. The girl doesn't exactly breed sympathy."

"Stand up."

He blinks. "Say what?"

"Stand up. Take a jog around the block."

He holds my gaze, his green eyes gleaming.

"Right," I continue. "You don't get up and go running because you can't. The same way Drew can't help making other people feel stupid—because compared to her they are."

He pauses. "Point taken."

"And now you owe me."

He frowns. "For what?"

"Insulting her like that."

He takes another swipe at his whiskers but this time cranes his neck, looking toward the truck. DeMott sees him and raises his hand, a gesture of hello.

"Who you got driving," Teddy asks, "Prince Charming?"

"Show me exactly where that batholith is exposed."

"Now?" he says, shocked.

"Right. Now."

TEDDY SITS ON the passenger side of the bench seat, held in tightly by the seatbelt. DeMott follows his directions and takes River Road down to the Hugenot Bridge. But we don't cross over the water.

"Turn here," Teddy says.

"Here?" DeMott says.

The road is rutted gravel, lined on either side by wild aspens. The wind blows a hail of yellow leaves from the trees. They flutter through the sunlight like hammered gold.

"What are we doing here?" DeMott asks, bouncing over the road.

"You mean, besides giving me a pain in the butt?" Teddy says.

I sit sandwiched between them. And I remain silent. Every time the truck bumps into another divot, I brush up against DeMott's right shoulder. I'm wearing a sweatshirt and he's got that jacket on and still I can feel heat from him. It's making it hard to breathe.

I steal one more sidelong glance at his perfect profile. But now his eyebrows are quirked up.

"What's bothering you?" I ask.

"That sign back there said No Trespassing."

"Not important," Teddy insists. "Let's talk about Raleigh. She seems tense."

"I'm right here, and I'm not tense."

"She just proved my point." He leans forward, straining against the seatbelt, speaking over me to DeMott, "Am I right or am I right?"

DeMott glances at me. "You do seem a little tense."

"I'm not."

"I said *a little*."

"Not even a little."

"It's official," Teddy says. "Y'all sound like an old married couple."

I feel the flush of embarrassment rising up my neck. I hold my breath as DeMott slides in the clutch and coasts to a stop. The blood is reddening my cheeks now.

But nobody speaks for several long moments. Each of us stares out the windshield. Right in front of us, the massive curve of rock rises fifty feet high and stretches hundreds of feet across. Mining has gouged the thick horizontal layers, including a band of pink-and gray stone that blooms between the layers like a gigantic frozen balloon.

"Welcome," Teddy finally says, "to the Petersburg Batholith."

"Wow," says DeMott.

"Glad you're impressed, son. Now get me outta this noose."

DeMott climbs out of the truck. He walks to the back, where Teddy's wheelchair sits folded on the flat bed.

"You could do worse," Teddy mutters.

"Stop it."

"Okay, a lot worse."

"There's nothing going on."

"Sure sign that something's going on."

DeMott opens the passenger door. Teddy grins at him wickedly.

"Is everything okay?" DeMott asks, looking a little concerned.

"With me?" Teddy asks. "Yeah. I'm great."

I grab my backpack and slide out the driver's side. If Teddy says something more, I don't hear it because I've already slammed the door, walking away.

"So you know what you're looking for?" Teddy calls out.

I turn around, ready to blast him, but I'm too stunned to speak.

DeMott stands behind the wheelchair—pushing Teddy forward. Even though this isn't the easiest ground to cover, I know Teddy can handle it. I've seen him operate on our geology field trips. He never lets *anyone* push his chair. The sight of this fractures something in my mind. I can only stare at them, unable to get one word out.

Teddy leans back, speaking over his shoulder to DeMott. "What's wrong with her?"

"Far as I can tell, absolutely nothing," DeMott says.

Teddy turns, looking at me with that wicked grin. "What'd I tell you?"

"You told me," I reply, suddenly snapping back to reality, "that you'd show me where Drew could've picked up pink rock in her bike tires."

"Yeah. Right back to business. Okey-dokey, have it your way, state the hypothesis."

"The Petersburg Batholith contains pink granite. But the batholith is only exposed at the surface in four places around Richmond. This location is closest to school and the most likely place for Drew because one, she hates to exercise, and two, you need to be nice and help me."

Teddy turns his head again, speaking to DeMott again. "Ain't I nice?"

"You seem nice."

"Thank you."

"You're welcome."

"Anytime."

"Okay, look," I say, "if you two are going to just goof around, leave. I don't need your help."

It's a totally stupid thing to say—obviously I need help—and for saying it, I only feel more mad and weird. Which leaves me with the only option for the self-respecting liar . . . I walk away.

I head straight for the rock wall. But on my way over, I pass a huge mound of excavated rock, piled beside a backhoe. It looks like half-sand, half-gravel. I kneel down, pinching a sample. The air right here tastes of minerals, earth—Chthonic. The word Teddy taught me this summer. He wants me to use it on Sandbag. Our Lit teacher asks for "challenge words"—we give Sandbag a word, see if he knows the definition. He always—and I mean *always*—does. Grinding the soil between my fingers, I glance toward the truck. DeMott and Teddy are still chatting away.

"Hey!"

Their heads snap. But neither makes a move toward the rocks.

I take a deep humbling breath and walk back to them, remembering how every time I act proud, I wind up feeling even more stupid.

"I need some help," I say.

Teddy nods. "Take a soil sample."

"From where?" I spread my arms out wide. "This place is huge."

"You already forgot," he says, without a trace of accusation. "What did you read yesterday?"

"You mean that story about the dead German woman?"

"Right. Strangled with her own scarf, left in the field."

"I'm sorry—what?" DeMott looks horrified.

"The reason I wanted you to read that," Teddy continues, ignoring DeMott, "is the whole principle behind transfer of material. Soil got transferred onto that German killer's clothes, right?"

I nod.

"So, you found Petersburg granite in Drew's tires. Now you look for any place her bike could've come in contact with the soil. You were on the right track a second ago—" he nods at the pile of sand and gravel. "Go look again. Flag anything that don't look natural. DeMott can help you."

I stare at the ground, watching the soil as we walk toward the pile of gravel and sand. I don't see any bike treads. But the taupe-beige sand covering the ground does remind me of the other stuff in Drew's tire treads. I see some sharp pink granite pebbles, but they're all too big for what was in her wheels.

At the loose soil near the backhoe, I see wheel marks. But they're about a foot wide. Car tires. Not bike. I also see the parallel teeth marks of the backhoe's tread. Yesterday's rain pock-marks and blurred everything, including some shoe prints I find walking around the pile. I kneel down, measuring each shoe imprint. Too big for Drew's feet. And whoever it was, they were heavy enough to compact the loose soil through a half-day of heavy rain. The guy who runs the backhoe probably.

I pull out my camera and take pictures of all the tire impressions, the backhoe's treads, the shoe marks. Then I keep circling the mound. I haven't seen one of those blood-red icicle shaped stones. Nowhere. And all this rock is metamorphic—hard rock. Those red things are sedimentary, soft rock, that dissolves its shape in water.

DeMott waits on the other side of the mound.

"You think she was here?" he asks, looking a little confused.

I shrug, continue past him, backtracking again.

"She's like that!" Teddy yells. "You'll get used to it!"

Pretending to ignore his comment, I glance up at the rock wall. Could she have ridden her bike on top of it? I don't see how she could've gotten up on that ridge. I lower my eyes, taking in the chunky layers of stone. They look as orderly as Legos, except for that purplish-pink plume of granite. Geologically, we'll probably never fully understand what happened here. We can guess. We can make theories, models, but the unknowing is part of the puzzle of the Earth. I scan the stones, searching for anything sedimentary. Anything that would account for those red icicles. But there is nothing.

I hear footsteps behind me.

"I'm not sure what you're doing," DeMott says. "But I'd like to help."

I nod, scanning the soil at our feet. The treads look different on this side of the mound. I kneel down, pinch the soil and rub it between my fingers. The rain's pummeled the sand but—

I look up at DeMott. "Can you tell him to come over here?"

He walks away. I watch his back, like Friday night, and decide there is definitely something nice about his walk. Straight back, but not uptight. Hands loose at his side. I feel a flutter right below my stomach.

He says something to Teddy that makes my geology teacher laugh. The flutter comes back to my belly button.

Once again, Teddy lets DeMott push his chair. I stare at the narrow rubber wheels, rolling over the soil, gathering grains in their treads. Why would Drew ride her bike down here? I have no answers. Not even a good guess.

Unless . . .

I stand up. A heavy feeling sinks into my chest. I can't breathe. What if she came down here for geology. I turn, running my eyes over the whole quarry. For me.

"You find something?" Teddy asks.

"Probably nothing." My voice is shaking. I swallow the fear, turn back to the mound of soil. "You said to flag anything that doesn't look natural."

"No, what I said was, anything that *don't* look natural. But that's why your parents pay hefty tuition, so you don't sound like a hillbilly." He grins.

I point to the backhoe, the tire treads, the big shoe prints. I stop on the small oblong divots. About six inches long, less than a half-inch deep. But regularly spaced.

"Does that look like steps, like somebody walking?"

"DeMott, git me closer."

DeMott pushes the chair nearer the impressions. Teddy leans forward.

"I see it. Good eye, Raleigh." He sits up. "Photos and a sample."

I take more photos, then swing my pack around, rummaging for my Ziploc bags. Teddy is leaning so far forward again that his thin body looks folded in half. I glance at DeMott, but he's already figured out the risk, leaning his own weight into the back of the chair, counterbalancing so Teddy doesn't topple forward. I like it that DeMott already knew to do this. I like it a lot.

I open a Ziploc bag as Teddy brushes his knuckles over the soil. His head is so low I can see a pale halo in his red hair. He's balding. I look away, pinch the soil, deposit it into the baggie. I hold it up to the sun. Pink granite pebbles. Each covered with a heavy dust of taupe sand. And silt. But again, no red icicles. I seal the bag.

"Grab it, will ya, DeMott?"

When I look over, Teddy is sitting up and DeMott is stepping around him.

"Careful," Teddy says.

DeMott pinches something on the ground. Dirty and brown, it looks like a string. He pulls. It's connected to something under the mound because the grains start to fall around it. DeMott tugs harder.

My heart clenches.

"No," I whisper.

He holds the string up. The object dangling at the end . . . it's a shoe.

Small, covered with soil. But the color, there's no mistaking it. Or the kind of shoe that it is.

Purple.

Converse All Star.

A purple Converse All Star.

CHAPTER TWENTY

"LISTEN TO ME," Teddy is saying.

DeMott's truck bumps over the rough road. Drew's shoe, sitting in my lap, jumps as if alive.

"Raleigh!"

I know things. Things no fifteen-year-old should know. All those many hours in my dad's courtroom, listening to vice-cops and detectives and coroner's reports. I know things that should scare kids but never scared me because I already had a mom who claimed I wasn't her "real" daughter.

But now?

All those things from the courtroom race through my head. And they scare me.

Teddy leans forward, speaking to DeMott. "Son?"

"Yes, sir."

"We're gonna make a detour."

"To the police?"

"Yeah, we'll get to them. Right after we check the shoe."

"Wait—is that the right procedure?"

On my left, I sense DeMott's worried gaze, running over the side of my face. But I can't turn my head. It's like the bad things have hypnotized me.

"Son, you need to relax."

"But I thought you're supposed to call the police," DeMott

says. "Right away. Not wait."

"Raleigh?" Teddy asks.

My mind tunnel-visions back to the mound of soil. This is Drew's purple high-top. No doubt in my mind. Buried under all that soil. Why? Why in a quarry I've never even heard of? And how? I look down at the shoe in my lap. Evidence. Just like all that evidence I saw tagged and bagged and paraded through my dad's courtroom, Drew's shoe is evidence.

"Raleigh?" Teddy pushes his weight against my right side. "You gotta get out."

I blink. We are parked at the gym at St. Cat's. There is Drew's bike. Still waiting. Waiting for me?

I feel sick.

DeMott helps Teddy into his chair.

"C'mon," Teddy says. "Don't waste opportunity. You know Drew wouldn't."

As soon as I walk into the geology lab, I bend over the trash can by the door and throw up.

"Go puke in the bathroom!" Teddy says. "Nobody's gonna be cleaning tonight!"

Saliva pools in my mouth, preparing for another round of up-chuck. My hair falls forward. I reach to grab it, but a hand gets in the way.

DeMott.

He holds my hair, at the base of my neck. I close my eyes. *Please. Make it stop.* Make. Everything. Stop.

"Are you okay?" DeMott asks.

"Fine," I mumble, spitting again.

"Fine," Teddy says. "What she always says. 'Fine, fine— I'm fine.' And yet, anybody with eyes in their head can see she ain't."

I force back the saliva, breathe deep, and force myself to be "fine." When I straighten, standing up, DeMott steps back. My knees feel soft, weak. My feet wooden. But I manage to walk over to the roll of butcher paper, tear off a sheet and carry it to the counter, all the while keeping my watering eyes focused on the floor. The clean and shiny and polished floor that is nothing like the dirty sand covering my best friend's lost shoe.

When I look up, Teddy's hand is shaking from the strain of holding the tip of the shoelace, clamped between his working thumb and his fingers stuck together.

I lay down the paper. He exhales, releasing the shoe—her shoe. He shakes out his wrist.

"Gloves," he says.

"What?"

"Put on some latex gloves. They're in the cabinet."

I snap on the gloves, which before I've only worn for testing acids.

"Turn it over, check the treads. But don't take all the soil out," Teddy says. "Like the bike tires, leave some soil in there. For the cops."

"So we are calling the police," DeMott says, still standing by the door. "Right?"

"You were the kid who always colored inside the lines," Teddy replies. "Right?"

I pick up a soil knife. My hands feel far away. The latex bunches on my fingertips. I can feel the sweat inside them.

"I just don't want us doing something illegal," DeMott says.

"What we're doing is geology."

"Yes but—"

"Geology is a dirty business."

"All puns aside, aren't we tampering with—"

"Tampering's when you cover something up. We're looking for clues."

"Are you sure the police will see it that way?"

"Raleigh," Teddy says. "Hurry up."

Something is happening to me. I've had this feeling before but only when my mom goes dark. It's a swallowed-up sensation. Like when people say "out of body experience." I think it's like this—I'm here and not here, all at once. I'm not even thinking, my hands just know what to do. I use the tweezers stored in the drawer to dig grains from the sole of her shoe. I faintly hear the dull rain of sand on the paper. I make a mental note of three tiny pebbles lodged inside the sand. I find a hair, short and brown. Pinch it, hold up the light, wonder if it belongs to Isaac Newton the cat. Or the person who—whose existence won't even let me finish that thought.

I set the hair aside from the soil.

When I go back to the shoe's treads, the icicles are there.

I turn the sole, pointing at the red shards so Teddy can see them.

He nods. "Stratigraphy. Write down the stratigraphy."

"Strati-what?" DeMott asks.

I pick a Sharpie from the drawer under the counter and draw a rough sketch on the butcher paper. I place the soils in the order we found them. Here and in her bike tires. In both cases, the red icicles were buried under the other soil. The soil that matches the quarry.

"Stratigraphy tells us the order of deposition," Teddy explains. "First soil you see is the last deposited. Deepest soil is deposited first. Make sense?"

"History, you mean."

I draw the order of soils vertically, showing the pink granite pebbles compacted by taupe sand covering the blood-red icicles. DeMott looks out the doorway.

"We should call the police," he says.

"We will," Teddy says. "And we'll tell them everything. Except this part."

"Hold on! You said this was okay!"

"It is." Teddy waves a clamped up hand, dismissing him. "The police don't have geologists on staff."

"How do you know?" he demands.

"Because I'm the guy they bring this stuff to."

"Oh."

"Only the FBI has geologists on staff. And believe me, we don't want them showing up."

I look over at my teacher. His forehead shines, a scrim of perspiration. I'm thinking about what he just said, how he said it. We don't want the FBI showing up . . . because . . . ? Because that would mean Drew's—

I wait for him to look at me. But he refuses. When I glance over at DeMott, his blue eyes have darkened. The color of the ocean when clouds sweep in front of the sun.

"It's okay, you can leave," I tell him. "Really, it's fine."

He only turns, continuing to stare out into that empty hall-way.

CHAPTER TWENTY-ONE

ORTY MINUTES LATER, DeMott turns into Drew's driveway. We both get out. Teddy stays in the truck.

I don't walk around to the sunroom. Even though I know that door is open.

Standing on the front stoop, holding the clear plastic bag that contains the purple All Star, I try to think of something to say. Once again, the words refuse to come.

Reaching around me, DeMott presses the doorbell. But his other hand rests on the small of my back, that certain kind of heat traveling up my spine. I feel that flutter, let out a breath.

"You okay?" he whispers.

But the door opens before I can automatically say "Fine."

On this late Sunday afternoon, when her daughter's been gone for more than forty-eight hours, Jayne looks perfect. Her brown hair is shiny, the trimmed ends barely touching the shoulders of her red cashmere sweater. She smiles.

"Hello, Raleigh. Who's your friend?"

God, forgive me. Again. I really want this woman to suffer.

I lift the plastic bag, dangling it in front of her face.

"We just found this, buried in a quarry. Right off Huegonot—"

"Sorry to bother you, ma'am—" DeMott interrupts. "I

know this is a shock."

His manners, unbelievable. I want to jam my elbow into his stomach.

But Jayne doesn't hear him. Her face is contorting, her features shifting from Miss Perfect to Screwed Up Mother.

She reaches for the bag.

I pull it back.

I've come up with some new hypotheses these last two days. One—Jayne can't be trusted. Two—ordinary things, like bike tires and shoes, hold extraordinary information.

And three—"You need to call the police. Right now."

I DIG THROUGH my backpack until I find Officer Lande's card, which I shoved way down, tucking under the bottom interior flap so my mom would never find it.

I hand it to Jayne. But she backs away, shaking her head.

I pick up the phone, dial the number and get voice mail, which tells me to leave a detailed response, or if this is an emergency, please dial 9-1-1.

"This is Raleigh Harmon, and this is an emergency," I reply. "But I'm not calling 9-1-1 because I want you to help us. And we need you right now."

Jayne is standing to my immediate right, so close I can hear her breathing. It's quick and shallow, like someone running hard.

"I'm at Drew Levinson's house. Her shoe was just found in a quarry off Huegonot Road."

When I hang up, Jayne isn't standing beside me anymore. She's moved over to the kitchen but stays in the threshold. I wonder how much she wants some wine. Behind her, the cuckoo clock clacks against its door, rapping four times.

Four o'clock.

In two hours, it will be dark.

✧　✧　✧

OUTSIDE, WE CHECK on Teddy. He's dug out one of his stinky cigars from some pocket.

"Hope you don't mind," he says to DeMott, still sitting in DeMott's truck. "And course, even if you did mind, all that high Virginia breeding wouldn't let you say it. So we're cool, I guess."

I go inside, DeMott follows. When I sit down at Drew's desk, turning on her computer, I feel like puking again.

"Who is that?" DeMott points at the poster over her bed.

"Richard P. Feynman." I type into the computer *Feynman*.

But that's not her password. I squint at the blinking cursor, my fingertips resting on the keyboard, itching. DeMott continues to gaze around the room, taking in the mobile of the solar system, the charts on the walls showing her math theorems. The books and books and books.

I try more passwords.

Physics.

No.

Fibonacci.

No.

"She must be really smart," DeMott says, standing behind me now.

"You have no idea."

I can feel heat from him, even from here. I push that idea away and type out the combination from her bike lock, 0 1 1 2 3.

"Why those numbers?" he asks.

"Fibonacci sequence."

"Pardon?"

"It's a math mystery. The next number in this sequence

145

will be the two numbers before it, added together."

"Always?"

"Forever."

"Whoa."

"It's beyond me too." I keep typing the sequence, following Fibonnaci because Drew loves this idea of order and mystery all wrapped together with numbers. I'm up to 5 8 13 21 34 55 89, doing the addition in my head. I'm starting to want a calculator, when I hit Enter and—

"Bingo!" I cry.

"Talk about a strong password."

On the black screen a quote appears in purple letters: "Science is the belief in the ignorance of experts."

DeMott reads it over my shoulder. "Did she come up with that?"

"No." I stare at the words. Like a message from the great beyond. "The guy on that poster over the bed said it."

I scroll through her files, opening every folder, only to find that every weird physics phenomena in the known universe has found its home on this computer. Quarks. Nutrinos. String Theory. All the baseball math that makes my eyes glaze over—statistics, more statistics, still more statistics—but a pang of remorse squeezes my heart. I should've paid more attention, I realize. Maybe she did tell me something, and I missed it. Too wrapped up in my own projects, trespassing in a tunnel, to listen to the person I miss so much it hurts. I keep searching the files, hoping hoping hoping I'll find something labeled: *My Plan To Run Away and Not Tell Anyone Even Raleigh.*

Nothing close.

I click on her photo album.

"Hey, look at you two," DeMott says softly. He is leaning down, so close I can smell the fresh air on his clothes.

I swallow and scroll through her pictures. And then, that out-of-body feeling comes over me again, like these are pictures of two girls I don't know. Pictures snapped at Big Man's Burgers on Friday nights. Pictures at ball games. In most of them Drew looks like a tiny professor—small and scholarly and disappointed by the dumbness all around her. I search for the photos where she is smiling. Like her hero Feyman. I decide people will look at a smiling face.

When I find the right image, I paste it to a blank page. Above it, I type some words. Erase them. Type again. Finally, I settle on:

MISSING GIRL.

The cursor blinks.

Waiting.

"Is something wrong with that?" DeMott asks.

I delete both words, then type HAVE YOU SEEN HER?

"You're right," he says, quietly. "That's much better."

But still not ideal. That question sounds like those milk carton kids, the ones who've been missing for so long that you can only stare at their adult progression image and marvel at how noses grow and chins widen and then you're not even thinking about the missing kid anymore.

Hoping to block that reaction, I write a short paragraph underneath her picture describing Drew Levinson, girl genius, wearing a St. Catherine's school uniform and possibly missing one purple Converse All Star.

I read the text three times. She will hate me for this. I hate myself for this.

I refuse to type Jayne's phone number. And since Rusty doesn't always answer his phone, I can't put his number. But no way can I put my home number, so I pull out Officer Lande's card and hand it to DeMott.

"Read me the phone number." I type carefully—I don't

want a single digit to be wrong.

Downstairs, a door slams. It slams so hard a percussive shake rattles through the bedroom floor. DeMott looks at me, eyebrows raised in alarm.

A man yells. He yells one word.

"Jayne!"

DeMott's mouth drops open.

"Rusty." I hit Print. Fifty copies. Scoop them up.

Downstairs, Rusty is yelling again.

"C'mon," I tell DeMott. "You can meet the Father of the Year."

CHAPTER TWENTY-TWO

A MELANGE, I decide.

We've formed a melange. All of us in Drew's driveway, like random stones cobbled together by outside forces.

That's the geological definition of melange, and we fit it.

Officer Lande, arriving right after Rusty's big entrance, stands between Drew's parents like a referee in the ring with prize fighters. I stand by the truck, trying to stay out of reach of the verbal punches and the jet stream of Teddy's cigar smoke. DeMott stands beside me, silent, watching, listening.

"This is all your fault!" Rusty yells, his finger aimed at Jayne.

"Here we go!" Jayne throws her arms in the air. "Blame me. Of course."

"You're supposed to be her mother."

"I am her mother!"

"When? The three hours a week you're sober?"

I glance at Officer Lande. Her cool gray eyes flick, following the words like uppercuts.

"You and your ambition." Rusty continues. "Is it that hard to pay attention to your daughter?"

"Me?" Jayne seethes. "Who're you—Father of the Year? You can't even crawl out of your hole long enough to take her on a vacation."

"Vacation?" He stabs a finger at her. It's sooted with modeling clay. "I can't afford a vacation because you want child support."

"It's called working for a living!"

Money. That's their big button. Way back when, Rusty actually worked at a bank. He was an executive. He wore pinstripe suits and short hair and that fake smile I hate so much. But one day he quit. He said he wanted to make pottery. They divorced within six months. Drew put it this way, "Jayne climbs and now Rusty reclines." Today, he's wearing flip-flops—even though it's cold—and a wrinkled shirt with cargo shorts whose torn pockets sag open, like they're trying to remind everyone he really is a starving artist.

"And New York!" he hollers. "I'll bet Drew was thrilled about that move. What did she say to you?"

Jayne glances at Officer Lande who is holding a notebook and pen, taking down every mean word.

"Did I mention we're moving?" Jayne asks.

Officer Lande flips through her notebook pages. "Two thirteen Saturday morning."

Jayne lifts her face, closing her eyes against the afternoon sun. She is beautiful. And she is ugly. All at once. I can't explain it except that it's like seeing a really successful person standing on the edge of ruin.

"I refuse to apologize for advancement," she says.

"Advance—"

"Hold on." I step forward, cutting off Rusty and turning to Jayne. "When did you find out about this 'advancement'?"

"I don't remember," Jayne says.

"Bull—"

I cut him off again. "Did you just find out?"

She hesitates. "They told me last month. In September."

"What?!" Rusty cries.

She whirls on him. "I couldn't say anything—in case it fell through."

"Or in case she ran away," he says.

"Hang on." Teddy exhales a cloud of smoke. "Let's have a show of hands. Who really thinks Drew ran away?"

The Levinsons both raise their hands. But me, DeMott, and Teddy don't. Officer Lande just looks at us, counting hands.

Teddy looks at me, giving me a signal to continue his point.

"Drew would argue first," I say. "She wouldn't run away, not right away." I look at Jayne. "Did she argue with you?"

Jayne just stands there awhile. The wind rustles the leaves. "Yes, she got mad."

"Of course she got mad," Teddy says.

"But did she point out the flawed logic?" I ask. "Did she tell you it made no rational sense to move to New York?"

"I don't remember."

But I know Drew. Her first line of attack would be to outwit her mother, get into a verbal battle, conquering through her IQ. That's why Jayne didn't tell her earlier. A knowingness goes through me. It's almost something I can touch, it's so real. Like the shoe I handed Officer Lande, now stashed in the police cruiser.

"She didn't run away," I insist. "And you know it too."

"This is a very big promotion," Jayne says, like anyone cares. "I can finally stop worrying about money."

"Great," Teddy blows smoke. "Now you get to worry about your daughter."

"But Raleigh's wrong!" Jayne says. "I told her about the move. Drew said, 'You'll be sorry.' "

Officer Lande asks, "When was that?"

"Thursday night."

"Interesting." Officer Lande again flips through her notebook. "You previously said you told her Friday. At breakfast."

Teddy mutters, "Why I like dirt. It doesn't lie."

"I don't remember the specifics," Jayne says, sounding defensive. "It's been so hectic. A lot of people wanted this position."

"Enjoy the climb," Rusty says, "because it doesn't end anywhere nice."

"Nice?" Jayne eyes are glistening with tears. "It's not supposed to be nice. It's called work."

"Are you saying I don't work?"

Officer Lande lifts her hands, calling the fight.

"Let's not go down that road," she says. "Let's focus on what Raleigh just turned up." We wait. The wind swirls. Rusty is breathing hard, but Jayne looks frozen. All except her eyes. They are melting.

Officer Lande's gaze lingers on Jayne.

"With or without your permission," she says. "I'm calling in a report. Just to be safe."

"What's that mean?" Rusty asks.

"It means your daughter Drew is officially missing."

CHAPTER TWENTY-THREE

EVEN THOUGH TEDDY'S cigar has burned out, that throat-coating stench lingers inside DeMott's truck.

But that's not the heaviest thing in here.

The silence is.

It's smothering. Choking. Dense.

As we drive away from Drew's house, my ears ring with it.

DeMott doesn't say anything until we're all the way down Grove Avenue.

"Are you alright?" he asks.

"I'm fine."

Teddy sighs. "I'm not. And I'm not pretending."

"I'm not pretending." I say.

"DeMott, is she pretending?"

DeMott nods.

Teddy leans back. Normally he'd be grinning right now, satisfied that somebody agreed with his accusation.

But when I look over, I don't see anything smug on his face.

We turn onto his road, heading for his worn-out house.

"I will never say this again," Teddy sighs. "So listen up."

I wait.

DeMott slows the truck to a crawl.

"Ask God for some help," Teddy says.

I study him, stunned a moment. "You told me you don't believe in God."

"I don't," he says. "But you do. And right now, that's what matters."

I just stare at Teddy, shocked at the cosmic crack that just split him open. The most self-reliant, stubborn, independent person I know just acknowledged we're helpless.

Only now I'm at a loss for how to respond. How can I tell him that I don't even know what to think about God, much less what to pray. I mean, if God loves all the little children, what's up with giving Drew parents like Rusty and Jayne? They're supposed to love and take care of her, not act like their lives are way more important. And what about my mom? What good would it do to tell Teddy how many times I've begged God to heal her—and yet that's never happened.

Finally, I say, "Teddy, I believe in God but I don't understand Him . . . or why He lets certain things happen. Like right now I'm . . . I'm . . . "

Teddy turns, stares out the window. I gulp for air and revert to logic—what we're both comfortable with.

"You taught me to pick the hypothesis, and gather the evidence. If that evidence makes the hypothesis look wrong, change the hypothesis. Right?"

He looks at me with a furrow between his eyes. "Right."

"I've been praying my brains out for Drew." My voice cracks. "Every day, every minute. I prayed in church this morning. And what did it get me? Her shoe. Buried in a quarry."

Silence smothers the car. I want to jump out and run—and run and run and run. But I'm trapped. In so many ways.

"Sometimes," DeMott says, "the answer isn't what we want to hear. But."

My eyes burn. "What."

"But we don't give up hope."

We drive with that silence, so heavy that DeMott cracks his window for fresh air. The wind washes into the cab, and suddenly I realize what this quiet feels like—a funeral.

Like we just attended a funeral, without a body.

DeMott pulls into Teddy's driveway. The neighbors are still toiling in their yards. The leaves are gathered into neat piles. Gathered so quickly the grass underneath is still green. In the fading sunlight, the whole thing looks like some bygone era where good and industrious citizens cheerfully completed their chores.

Teddy glares at them. They look away.

"You believe in God, I get it," he says. "But you want to hear one good reason why I don't?"

Desperately.

So desperately I don't dare open my mouth.

"Every Sunday morning, all of these neighbors of mine go to church. Then they come home, eat supper, and work on their yards. At Christmas they light up the trees and on Easter they gussy up and strut around like hens. But not one of them has ever walked up to my door and asked if I needed help. Not one. These good Christian folks, you know what they do? They call the city and complain about my yard. Say I'm ruining their property values. Now you tell me, why would I want to have anything to do with the God these people follow?"

The three of us sit there, staring at the neighbors who continue to steal glances at DeMott's truck. But they never stop working.

The funeral feeling gets worse. So bad my heart aches inside my chest.

"You know what my dad says?" I finally ask. "He says, 'If

you think they're bad now, imagine if they weren't Christians.' "

"Huh." Teddy says. "Judge's got a point. But I think I got one too."

DeMott climbs heavily out of the truck, quietly closes his door. I stare straight ahead, at the hanging shutters. My heart feels so fragile right now, it's like if I turn my head, the whole thing will shatter. There's a long metal scrape in back as DeMott takes the wheelchair out of the truck.

"Right nice dude," Teddy says. "You like him."

"He belongs to Tinsley Teager."

"Ain't no way on God's green earth that's right—not that I believe in God."

The passenger door opens. Teddy turns to DeMott.

"Son, I feel as beat as the lead dog after the fox hunt. You mind liftin' me?"

There isn't one second of hesitation. DeMott reaches out, slipping his right arm under Teddy's limp legs. His left arm goes behind his back and when his hand touches me by accident, a hot flash sears into me. My heart reacts like it got hit with those electric paddles they use to revive dead people.

DeMott lifts Teddy, sets him in the chair.

Just like that.

Like he's done it a million times.

I turn my head, glancing at the neighbors. Their heads are bowed over their duties, but they're stealing even more glances.

At the top of the wheelchair ramp, Teddy fishes in his pocket for a key. It takes him a long time. In all the time he's been my teacher, Teddy's never really seemed handicapped. He barrels through life, hollering, bellowing, greeting every day with so much gusto he intimidates everyone.

DeMott pushes the front door open. But when he comes

back behind the chair, he pauses. I see him kneel down, looking up into Teddy's face. His voice, sliding through the truck's open window, sounds calm.

"I believe in God," he says. "Someday I hope you will too."

If Teddy replies, I don't hear it.

DeMott stands, and pushes the chair though the door.

I lean forward. I put my hand on my heart, trying to stop the pain. When I look up through the windshield, the sky is amethyst blue. That first whisper of dusk.

WITH THE LIGHT that remains and the flyers printed in Drew's bedroom, DeMott and I cover the entire neighborhood around St. Catherine's. I hold the paper, DeMott slams his palm into a stapler borrowed from Teddy.

Every telephone pole.

Every sidewalk tree.

Every bulletin board outside the cafes on Grove Avenue.

We even walk into the Country Club of Virginia, down the block from St. Catherine's. The receptionist at the front desk smiles at DeMott.

"Hello, Mr. Fielding."

Mr.?

"Hi, Mary," DeMott says. He hands her a flyer.

She looks at it, then looks up. There is so much sadness on her tan face.

"I'll have to ask the manager," she says. "He'll be in to-morrow."

She sets the flyer aside. I stare down at the page. Drew grins up from it. She's pretty in a bookish way. Big brown eyes, so bright that it seems the headline reads like a joke— HAVE YOU SEEN HER?

I want to grab this woman Mary and scream, "Don't wait for management—hang the thing up!"

It's our last flyer.

But instead of screaming, I turn away, walking beside DeMott to the Country Club's parking lot.

"I've got a flashlight," he says. "We could print some more, go hang them."

Dusk is gone. The night is so chilly that his words ride on silver clouds of condensation. I shake my head. Maybe I even shivered, because when I get in the truck he offers me his Carhartt jacket. And I accept it. The rough material still smells like clean laundry done by servants. But there's another part, too. The sweaty boy part. And it smells fine.

"What time is it?" I ask.

"Close to seven."

"I need to get home."

There is more silence in the truck. But it's different now. Tense. Anxious. I'm thinking about tomorrow, and about what the chances are my mom will see one of those flyers. Maybe there's one good thing about her going into another episode— she won't leave the house. The voices in her head keep her inside, scared.

When I glance up, DeMott's driving around the Robert E. Lee rotary. Standing in the floodlights, the general and his horse Traveler shine.

"Raleigh."

I'm staring at our huge house. Through the magnolia leaves I can see lights inside. I am dreading going in there, dreading telling my dad this new development with Drew, dreading the maneuvers we'll have to devise to keep my mom from knowing.

Maybe this is why, as a kid, I never liked playing hide-and-seek. That never seemed like a game to me. It was my life.

"Raleigh?"

He's stopped at the curb outside our front entrance. The grand entryway facing the even grander avenue.

Once again, it feels like I can't turn my head. My heart, hurting more. But I force myself.

The glow from his dashboard, the soft light of the streetlights, they make his features look even more like a sculptor's version of the perfect face for a young man.

"If you need anything," he says, "and I mean anything, don't hesitate."

I nod, open the truck's passenger door. The dome light comes on. His eyes, they're dark again. Like all this hard reality—evidence and police and missing-person flyers—settled into him.

A thought, a memory slips through my mind. Something my sister Helen once said. She was classmates with DeMott's older sister, Jillian. One day her art class toured the Fielding's plantation house, Weyanoke. Helen came home and said, "Those Fieldings live completely insulated from reality."

Not anymore.

"Thanks," I tell him, wishing I could dredge up more warmth in my voice. But I can only maneuver out of his jacket, offer it back to him.

He doesn't take it. "You want to get some dinner?"

"Now?"

"Or whenever," he adds quickly. "And we don't have to talk about . . . you know. Unless you want to."

I lay the jacket on the seat between us. When I grab the door, not opening it further and not closing it, I can feel the night air. It brushes into the warm cab and I wonder if maybe this moment will be *Before*. Before I hear something really awful from the police. And then everything will be *After*.

After life is never the same again. And what's even weirder is, I can feel this moment, another real-but-invisible thing, like what my dad tells me about an invisible stitching that holds the world together.

"Thanks," I glance over at DeMott again. "Thanks for the offer, but I don't think I'll be very good company tonight."

"Maybe another time."

"Maybe." I take my backpack from the floor and step out on the sidewalk.

"Hey," he says, leaning to speak through the open door. "I hope this doesn't sound wrong, but in spite of everything bad that happened today, I liked hanging out with you."

It does sound wrong. But the odd thing is, I actually enjoyed having him around. And that's totally not like me. I like solitude, especially if I'm upset. And yet, my back still feels warm where he put his hand on it when I had to talk to Jayne. And I can still feel the warmth from his jacket, like a blanket over my shoulders.

But I have no idea how to say any of that.

"Okay," he says, glancing away. "Guess I'll see you around, somewhere."

I nod, close the door, stand on the sidewalk as his truck rumbles down Monument Avenue. At the JEB Stuart rotary, his taillights flash red, shimmering in the dark. The truck circles the rearing horse, and then it is gone.

"Yeah," I whisper. "See you around. Somewhere."

CHAPTER TWENTY-FOUR

M Y ONE HOPE—my last hope on this awful day—is to reach the back stairs without being seen so I can run to my bedroom and check my email, find some message from Drew.

But the kitchen tonight smells of beef and salt and my mother's frantic attempts to pretend she's normal.

"Your jeans are dirty," she says the second I step through the back door.

I look down. I've left my All Stars outside, as a precaution, but now I see the quarry dirt is smeared into my jeans, where I knelt down to take soil samples, photographs. The image of Drew's purple Converse flashes through my mind.

When I look up, my dad is wearing that expression which says Blessed Are The Peacemakers.

"Hiking," I say.

"Hiking?" she repeats. "You went hiking?"

It doesn't matter how much heat is radiating from the oven, how much our old windows are sweating from her stuffed domestic efforts, the whole room freezes. Nobody breathes, each of us waiting for the very next words that will determine whether this night goes up or down, light or dark, forward or back.

"DeMott."

That's all I come up with.

Her eyes are moving quickly, her mind adding everything up, but two plus two will never equal four.

And my own mind is scrambling, ransacking for one full sentence that isn't also a lie. "DeMott," I repeat. "He wanted to show me around Weynanoke."

It's true—he wanted to, I just didn't go.

In the next frozen silence, I walk across the room and set my pack down on the bottom of the back stairs. I am too tired, too distressed, too defeated to make another attempt at explaining what can't be explained. I want to run upstairs, slam my bedroom door, lock it forever. I saw the look on my dad's face. No way can I talk to him tonight about Drew. He's got his hands full.

Without replying, my mom turns and opens the oven door. My stomach growls but my head overrides it, wondering what she's cooking.

"DeMott seems like a good guy," my dad says.

I don't say anything.

"Do you like him?" he asks.

She answers for me. "He's going to marry Raleigh."

I look at my dad, horrified. He laughs.

"Does Raleigh have any say in this?" he asks.

"Yes." She pulls the casserole dish from the oven. "God told me she's going to say yes."

I feel sick. My dad laughs again, so relieved that she's taken this new track with the conversation. But she doesn't get that. She looks over at him, confusion clouding her face. Somehow it hits her that she's apparently made a joke. She laughs, tentative. But it's enough to get them chattering. I push a smile on my face, take my place at the table. That familiar lump camps in my throat. It won't help me choke down whatever is under the muddy-brown casserole sauce.

She serves us. We pray. My dad takes a bite, tells her it's delicious. She tells us—happily—that it's meatless meatloaf.

My first bite tastes like somebody made a brick out of oatmeal then coated it with burnt ketchup.

I try to swallow that bite, pushing the food around my plate. Suddenly I miss Drew so much my eyes sting. She's the only one I could describe this meal to, then laugh.

And even though he's sitting right across the table, I also miss my dad. Somehow I was stupid enough to expect I could come home and tell him what happened today.

"Raleigh."

I push back the burn in my eyes. Then look up.

His gaze is locked on me. "You're awfully quiet."

I drop my eyes. His plate, it's clean. He's eaten every bite of the oat-brick.

"Just tired," I tell him. "May I be excused?"

"You're not hungry?"

"No, sir."

He frowns. "Hope you're not getting sick."

Normally, if my mom hears we're coming down with an illness, she leaps up to make herbal concoctions that supposedly boosts our immune systems. And my dad and I both look at her, waiting for her reaction.

She remains silent.

And why not?

If I'm not her real daughter, my health is my problem.

CHAPTER TWENTY-FIVE

ONDAY MORNING MAKES me wonder if I'm turning into my mom.

I can feel people watching me, looking at me. All through my first three classes—History, Latin, Biology—their eyes are on me. But whenever I turn around, nobody's looking. But still some invisible hand keeps tapping me on the shoulder.

By lunch I feel rattled walking into the cafeteria, tossing my sack lunch in the garbage because—in yet another med-induced mania of domesticity—my mom has packed me a sandwich made of meatless meatloaf, slapped together from last night's leftovers. When my dad saw it, he slipped me money for lunch. I buy a grilled cheese sandwich from the cafeteria and carry it across the lunchroom, sitting at our usual spot by the back windows.

I can't taste the food.

Loneliness. Worry. Fear. It's all there.

But there's this other thing, a feeling in the air. Even if I can't name it, couldn't describe it if a knife was held to my throat, it's here—in the atmosphere.

And it scares the crap out of me, because I'm pretty sure this is how life feels for my mom all the time.

I want to leave the cafeteria, but lunch isn't over, and Tinsley's table of rich girls camps right by the exit, to check out everyone coming and going. There's no way around them.

Tossing my lunch in the trash, then taking a deep breath, I walk toward the exit. Suddenly they stop talking. And just as suddenly I can feel every pleat in my plaid skirt, every seam in the white blouse. Like my skin's too alive.

"Don't forget your promise, Raleigh," says Tinsley.

I bite down on my tongue, shove open the door.

The hall is empty.

At my locker, I stare at Drew's combination lock. That white arrow isn't pointed at zero. It makes me feel ashamed, how petty I was being Friday night. I turn the dial, slowly ticking past each number.

What about a message, I wonder.

A note.

What if Drew did run away, but snuck back into school? Took her books? My fingers start to shake, twisting the dial back and forth, clicking through her combination. A note that will explain the missing shoe, apologize for not telling me about the move, reveal where she's hiding—I yank open the locker.

The textbooks stand at attention, each one waiting alphabetically for her return. Inside the door, Richard P. Feynman grins at me.

I slam the locker, spin the dial. My eyes burn so hot it's difficult to see that white arrow. I replace it the way Drew would want it, straight up. When I paw through my locker, those three words hammer through my head—*Do Not Cry*. I have Lit next and Tinsley's in there and if she sees one trace of a tear, it'll be the end.

I grab Rossetti's poetry and hold the book to my chest like a shield, work my way down the now-crowded hallway. I feel eyes again and the bitter memories leap up, begging to be recognized. It feels like the first day of school. No, worse. It feels like the day in second grade when I overheard some other mothers talking about "Nadine." We were backstage at a Thanksgiving play. I was waiting in the wings, unrecognizable in my costume. One of the moms said Nadine "wasn't all there, bless her heart." And they talked about how we'd been "dirt poor" until David Harmon came along.

Drew is the one girl who's never judged me for anything that wasn't my fault. I stare at the floor. My shoes. *Do. Not. Cry.* When I reach the corner, I look up to avoid bumping into anyone.

That's when I see the tall man.

He's way over six feet tall, towering over this sea of girls. Also he has a face that looks like a wooden mask carved by angry natives.

But it's his eyes that stop me. Pin me to the floor. Most people haven't spent their formative years in criminal court listening to police testimony, so most people would miss his eyes. This guy's got the scan, the veteran cop look-around. The way cops barely move their heads but their eyes are seeing everything.

He walks right up to me. My pulse thuds.

"Would you happen to be Raleigh Harmon?" he asks.

He wears a sports coat with jeans. Probably to cover a gun.

"I'm Detective Mike Holmgren," he continues, knowing full well who I am. "I'm with the Richmond Police."

The crowd swims around us, but it's lost the usual frantic commotion of fourth hour. When I glance over my shoulder, Tinsley's group is standing in a half circle, gaping at us. I can't really blame them. He's a Big Scary Dude.

The good news, I decide, is that I'm not paranoid like my mom. People really are watching me.

The bad news? My throat's closed. I can't speak.

"It's okay," the detective says. "I talked to your headmaster. He says you can show me that quarry."

THE DETECTIVE DRIVES a Camaro, black and shiny as obsidian. But it smells worse than Teddy's van.

I hold open the door, coughing.

"Sorry, clove cigarettes," he says. "I'm trying to quit smoking."

"By smoking something else?"

"I never claimed it made sense."

The smell is so ghastly, I take my time getting in. Well, that, and I don't want to get in.

"Did you call my parents?" I ask.

"Mr. Ellis talked to your dad."

Oh, crap.

I sit in the bucket seat, so low I'm eye-level with the dash. The detective fires out of the parking lot, slides through two stop signs and guns the engine between stoplights. The trip seems to take two minutes, yet he manages to ask dozens of questions. What is Drew like, how did she feel about moving to New York, how did I happen to find her shoe yesterday? He even asks me about Burgers & Brains—our Friday nights at Titus's place. The detective knows so much about us that when we pull up to the quarry, I feel spooked, like he might know about me trespassing in the tunnel, too.

He parks the shiny car at the far edge. "You alright, seeing this again?"

"Fine." I open the door.

There are so many people here it almost doesn't look like the same place as yesterday. Dusty-looking guys wearing ball caps stand beside the big equipment. They look like quarry workers. But there are also two police officers near a Richmond cruiser, and a woman stepping out of a white panel van which is unmarked, except for the seal on the door that shows Blindfolded Lady Justice holding her scale. Richmond's motto runs around her in Latin.

Sic itur ad astra.

I know Latin, and I know that motto because it's in my dad's courtroom too.

Thus one goes to the stars.

For the first time, those words make me shudder.

The other huge difference from yesterday is yellow crime scene tape has been staked around the mound of quarry soil. Which isn't a mound anymore. The soil's been spread out. I see one plastic marker, right about where we found her shoe. It has the number one on it.

I follow Detective Holmgren over to the tape. I see another person, a guy with a camera. He wears hospital scrubs over his clothing. The woman from the van also wears scrubs. She is kneeling near where we found Drew's shoe.

"Mary Wade?" Detective Holmgren calls out.

She looks up, an annoyed expression on her face. But as soon as she sees me, she smiles.

The detective introduces us. Mary Wade Cavanaugh. She is with the Evidence Collection Unit.

"Mary Wade used to be a detective," he adds. "Now she does honest work."

She ignores his comment and starts asking me a bunch of questions. Some of them are repeats from the car ride over. But she seems way more interested in where, exactly, the shoe was found. Naturally, if she's collecting evidence.

Only by the fourth or fifth question, I realize she's more interested in how I found it than where.

"The soil looked unnatural," I tell her.

"Unnatural." She glances at the detective.

"Not like the rest of the soil around it," I add.

"So you've been to this quarry a lot?"

"No."

"Then how did you know something looked . . . unnatural?"

I don't want to get Teddy in trouble. Or DeMott. So I say, "I study a lot of geology. I know a little about rocks and soil."

Mary Wade smiles again. I don't like her smile.

Detective Holmgren opens a notebook, just like the one Officer Lande wrote in when listening to Jayne and Rusty.

I tell myself that I am not paranoid.

"Raleigh," Mary Wade Cavanaugh says, "does Drew have a boyfriend?"

"What—? No."

"How about online? Does she meet guys online?"

"No!"

"But you really wouldn't know if she was in some chat room, would you? She could've met some guy. Romantically."

"Drew's interested in one guy."

Mary Wade's eyebrows shoot up. "Name?"

"Richard P. Feynman."

"How do you spell that?" asks Detective Holmgren.

"Don't bother," I tell him. "He's dead."

They both looked stunned, so I explain who Feynman is and that Drew is, in fact, totally infatuated with him.

Once again Mary Wade Cavanaugh is giving me that condescending smile. "You girls sure sound smart."

"Drew's smart."

"And you're humble," she says. "Do you remember what time you came back?"

"Back, where?"

"Sorry." Her smile's probably supposed to look friendly, but to me it looks more like she's trying to cover up a toothache. "Officer Lande's report said you went looking for Drew on Friday afternoon. You checked the school. Then you came back that night."

"That's right."

"And you saw Drew's bike when you came back the second time?"

I nod.

"So what time did you come back?"

"Exactly?"

She smiles. "As close as possible."

"I left my house around eleven thirty, I think," I tell her, skipping right over the sneaking-out part.

"On foot?" she asks.

"I ran."

"How far is it from your house to St. Catherine's?"

"Two miles."

Holmgren asks, "How long does it take you to run that?"

"I was tired, it was late. So probably fifteen minutes."

"Fast," he mutters.

Mary Wade smiles. "And then what happened?"

"The dance was going on. You know, Homecoming. I saw her bike. And it wasn't there before. And I knew she wouldn't go to the dance."

"Because she's infatuated with a dead scientist," Mary Wade says.

I hesitate, not sure of her tone. "I asked for, uh, permission to go into the school to find her." This is not a lie—I did ask. "When I got to the Physics lab, I saw her jacket and stuff. But I couldn't find her, anywhere. I came back outside, her bike was still there. And that's when I noticed the lock wasn't right."

"Not right, how?"

"Drew always twists the cable twice, to make the sign for

infinity. You know, a figure eight?"

She smiles. "I'm aware of what the sign for infinity looks like."

Right.

"But the cable only looped once through her spokes. Plus the combination's numbers weren't set at zero. Like she always does."

When I glance at Detective Holmgren, he stops writing. I get that paranoid feeling again. If life is like this for my mom, I really feel sorry for her.

"And you're positive her bike wasn't at school when you came by in the afternoon?"

"Positive." I describe the plumbing truck.

"Did you get a license plate?"

"No."

Mary Wade says, "Funny you would miss that, being so observant and all."

"What time was that?" the detective asks. "When you saw the truck?"

"Around five thirty."

Mary Wade asks, "Five thirty—exactly?"

"Five thirty-ish."

She smiles. The time seems really important to her. And with each question, she smiles even harder. The questions start making me doubt my own memory. Maybe it was closer to six p.m. Maybe I didn't come back around 11:30. Maybe earlier. Or later.

"If you need the exact time," I say, "you should check the time logs."

"What time logs?"

"In the limousines. Everybody rents those things for the dances and I'm sure the drivers have to report where they are and what time. I saw a white one pull up right after I got there.

A girl named Mackenna Fielding was riding inside."

They look at each other. Mary Wade stops smiling.

"Is something wrong?" I ask.

"Oh, no," Mary Wade says. "It just goes along with what we heard about you two."

I feel that cold thing icing my spine. "What did you hear?"

"Your headmaster says the two of you like doing experiments."

The cold thing sinks deeper.

"Raleigh," asks Detective Holmgren, "why do you say Drew didn't run away?"

"Because she didn't."

"She's run away before."

"Just because somebody does something once, they don't automatically do it again."

"No," says Mary Wade, slowly, "but that behavior is what we call precedent. You might not know what that—"

"I know what precedent means. For a crime. But whatever happened to innocent until proven guilty? Doesn't that rule higher than precedent?"

Detective Holmgren laughs. Mary Wade shoots him a look. He stops.

"Sorry," he says. "I think Raleigh would make a good detective someday."

"Yes." Mary Wade smiles. "In fact, maybe she wants to be one now."

I freeze. Totally freeze.

"Wouldn't it be fun," she continues, "to see how long it took the silly adults to figure out what you two did?"

"No."

"You're keeping secrets."

My blood betrays me, flushing into my face. I have secrets—but not the ones she thinks. And I can't tell her that. So

I stand there, my face getting redder and redder.

She smiles. "Raleigh, is there something you want to tell us?"

"I don't think so."

"This whole place." She opens her arms. The latex gloves covering her hands are dotted with grains of soil. "We haven't found any more evidence. At all. But somehow you knew to look under that giant pile of soil. So maybe you could tell us, *What should we do next?*"

My dad's courtroom has taught me a lot of things. I could say the same for dealing with my mom. Because among the most crucial, vital, important things a person can know is when to take the Fifth.

So I stand there, and say nothing more.

Mary Wade Cavanaugh gives me another smile.

Which really isn't a smile at all.

CHAPTER TWENTY-SIX

W HEN THE DETECTIVE drops me off at school, seventeen minutes remain in fourth period. And wouldn't you know, Parsnip is waiting at the front entrance.

"Straight to class, Miss Harmon," she says.

I walk down the hall, slow as cold sap dripping down a tree. My Rossetti poetry book smells like the clove smoke from the detective's car. The musky odor wafts around me, telling me that what just happened wasn't a dream. Though it sure felt like a nightmare.

At Sandbag's classroom, I peek through the side window. He stands front and center, pontificating. I know what will happen if I open the door.

"Miss Harmon!" The voice skitters down the empty hall.

I turn to see Parsnip, glaring from the other end.

Somewhere in America, a prison is missing its warden.

When I open the door, Sandbag is mid-sentence. He stops talking and I step inside, keeping my eyes on the polished floor, walking toward my desk, praying to become the definition of unobtrusive, obsequious, any of the vocabulary words he's thrown at us.

But, no.

"Well, well, well," he says. "Miss Harmon. How lovely. But please don't take your seat. Come. Stand at the front of the class."

Oh, God. Help!

"Since you've inserted yourself into the classroom so as to receive full attention, I presume your homework is completed. Do give us the honor, won't you? Please recite Christina Rossetti's fabled lines of lyricism."

I know, I'm supposed to acknowledge alliteration—recite Rossetti lines of lyricism—but my brain's first trying to recall the poem.

Nothing.

In the heavy silence that follows, Cassandra Jameson raises her suck-up hand. Sandbag lets her recite the lines.

"Extremely well delivered, Miss Jameson."

I fix my gaze on the empty chair in the back row. Drew sits there. Only now the chair looks so wiped down, so washed clean of every trace of her, it's like she never existed. Which would be fine by Sandbag. He probably hates Drew even more than Ellis and Parsnip. Suddenly I look at him. He was here Friday night. He saw her. And it was here, in this same classroom, that Drew showed him what she's made of—and he isn't. Three years ago. The Monday after she'd run away and Sandbag, purposefully, made sure to post two new vocabulary words on the whiteboard: impudent and vainglorious. He stood here in front of our then-sixth-grade English class and enunciated each syllable, all the while looking directly at the girl in the back row with the wild brown hair doodling out a math theorem on the pages of her Norton Anthology.

"Miss Levinson," he had intoned. "You—more than anyone—should memorize the definitions of impudent and vainglorious."

"Sure," she said, not looking up. "And when you're done talking, I have a challenge word for you."

Challenge words. Sandbag's way of showing off. We brought words to stump him. He always knew the meanings.

"Oh, pray tell," he replied. "What could your challenge word possibly be, Miss Levinson?"

"Catachresis."

There followed one of the most significant silences of my life. Weighty and delicious. Like some Christmas fruitcake that could be used as doorstop. That heavy. We waited. And waited. And I remember looking from Sandbag over to Drew. Back and forth.

The clock ticked.

"At this particular moment," Sandbag replied, finally, "I cannot recall the definition."

Drew looked up. "Catachresis."

Then she spelled it—enunciating each letter like a champion at the national Bee. "Catachresis, the misuse or strained use of words, sometimes for rhetorical effect."

Right there, I knew she was great.

Not good. *Great.*

And now she is not here. Not anywhere.

"Open your poetry book, Miss Harmon."

I open the pages. The scent of cloves rises and suddenly I see the quarry, the sand, Mary Wade Cavanaugh smiling at me.

"Begin at the third stanza," he says.

My throat is closing. I force out the words. " 'Shall I meet other wayfarers at night? Those who have gone before.' "

"Continue."

" 'Then must I knock, or call when just in sight?' " I clear my throat.

"Continue!"

" 'They will not keep you standing at that door.' "

I stare at the page. My eyes sting. The words are suddenly

blurry.

Do. Not. Cr—

"Look at me, Miss Harmon."

I squint, holding back the water in my eyes.

He peers over his half-glasses.

"We, in the royal sense of the plural pronoun, would appreciate your assenting to join our conversations at their appointed times. Your tardy arrival now means you will explain this stanza's enigmatic envoys."

"Assonance," I whisper for enigmatic envoys.

"Correct. I've used assonance. Now what is Miss Rossetti telling us?"

I run my eyes over the words. The words shift. Pop up. Rhymes out of context. Night. Before. Call. Door.

"Hellooooo," he says. "Earth to Miss Harmon, come in, Miss Harmon!"

I hear their giggles.

"I think," I clear my throat. "I think what Rossetti is saying is, you want something done, do it yourself."

I hear laughter now. His face is filled with merriment, mockery.

"What a prosaic interpretation, Miss Harmon, particularly given this poem's powerful lyricism."

Stuff your alliteration, you windbag.

He lifts the book of poetry over his head, holding it like some holy sacrifice.

"What Miss Rossetti is saying is an admonishment—Ask! And she says it shall be given. Seek! And you shall find. Knock! And the door will be opened—"

I walk toward my desk. Sandbag keeps crying out, giving one of his all-time hysterical performances. Everyone is scribbling, committing his words to their notebooks because the best grade goes to whoever can repeat exactly what

Sandbag says. Not what Rossetti wrote.

"Seize the opportunity—"

I sit down and open my own notebook, scribbling down one line:

That's what I said.

WHEN THE FINAL bell finally rings, I head straight for the bathroom, slide into a stall and wriggle out of my uniform. Changing into jeans and a T-shirt, I dance around to avoid all the toilet paper on the floor.

As I open the stall door, I see that somebody's left another giant lipstick kiss on the mirror. Once again, it feels like some kind of personal jab, a joke about kissing my life goodbye. Then again, maybe I really am paranoid.

I don't find Teddy in the Earth Sciences lab. But judging by the crystallized white foam on the counters, he just finished teaching middle schoolers about erosion rates for calcium carbonates. I sweep up the gritty aftermath produced by dripping vinegar and lemon juice on marble and limestone, and empty the dustbin in the trashcan. I bang the bin on the can's side, over and over again.

It feels so good to hit something.

Then I twist my hair into a pony tail, rip off a sheet of butcher paper, and lay it on the counter. I am digging through my backpack for the film canister that holds the soil from Drew's shoe when Teddy rolls into the room.

"Okey-dokey." His red hair lifts off his forehead, unfurling like a stiff flag. "You know what to do, right?"

"I'm not sure."

"Then I did too much last time."

"Bullcrap."

His eyebrows shoot up. "Well I'll be a horse at the races—

Raleigh Harmon speaks an unvarnished word."

"I've had it."

"Good!"

"Stop it—you know something's wrong. You knew we needed to get this soil from her shoe. So stop teasing me and start helping."

"Anybody ever tell you deduction suits you?"

"I mean it." I snap open the film canister, grab the tweezers, pour the soil on the paper.

"Let's consider your hypothesis," Teddy says, rolling closer. "In fact, let's consider your scatoma."

"My . . . what?"

"Blind spot. Drew's got every reason to run away. You heard her mom. They're moving. The woman isn't changing her mind."

"The woman's a drunk."

"More unvarnished words. It's good. Just don't get biggidy with 'em."

Biggidy. That's Hillbilly for "pride."

I scrape the canister with the tweezers. Less than an ounce of soil, and the grain sizes are all over the place.

Teddy leans over. "Sieves," he says.

I crawl into the bottom cupboard. Unlike the Physics teacher, Mr. Straithern, Teddy doesn't have one compulsive bone in his wounded body. So order isn't his priority. The cabinets with geology equipment are as chaotic as the back of his van. I have to shove aside boxes and boxes of donated film canisters and more boxes of thin sections for the microscopes. Some sample minerals. Then old microscopes, the ones we used before he won the scopes with polarized light.

"Bumfuzzled, are ya?" he says.

"No!" I yell from inside the cabinet. "I'm not confused! The problem is you're—" I yank my head out, holding the sieves I've been searching for, and stand up. "—you're a mess!"

But then, suddenly I am confused.

DeMott Fielding stands in the doorway, like he's waiting for permission to enter. My mouth is still hanging open when Tinsley appears beside him, wearing an expression that says if I don't keep my promise to stay away from him, there will be consequences. Serious consequences.

"I have this same speechless effect on the ladies," Teddy says. "It's amazing."

Just for that, I recover. "What're you doing here?"

"I was wondering if you heard anything about your friend."

He steps into the room, followed by Tinsley who's also ditched her school uniform but isn't wearing baggy jeans and an old T-shirt like me. Tinsley wears skin-tight brown jeans with a fluffy white sweater. A marshmallow roasting on a stick.

"Bless her heart," she begins, putting me on notice, "Drew has really pulled off a good trick this time. Like they say, practice makes perfect."

I have a sudden fantasy about a fire and marshmallows turning black from the flames.

DeMott is standing near enough to see the counter. "Is that . . . ?" He points to the soil. "From the . . . ?"

"Yes."

"And you plan to . . . "

"Yes."

Just like yesterday with my mom, he's quick with the clues. Not only will Tinsley have a horseshoe if she finds out he drove me in his truck, but she'll blab all over school about Drew's shoe being found in the quarry.

"Y'all done jibber-jabbing?" Teddy says. "Because we got

work to do."

But DeMott doesn't seem to hear him. He's reached out and picked up the tweezers, using them to spread the soil out across the paper. I glance once at Tinsley.

She mouths words at me—*You promised.*

"I've seen this stuff before," DeMott says.

"Yes," I say with emphasis. "We know." Trying to send him another clue, namely, *Shut up.*

"I mean, from before that."

Tinsley takes a deep breath and heaves a steaming sigh. "Isn't somebody supposed to be at cross-country practice?"

"No," Teddy says. "They don't allow wheelchairs."

She gives him a quizzical look.

DeMott, still holding the tweezers, pinches one of the grains. He lifts it up. "I'd know these things anywhere. They're totally evil."

"Evil-Stone," Teddy says, rolling his eyes. "Only in the South."

I look at the grain. It's one of those red icicles. The color of dried blood.

"I'm serious," DeMott says. "They stick in your socks. You have to pick them out one by one." He turns to Tinsley. "Remember, when you walked on the diamond and got some on your—"

"Ohh," she says. "I hate those things, they—"

Teddy lifts his hand, cutting her off. "Son, start over. You've seen 'em before?"

"Yes, on the field."

"What field?"

"The baseball diamond. At St. Christopher's."

My wrists tingle. "Baseball?"

Drew.

"I soooo despise that dirt," Tinsley whines. "If DeMott

wasn't playing varsity, I'd never go near that field. But he made varsity even as a freshman. And varsity cross country, which might change if he—"

"Darlin'," Teddy says, "close your mouth. DeMott, where's this field?"

DeMott sets down the tweezers. But he says nothing.

"Son, spit it out!"

He looks at me a long moment. He almost looks like he's going to apologize.

"It's just down the road," he says. "Right near the . . . "

He doesn't need to finish.

I know what he's going to say.

Right near the quarry.

CHAPTER TWENTY-SEVEN

WATCH TINSLEY picking her way over the baseball field's grass. She looks like a pampered cat being forced to touch water.

Suddenly DeMott grabs my arm and yanks me to the ground.

"Duck!" he yells.

The baseball whizzes overhead, slamming the chain link fence. The metal shivers after the impact.

"Oh! My! Gawd!" Tinsley screams. "Oh my God! Oh my God! I almost died!"

Of course, she was nowhere close to the line of fire, but she continues to cry out to God. Since we're made in His image, I imagine God is rolling his eyes, like me.

"DeMott!" she screams. "What if that baseball hit me?!"

Oh, the fantasy of it.

But DeMott ignores her question, lifting me from the turf. "You okay?" he asks.

I nod.

He lifts his hand and calls out to the players on the field. "Hold fire!"

The catcher threw that wild ball, missing first base by a good ten feet. He's a scrawny kid, the face mask making his head look out of proportion with his narrow body. His maroon-and-white uniform—for St. Christopher's—bags around his knobby knees.

DeMott picks up the ball, waiting for the catcher to hold up his big mitt. When he throws the ball back, it sinks into the leather mitt with a *thwack*.

The kid winces. Then checks the mitt. He sees the ball. A smile breaks across his face.

"There's different dirt on every turf," DeMott is saying, not realizing he's just made that kid's day. "At least, they look really different to me. You're the geologist. You tell me."

"What do you think is different?"

"Well, over in the dugout, for instance, there's gravel. It's like the rocks we use at Weyanoke to fill in old wells. Or if we need really serious drainage."

I glance over at the dugouts. Tinsley stands near it, leaning into the chain link. She lifts her cell phone and calls out. "Why don't I call your coach and tell him you'll be late for practice?"

"And this stuff," DeMott reaches down, scooping the soil along the first base foul line. "There's no gravel in it. It's just . . . dirt, I guess."

He opens his palm, showing me the soil.

It's dark brown, nearly red, and so fine and soft it must be mixed with silt, which is even finer than sand. I also see those red icicles. I pinch one from his palm and hold it up to the afternoon sun. Those ragged edges, they make me wonder what's in this stuff.

I look back at DeMott, but he's watching one of the coaches barreling toward us.

"Hey, you mind?" the coach barks. "We're about to start a game here."

"Hi there, Coach."

"DeMott? Is that you?"

The coach wears a St. Christopher's uniform, the same maroon-and-white as the catcher, but as he shakes DeMott's hand, he lifts the baseball cap from his head, giving me a lightning-fast once-over. I realize now why DeMott picks up clues so quickly—baseball. He reads signals. And he reads the coach's here.

"Coach, this is Raleigh Harmon. From St. Catherine's. She need to look at the turf." "Now?"

"It'll only take a couple minutes," he says, turning to me. "Right?"

I nod.

"We've got a game," the coach protests.

"Yeah, I see your catcher," DeMott says, nodding toward the scrawny kid. "How about a trade. My time for your time?"

The coach pivots to look at the catcher, who has just missed an easy pitch over the home plate. Scrambling for the loose ball, the catcher trips over home plate, landing on his glove.

"He needs more than five minutes," mutters the coach.

"Twenty," DeMott says. "And you give Raleigh ten around the diamond."

"Done. But step on it. Game starts in forty."

The coach walks away, whistling for his players to meet in the outfield.

"Thank you," I say.

"Thank me later." DeMott points to the parking lot. Dozens of boys in kelly-green uniforms stream from a yellow school bus. "I don't have any pull with the coach from St. Benedict's."

I jog over to home plate, swing my pack forward, and kneel in the dirt. DeMott waits beside me, which feels sort of awkward. I feel obligated to make small talk. "How long have you played baseball?"

"Third grade."

"You must be good."

He seems about to answer, but Tinsley appears again. This time her fingers are laced into the chain link above the backboard. All I can see are the shoulders of her white sweater and her face. It reminds me of those empty plastic shopping bags that the wind blows into fences.

"DeMott," she says in a baby voice, "I'm sure Raleigh would like to do whatever she's doing by herself. You need to get to practice."

His back is to her when he says softly. "Baseball is my best sport. I've made all-state for three years."

I look up, startled to hear him boast. Not only does he not seem the type, but it's very non-Virginian to brag. He kneels down beside me.

"But I'm not very good at cross country," he continues. "I don't like running. That's how life works, isn't it? We're good at the stuff we like, so we do even better—because we like it. But we only get worse at the things we don't like."

I take one of Teddy's canisters from my pack and skim it over the soil, filling the container. "If you don't like to run, why are you doing cross-country?"

He glances over his shoulder. Tinsley isn't looking at us anymore. She's checking her cell phone.

"Because other people want me to."

I take a pinch of the soil, rubbing it between my fingers. Definitely silt in this stuff. It feels soft as talcum powder—silken, buttery—but there's also sand. That part feels gritty. Also, I now see the soil isn't red but orange. Probably full of iron.

"You're like that," he says.

I stare at the soil. The red icicles, I decide, are probably clay. But I can't tell if they're manufactured like bricks, or if they were naturally formed.

"Like what?" I ask.

"You do things because other people want you to. You like to make other people happy."

I lift my gaze, meeting his eyes. Home plate sits between us, but the afternoon sun falls against his back, casting his shadow toward me. When I drop my eyes again, the dirt holds our dark outlines. Our foreheads look like they're touching.

I nod. Our shadows kiss. I feel a flutter below my stomach.

"You're right," I manage to say. "I am like that."

I take a Sharpie from my pack and write the soil's location on the canister—HOME. Meaning, home plate. But as I write out the letters, my mind goes home, to the place where I do all the things that make other people happy. Like, hide my real life. Eat really bad meals. Pretend Friday night dinners are still held at Drew's house. I do all these things for my dad. And for my mom.

DeMott scoops another handful of soil, shaking it until only the red icicles are in his palm. "You know what these things are? Pernicious."

"Good word." I nod, watching our shadows kiss again.

"I'll bet there are still some stuck in my knee pads from years ago."

"Knee pads—you were a catcher?"

"My white socks turned orange in the wash." He lifts his hand, and his shadow seems to caress my face. The feeling in my stomach is so strong I have to look away.

"And I've played just about every field in town," he says, dropping the stones. "I've never seen another field with these mean red things."

I stand up, shattering our shadowed embrace, and take a deep breath to remind myself why I'm here—Drew.

Picking up my pack, I walk down the foul line. The St.

Benedict players are dumping their gear in the visitor's dugout. DeMott follows me.

"I thought baseball was a spring sport," I say.

"Not for the little guys. Elementary school and younger. The city doesn't have enough fields for everybody to play in the spring."

At first base, I scoop soil and mark the new canister. DeMott stays right next to me, glancing to the outfield where the St. Christopher's players have paired off to throw and catch. I glance over, capping the canister. They're such little kids. Pipsqueaks. Why would Drew come here, to watch kids who can't even catch right? The only reason she even watches the Braves' minor league is because every once in a while a player gets called up to the majors—somebody like Titus—and Drew already has the guy's stats going. She gets all wiggy with math-joy about that head start on numbers.

But these kids?

"Have you ever seen her, watching the games?" I ask.

"Who?" DeMott stares at me.

"Drew."

He's still staring.

"My friend, Drew?"

"Oh. Right. Sorry." He's blushing for some reason. "From the pictures I saw on her computer, I've never seen her before. Then again, I never really look at the stands. But Tinsley might know. She's always up there. Gabbing on her phone."

We both glance over. Sure enough, Tinsley's yakking on her cell phone and hopping foot-to-foot in her cute ankle boots. Like she's cold and trying to get warm.

"I hate those things," he says.

"What things?"

"Cell phones."

"Me, too."

He smiles. "That's two things we have in common."

Now I'm blushing, so I grab my pack and quickly make my way around the diamond. DeMott follows but says nothing more. I take soil samples from all three bases and find a dry top layer, almost flaky, but Saturday's heavy rain has percolated through to the next layer, depositing silt. Eluviated, that's the word. When water carries material through soil. When something's deposited on the lower levels, the prefix changes—illuviated. The same leaching process that forces my dad to add new topsoil to the garden every spring. I keep thinking about geology because it takes my mind off DeMott, standing so close I swear I feel heat from his skin.

"She's going to be okay," he says, suddenly.

I don't look up.

"You know that, right?" he says. "She's going to be okay."

Finally, I dare to look at him. That steady blue in his eyes never flickers. No wavering. No doubt or pleading or pretending, and a sense of relief floods through me. I keep staring into his eyes, not wanting to break contact, and then I see something else. Sadness. A deep reserve of sadness, going so far down into him it never reaches the surface. I want to tell him we have three things in common.

I look away, trying to get the courage to speak. I cap the canister, swallow my pride, and the moment is gone.

"What an honor!" The St. Christopher's coach comes barreling toward us again. "Such a huge honor."

He's got his hand out, like he's going to shake DeMott's hand. I step back slightly.

But the coach walks right past us.

DeMott turns, watching him. "Holy Moley!" he exclaims.

I turn to see what's going on, but the sunlight stabs my eyes. Still holding the Sharpie, I lift my hand to block the light. All I see is a black shirt and skin as black as the shirt.

"The boys are over the moon." The coach pumps the black man's hand. "We can't believe you're our umpire."

The umpire, wearing the black shirt, smiles. He sees De-Mott walking toward him with his hand out too. Then the man looks over at me.

His smile falters. He looks uncertain.

"Raleigh," he says. "What're you doing here?"

CHAPTER TWENTY-EIGHT

TITUS.

The umpire is Titus. He walks toward me. The coach and DeMott shift to either side of him, like he's Moses parting the Red Sea.

"Drew with you?" he asks.

Her name, on his lips. It makes me even sadder. But also because I've never seen Titus looking like this. He looks . . . happy. And the man is never happy. Ever. If someone cracks a joke in the diner, he never laughs. He doesn't even smile.

But right now his eyes shine, his teeth glowing in a wide white smile.

"You don't know," I whisper.

"Say what?"

"You don't know."

"Girl," he shakes his head, "plenty I don't know."

"She's missing."

"Missing—the game?"

"She's gone, missing. Nobody's seen her since Friday."

His smile falters. He turns his head, eyeing me like there's more, like I haven't gotten to the punch line.

DeMott picks up another clue. He turns to the coach, "I'll go work with your catcher."

The coach nods, whistles for his players again. I watch the

catcher come loping over the green grass, a puppy getting used to his big feet. DeMott lays an arm across the boy's thin shoulders, leans down to speak with him, guiding him toward home plate.

"Raleigh," Titus says. "Talk to me."

His huge frame seems to swallow the sun. His gaze has gone back to its default setting, a dark heavy expression that's so serious and grave you want to confess every bad thing you've ever done.

"Remember when I left your place on Friday? I've been looking for her ever since. It's like she disappeared. Her stupid parents think she ran away. But I know she didn't run away, that's not what happened. I know it."

He frowns. "You know?"

Just what I need. Another skeptic.

"Okay, fine. You know those purple Converse tennis shoes she always wears? I found one, buried in a quarry down the road from here. And her bike—"

He holds up his hand. The palm is pale pink. "You found a shoe—one shoe?"

"Maybe the police found the other one, but they're telling me they didn't find anything else, which makes no sense. I mean, they were searching that quarry all morning."

"The police." He takes another step back. "The police are involved?"

"Titus—she's missing! Officially missing. Why isn't anybody listening?"

His dark gaze roams over the field. The two teams zip balls back and forth, their bright white socks flickering as they run. Titus's eyes begin to dart, like he's trying to follow every baseball, every player.

"I need to go," he says.

He turns, walking fast to home plate. Over his shoulder he

carries a black bag. When he reaches the plate, he opens it and removes a small broom. He begins sweeping the plate marker, brushing it with furious energy, rubbing and rubbing. I can see the dust and debris and little red pieces of clay flying in the sunlight. He cleans until the plate is nearly white again.

"Are we done here?"

I turn around. Tinsley is standing behind the fence at third base, the phone still in her hand.

When I explain that we need to wait for DeMott because he's helping the catcher, her sigh hisses like the steam radiator in my upstairs bedroom. I turn my back to her again, watching DeMott. He crouches along the first base foul line. Beside him, the boy imitates his stance. With their large gloves raised, they look like some human breed of bicuspid, both of them hinged on their love for this game that I will never understand.

Fifteen feet away, the pitcher stands waiting. DeMott gives him a signal. He winds up, fires the ball.

Thwack!

Right smack into the kid's glove.

DeMott springs up. "You did it!"

The catcher stands, slowly lifting his wire mask, staring into his glove. When he looks up at DeMott, his awe dissolves into a huge smile.

"Told you could do it," DeMott says.

Tinsley releases another sigh.

"Seriously?" she says. "This is what he skipped practice for?"

WE WALK BACK to DeMott's truck—me, DeMott, Tinsley pussyfooting between us.

"So, let me get this straight," he says. "You don't even like baseball but you're on a first-name basis with Titus Williams?"

I shrug. Not to be rude, but because I'm puzzled by the grass. If Drew was here, shouldn't I have found blades of grass in her shoes?

"Raleigh, that guy's a living legend."

"We eat at his restaurant."

"He's got a restaurant?"

Tinsley heaves another hissing sigh. And just for that, I explain the whole thing—how we found Titus's restaurant on Opening Day, how Drew immediately recognized the big guy behind the grill, how Titus gave us free shakes that day and how Drew won another one every week after that because she always beat me there. "Until this Friday. When I really wish she had beat me there."

There's a moment of silence before he says, "She sounds like an amazing girl."

"Amazingly troubled," Tinsley says.

"And you two hang out with Titus Williams?" he asks, ignoring her comment.

"No. Nothing like that."

"DeMott," she says, "if you hurry, you can still make practice."

He checks his watch. Looks at me. "Need a ride home?"

"DeMott! What did I just say?!"

"I heard you." He gives her an odd smile. Kind, but sort of pitying too. "I always hear you."

Yes, the grass is certainly puzzling, but the other enigma is DeMott and Tinsley. Obviously they're dating. I mean, they went to Homecoming and all that. Tinsley could have any guy, and she picked DeMott. Oh, did she pick him.

In the parking lot, she stops at a puddle leftover from Saturday's rain. "DeMott?" Her voice sounds like a child's. "I need your help. I don't want to ruin my boots."

He picks her up like she weighs nothing—because she does—and sets her down on the other side of the puddle. When he turns, apparently coming back for me, I leap over the water. But my landing is off.

"Oh!" Tinsley cries. "You splashed my boots."

"Sorry."

I wait as the two of them deal with Tinsley's suede boots. Frankly, I can't see any water on them, and DeMott says he can't either, but that doesn't stop him from reaching into his truck, taking out a towel, and wiping her boots while she tells him he's a true gentleman.

I watch this whole production with mixed emotions. Helen tells me guys like girls who are a little bit helpless. Needy. If that's what they want, I will never have a boyfriend. It's that simple. I hate relying on anyone. Ever.

"Sure you don't need a ride?" he asks.

"I'm sure."

Tinsley looks over her shoulder, and smiles.

CHAPTER TWENTY-NINE

So I RUN back to school, instead of getting a ride from DeMott.

I sneak around the back, because we're not supposed to go inside this late. I find the entrance to the Lower School is unlocked, and wind my way through the empty halls. As I'm rounding the corner to the Upper School connection, I see John the janitor and his rolling cart. I try to jump back, but he sees me. I stand, frozen, waiting to get busted. But he gives me one hard look then goes back to his work.

I run for the lab.

Teddy's parked his wheelchair in the corner farthest from the door. His arms are raised as far as they go, his wrists are curled, his slanted hands gripping a wad of paper, poised for a three-point shot to the trashcan.

"What letter are you on?" I ask.

"Second A, get out of the way, I haven't dropped one yet."

His slanted fingers release the ball of paper and my eyes follow. The paper backspins over the microscopes, sails across the desks, and slips into the trashcan with barely a whisper against the plastic liner.

"MAGMA!" he calls out.

Our version of HORSE. Teddy always wins. He's got an incredible shot from anywhere in the room.

I walk toward the microscopes, slip off my backpack, and tighten my pony tail which has gone loose from the run back to school. I'm ready to check the soil, but Teddy drops an atomic bomb.

"Your dad just called."

I hold my breath.

"He wanted to know where you were. He sounded a little . . . upset."

Sure, because Ellis called him when the detective showed up. So he must know about the quarry. Which means my dad also knows I didn't tell him about it and there's no explanation for my silence—*You're too involved with mom's problems*? Right.

"Now you owe me." Teddy rolls over to the scopes. "He says you need to get home. But I said you were in the middle of a very important geology project."

"That was true."

"Course it was true." He narrows his eyes. "You lying to your daddy?"

I shake my head, unzip my backpack, and set the canisters on the counter.

"He says you have to be home by six."

I say nothing.

"You be grateful," he says. "You got a dad who cares. Look what Drew got."

Sure, my dad cares—about my mom. He cares about her not hearing anything about Drew's disappearance. That's why he called. He cares that I don't come home late tonight because she's back in some paranoid cave.

"Yeah, he cares." I snap open the canisters.

"In West Virginia, we got a phrase for people like you."

"Just one?"

"We say *Nobody slides on barbed wire*."

"Whatever that means." I hold up the soil sample. "Can we please return to reality?"

I deposit the soil from each of the film canisters on the butcher paper, then circle each with a Sharpie, labeling them 1st, 2nd, 3rd and HOME. The last word brings up an image of Titus, brushing the plate marker. He was so abrupt with me. Just walked off. Maybe he's bothered about Drew. Or obsessive like Drew, and needs to see that plate really clean.

"Sure nice of DeMott to drive you over there," Teddy says.

I take a deep breath, tasting the Sharpie's ink-and-ether. I point at the soil. "First impressions?"

"You don't have much to work with."

"But you told me to leave most of the soil in her shoe."

"Oh, the soil? I was talking about DeMott."

I point, again. "I'm talking about the soil."

"You don't want to talk about DeMott?" He shrugs. "Your call. What's your first step?"

"Test the chemistry, looks can be deceiving."

He smiles. "Sure we're not talking about DeMott?"

"Yes. I'm talking about minerals."

"Okay, you want to test the chemistry. How?"

"First wash the samples. Like I did with the bike soil. It's from a baseball field. Who knows what's in there. So if I wash each sample, and remove the unnecessary debris, then I'll be—"

"Wrong," he says.

"Why?"

"Think."

"No, just tell me!"

"Use your noggin, Raleigh."

"But I don't see why I shouldn't wash the soil. How can I compare the chemistry if I don't clean the minerals first?"

"Good question. But not for your first step."

I glare at him. Then glare at the soils. The Sharpie marks on the white butcher paper look urgent, frantic. And the feeling's increasing. My jaw tightens. "Tell. Me."

"But then you won't remember it later."

We are still locked in an aggressive silence when John the janitor steps into the room. He gives Teddy a nod, Teddy nods back. When John sees me, the recognition is palpable—*Not you again.*

"Don't worry," Teddy says, picking up on it. "She's doing some extra credit. She'll be out of here before six."

"You cleared it with Mr. Ellis?" John asks.

"Actually, I cleared it with three people. Me. Myself. And me-self."

John lifts the garbage can and pours Teddy's paper basket-balls into a larger can on his janitor's cart. "Just don't bring me into it."

"You have my word." Teddy turns back to me. "Figure it out yet?"

I shake my head, too angry to speak. It's almost five o'clock and I have to be home by six. I don't have time for games.

"I'll give you one clue," he says. "Clay dissolves in water."

"I know that."

"No more clues."

John calls out, pointing to the whiteboard. "You finished?" he asks.

"Scottish, actually." Teddy laughs at his own joke.

I'm not amused. And John stares at him like he's got something wrong with him.

"Sorry," Teddy says, not sounding sorry at all. "Yes, I'm finished with the whiteboard. Wipe away."

John lifts a spray bottle and squirts. The words on the board bleed—*migmatite* into *foliated*. The sharp scent of alcohol cuts the air, clears my head. I glance down, searching the piles of soil. The red icicles freckle each sample. They're in each pile so I need . . .

"Proportions."

"Getting warm," Teddy says.

"Relative proportions."

It must be the correct answer because Teddy rolls away.

"So sieve it?" I call out. "Like I was already doing before?"

But he's already chatting away with John, getting into a discussion of the playoffs. I glance back at the soil. The key is in the percentages. How much red clay is in each sample?

"That pitcher," Teddy says. "Guy gives me a heart attack every time he takes the mound."

I scoop up the soil from her shoe, still waiting for me, and deposit the grains on the standing scale, cataloguing its total weight. I return the soil to the paper, clean the scale for the next sample and weigh it. I weigh every sample.

"Maybe the Braves should lose," Teddy says. "Winning thirteen titles, that's unlucky."

"Luck doesn't exist," I call out.

"Then again," Teddy says to John, as if he's heard nothing, "winning thirteen titles would prove luck exists."

I grab the sieves and clank them—hard—on the counter. Outfielders, they're discussing outfielders now.

For a guy who can't run, Teddy sure is obsessed with sports.

I unsnap the sieves' brass buckles, making sure to be extra noisy. But neither of them even glances over.

Geology sieves are made of brass. They're round and this set is four inches in diameter. When they're all buckled together, they look like a bronzed wedding cake, tall and regal. Inside each one is a screen, and they run in descending sizes—largest screen at the top of the tower, smallest at the bottom.

I begin pouring the first sample into the top of the sieve. I buckle the lid, pick up the entire two-foot tower and shake the thing. Shake and shake and shake. The janitor leaves and Teddy goes to work at his desk. I keep shaking, relishing the sound of soil sluicing against the brass like a percussion instrument.

Teddy rolls out of the room.

I unbuckle the top pan. It's empty. The second pan holds the red icicles, which have slipped through the opening in that first filter. I place those grains on the scale, record their weight and repeat the same procedure for each filter. The bottom pan holds the very finest particulates of soil, dust that is almost weightless.

I repeat this same process for each sample. It's tedious work and the weights come to decimal points in the hundreds of thousands. Fractions upon fractions. Thirty minutes later, I've got a headache, and Teddy rolls back into the lab.

"Can I round off these numbers?" I ask.

"You plan to work for the government?"

"What's that got to do with anything?"

"Bureaucrats might be fine with rounding off. But trust me, Raleigh, you ain't no government bureaucrat."

"That's a double negative."

"Maybe I'm wrong about you."

I don't round off, and it makes for difficult mathematics. Finally, when I've calculated each sample's relative percentage of clay, sand, silt and dust, Teddy comes over.

"Lemme see."

I've subtracted each individual pan's weight from the total weight, converted that fraction into a percentage. As Teddy reads over the numbers, I realize how deliriously happy this math would make Drew.

Math—plus baseball.

My eyes burn. Where is she?

"Sedimentary, my dear Watson."

I bend down, pretending to search for something in my backpack. Anything. I can't bear any humor right now.

"Hey, I'm making a Sherlock Holmes pun," he says.

I nod, so vigorously my pony tail bounces.

"Did you know Sherlock Holmes is the father of forensic geology?"

"He's fictional."

"Don't get biggity with me, I know he ain't real. But go read *A Study in Scarlet*. It'll show you—"

"No!" I spin on him. "I'm not reading anything. She's gone, I need help, I don't need more breadcrumb clues or jokes—I need help! Can't you just help?" My eyes feel like they're on fire, my throat clamped in a vice grip. Any second, I'm going to lose it.

He stares at the page with my calculations.

I can hear my breathing. I'm almost panting. I close my mouth, holding my breath, feeling my heart pound against my chest. I focus my eyes on his strange fingers, he's running them up and down the numbers, muttering under his breath. Then he sets the paper on the counter.

"Third base," he says.

I pick up the paper, reading my numbers for third base. That soil contained twenty-nine percent red icicles.

"Now check the shoe sample," he says, quietly.

The shoe sample had thirty percent red shards.

"That's your closest match," he continues. "Next is the pitching mound, but that's got forty-five percent. Quite a jump. Second base is only eleven percent, home plate is near sixty percent. So let's go out on a limb. Drew was near third base."

I nod. But I can't look at him.

"What's with the tears?" he says.

I lift my hand, covering my face.

"Well," he says after a long moment. "At least you didn't say you're fine."

I wait for the burn in my eyes to recede. Wait for my throat to open. I take a deep breath, stilling myself. My voice is still wobbly.

"I still don't know why she was there. Or why she was at the quarry."

I pause, wondering about telling him my theory. That Drew went to the quarry for me, for geology. How guilty I feel. But he nods at the clock.

"We'll try again tomorrow," he says. "I gotta get you home or the judge will hold me in contempt."

I CLIMB INTO his stinking van, listening to him muttering about my dad throwing him in the "hoosegow," whatever that is, if we're late. But when he turns the ignition, the radio drowns out his mutterings. He's got the thing turned up full blast and some woman's reading the news, which means we're in trouble because the news is always only read at the top of the hour. Six o'clock.

Teddy drives quickly out of the parking lot, but we get stuck at the extra-long stop light at Libbie and Patterson.

"The judge," he hollers over the news reader, not even considering turning it down. "Is he the forgiving type?"

My dad says mercy triumphs over justice. But mostly that's true for my mom and Helen. Not so much for me. But maybe Teddy can charm him, let him know we tried to be on time. I look over, about to ask him to remove the bandana he's tied over his red hair, when the lady on the radio says, "Breaking news tonight regarding a missing West End girl."

Our heads swivel toward each other.

"Drew Levinson, a tenth-grade student at Saint Catherine's School hasn't been seen since—"

A car honks behind us. Teddy yanks the lever for his gas pedal. The van leaps forward.

"—and today police took into custody a person of interest in the girl's disappearance. Jayne Levinson, the girl's mother, says her daughter had been visiting places in the city behind her back."

"What?" I say out loud.

The next voice is Jayne. "I want some answers. I want my daughter back."

"She's lying!" I yell at the radio.

Teddy only stares down the road.

"According to police, the girl was dropping by Big Man's Burgers, a diner in the Scott's Addition neighborhood. It's owned by Titus Williams. A Richmond native, Williams played three seasons with the Atlanta Braves."

The next voice that comes on sounds serious and stilted. Like a person reading a statement. "Mr. Williams has been taken into police custody for questioning. We will release more information as it become available."

"That was Richmond Police Chief Ed Shaunnessy," the news lady says. Her voice shifts. "Tomorrow's weather looks sunny and cold. Temperatures in the—"

Teddy punches the knob, silencing her.

I have no words. He says nothing either.

His van comes down Monument Avenue and circles Robert E. Lee. When I glance out the window, the night lights flash on the bronzed figures. I stare at the general, his horse.

They are right here, yet somehow they look distant and faraway, like sepia figures who have wandered home from the war, much too late.

CHAPTER THIRTY

I N THE FRONT parlor, our heavy velvet drapes block any view of the outside world. The grand piano grows dust as thick as gray fur. And in the far corner of the big room, an ancient record player slowly spins a tune, a song about how much one man can love one woman.

In sickness and in health, for richer, for poorer, 'til death do they part, my parents slow-dance on Monday nights. My dad claims it puts the rest of the week in perspective. But as I stand in the parlor's doorway, panting from racing out of Teddy's van to the front door, I feel totally out of sync.

My mom's eyes are closed and she leans into him, melting into his chest. His eyes are open, staring at me over the top of her head with an expression that repeats what he told me in the cellar Friday night—the situation is serious but not hopeless.

He speaks into her hair. "Somebody's watching us."

She pulls back, startled, but laughs when she sees me. Not a happy laugh. More like relief.

"Sorry," I say. "Mr. Chastain got caught in traffic."

My dad doesn't want me calling Teddy by his first name. And Teddy hates hearing Mr. Chastain. So when in Rome . . .

My dad takes her hand, kisses it and says, "We'll be right in for dinner. Give me one minute with Raleigh."

When she passes me in the doorway, she hesitates. One

moment. Two. I count them, sensing a clicking mechanism inside her head, the thing shifting like a tumbler in a revolver, searching for the chamber that holds the bullet.

I lift everything inside of me, and smile.

She walks down the hall.

When her steps fade into the kitchen, he asks, "Why didn't you tell me?"

"Mr. Chastain said he told you—I was working. In the lab."

"Not that." He opens the big wooden armoire by the front door, rummaging in his coat. He pulls out a newspaper, folded tightly to show only one headline.

MISSING GIRL. I see Drew's name below it.

"I did tell you!"

"Keep your voice down," he says.

"In the cellar," I whisper. "Friday night? I told you Drew was missing, you just didn't listen."

He hands it to me. "Read it."

I read it alright, but after the first paragraph it's like I'm looking through the wrong end of a pair of binoculars. The words shrink. I can see her name there, our school, a quote from Detective Holmgren asking for any information. But no mention of her shoe at the quarry. That means the cops are probably withholding that detail. For later. For when they catch somebody. But just as I'm coming back to normal, I see a small gray box to the right of the story. It shows a timeline for last Friday, the day "the missing girl, Drew Levinson," didn't show up for her regular weekly dinner with her best friend—at Big Man's Burgers.

Even though I'm done reading the story, I continue to stare at the newspaper. My heart can't hold any more dread right now, but here it comes, stomping toward me like a black-booted mercenary, kicking down all that righteous anger I just flung at my father.

He listened.

He's a judge. My dad listens to everything.

I hand him the paper.

"Because you wouldn't let me go."

"So you decided to lie?" he asks.

There is nothing to say. He pushes the paper back into his coat. Then takes several deep breaths, calming himself.

"How long?" he asks.

"How long . . . have we been going there?"

We both know that's the question. And we both know I'm stalling.

"For a while," I finally say.

"Raleigh . . . "

"Opening Day."

"You've been lying to me since Opening—that's—April?"

I don't move. I don't even blink.

"Two girls hanging around Scott's Addition? It's one of the most dangerous neighborhoods in the city. Raleigh, you were not raised to be this naive."

"I'm not naive."

"Oh no? Look what happened. Drew's disappeared."

My battered heart gives a sudden kick. And it sends out that mean little lawyer who lives inside me. She mounts a stubborn pony, rides to my rescue, waving her point.

"So you were wrong," I say.

"Pardon?"

"You were wrong. You said Drew ran away. That's what you said, on Friday. So you were wrong."

"Yes," he says. "I was wrong. Because you lied."

That last word hangs in the silence. It should shut me up. But that tiny attorney is still riding fast.

"How can you accuse me?" I protest. "It's not any different from the stuff you tell Mom."

"Do not attempt that comparison, young lady."

"The point is—"

"The point is you're grounded."

"What?!"

"Quiet," he says. "Grounded. For two weeks."

"I can't stay in this house for—"

"Alright, three weeks."

"That's not fair!"

"How about a month?"

I clench my teeth, restraining that galloping attorney. But she kicks, demands to make one last point.

"If you ground me," I say, "how am I supposed to find Drew?"

"Find her?" He glances down the hall, making sure Mom's still in the kitchen. "You're not supposed to find her. The police are." He reaches into his coat again, and pulls out a small black rectangle. "And from now on, you're carrying this with you at all times."

He hands it to me. A cell phone.

"If you don't know how to use it, Helen can show you. She's coming home this week."

"What?!"

"Keep your voice down," he says, not even correcting me with *pardon*. "Your mother. She needs to see Helen."

In my hand, the phone feels like a cold stone. My mother needs to see Helen, because I'm not measuring up to her insane standard. With one finger, I jab the phone, releasing the sharp electronic sound that makes me hand it back to him.

"Forget it. I'm not using that thing. I don't even like ordinary phones."

"This is non-negotiable, Raleigh."

"Why?"

"And since your mother isn't ready to hear about wireless communication," he says, ignoring my question, "keep the ring on vibrate instead of sound. I had the tech people put my number in there, at the courthouse, along with Helen's. But you can always dial 9-1-1 if—"

"If paranoia is contagious."

He glances down the hall again. It's a long moment before he turns toward me again.

"Titus Williams has a record for statutory rape."

"What?!" I jerk back, like I've been kicked in the gut. Then stabbed in the heart. "No. That's . . . I can't . . . no— that's impossible." But dad, the judge. I can't deny it—he would know.

"You're being naive, Raleigh."

"I'm not!" My voice is rising. *But this can't be true.*

"Please keep your voice down," he says. "His niece. She was fourteen. That's who he violated. Remind me, how old is Drew?"

I can see the anger flaming his eyes. But something is splashing against the fire, dowsing the heat. Sadness, almost apology. And fear. He knows how old Drew is. Fourteen.

"Then why wasn't that in the paper?" I finally ask.

He doesn't reply.

"Dad, what did you do?"

"I did some checking."

"Without talking to me first?"

"Now we're even." His eyes glisten. "Terrible. Isn't it?"

I feel desperate. So desperate. Not Titus—not Drew. "Just because somebody says it, doesn't mean it happened. You've told me that a hundred times, accusing someone is not the same as evidence."

"The girl's mother—his own sister-in-law—got a restraining order. And Titus violated it. No minors were supposed to come into his restaurant."

"Dad, he never touched us."

But as the words leave my mouth, I see Titus. At the baseball field. The same field where Drew apparently was, right before she disappeared. Anger comes suddenly. A volcano of frustration and hurt and I don't even know what, but I want to hit something.

"You're the reason he's in jail!" I yell.

He doesn't even turn his head, because there's no sound coming down the hall. Like some sixth sense, he seems to feel her presence. I glance past him. My mother stands, her wiping her hands on another Betty Homemaker apron. Bright yellow, some giant flashing traffic light that says, Caution: the Cook is Insane.

I slide the cell phone up my sleeve.

"Jail?" she says, in a high trembling voice. "What's this about jail?"

My mom's got trigger words. "Jail" is a big one. When she was sixteen, her mother threw her in jail for being crazy. At that time in rural North Carolina, parents could punish their kids however they wanted, even putting them behind bars. As soon as that cell door opened, my mother lit out for Virginia. Helen was born the next year. Whatever happened to my mother in that jail, I don't know. But the word strikes terror in her.

And now that I've thrown out the trigger word, I have to clean up the mess.

"Dad said if I don't wear my bike helmet I could go to jail."

He gives me a sharp look. But my statement is a lie. But I look back at him, trying to remind him of his lecturing me on the helmet laws. Once. Long ago.

My mom keeps wiping her hands on the apron. When she

speaks, her voice is that pitched tremolo. "Helen is coming home Thursday, her bus arrives at three-forty-five. See how the numbers align? Three. Four. Five. It's all lining up."

Gently, he takes her arm and walks her to the kitchen. I stand there, feeling like I've been beaten up inside and out, and watch them until they disappear into the kitchen.

In the silence, the old phonograph plays. But the song is over. The record is spinning, the needle winding around and around until somebody makes it stop.

DINNER IS A lentil stew. It looks like tree barf.

I choke it down then go upstairs and ignore my homework.

I type into my computer's search engine "geology baseball soil."

I'm stunned when the results show up. Its proper name is "ballfield dirt," and there's actual science with it.

Who knew?

When clays and silts get wet, they turn into mud with the consistency of melted plastic. But baseball fields need clay and silt because they keep the surface soft for running and sliding. To make the right kind of ballfield dirt, geologists mix specific ratios, always adding sand because it helps keep the wet stuff from getting too sticky. But I don't see anything about those weird red icicles in the St. Christopher's soil until I do another search.

It's a special product called vitrified clay. Vitrified basically means the clay is roasted at a super high temperature that drives out all the moisture. But it's an expensive process and most ball fields can't afford to use the stuff. But it works to keep all the other soils from getting clumpy, especially in heavy rain.

I can actually see some donor paying for that stuff for the

St. Christopher's field—maybe even DeMott's wealthy family. Richmond experiences heavy rain in spring, which must mess with baseball season. And now it makes sense that there were more red icicles around the pitching mound and batting area—where every person needs secure footing, not sticky mud.

I copy all the information and send a file to Teddy's home email.

When I walk downstairs, it's just past nine p.m. and my parents are cuddled on the couch. An old black-and-white movie plays on the television. Which is also black-and-white. Sometimes I swear this whole house is stuck in 1950.

But worse is my mother's eyes. They're glassy now. Like the meds have taken over. She doesn't even look at me.

"Goodnight," I say.

"Want to watch?" my dad asks.

"Thanks, but I have to get up early."

I walk back up the stairs, telling myself that is not a lie.

My alarm is already set. For 1:00 a.m.

CHAPTER THIRTY-ONE

THE NIGHT AIR is so cold that silver clouds bloom out of my mouth as I run down our alley. I cross Monument Avenue—the road is deserted—and hide behind Stuart Circle Hospital.

Taking out my new cell phone, I punch in the number for Officer Lande. My fingers are cold, stiff. A shiver rattles down my back as I hold the phone to my ear, thinking about how much Drew hates being cold. Not just the temperature, but that it represents a lack of thermal energy.

Please, wherever she is, keep her warm.

"Officer Lande speaking."

"It's Raleigh."

The pause is long enough for me to guess what she's thinking. *It's 1:16 a.m.—why are you calling me*? So I answer.

"I'm calling because I need to talk to you. Now."

THE BLACK-AND-WHITE POLICE cruiser swoops down West Avenue, creeping behind the hospital until she sees me jump out of the bushes. I yank open the back door, drop into the hard plastic seat, and feel the heat shroud me like an electric blanket.

One last shiver creeps up my back.

Officer Lande turns in her seat, studying me through the metal cage separating the front and back seats.

"And your parents know you're out here, again?"

"And you're going to law school?"

"Law school?" She frowns. "No. Why do you say that?"

"Because my dad says lawyers only ask questions they already know the answers to."

She has the kind of skin my mom is deathly afraid of—freckled from too much sun—and when she smiles, the freckles rise like bubbles.

"It's an honest question," she says. "I'd like an honest answer."

"My mom isn't all . . . " I hunt for words, avoiding the words I've learned not to say. "My mom doesn't think I'm her real daughter, okay?"

Another frown. "Who does she think you are?"

"Some spy. An impostor. Is Titus Williams in jail?"

"Now you're the lawyer." She turns around, facing the windshield.

"I know he's in jail," I admit. "But I don't know why."

"Titus Williams is a person of interest in the disappearance of Drew Levinson."

"If I wanted an official statement, I could read the newspaper."

She barely hears me. Her radio is crackling, bursting with the letters and numbers I used to hear in court when people read police transcripts. The Hundred Code, according to my dad. Officer Lande's radio is talking about a "possible four-one-five" in Jackson Ward. She seems to be listening to the report, so I glance out my window. I've been worried one of our neighbors will see me out here. Or see her cruiser—and me inside the cruiser. They're sure to ask my dad what's going on.

I slide down in the seat.

The radio goes quiet. She turns in her seat again.

"It's very serious, Raleigh."

"No kidding, that's why I'm out here in the freezing cold."

"I mean, about Titus."

She waits for me to say something.

I give her what she wants. "He always seemed like a nice guy."

"Yeah, well, professional athletes think they're above the law."

"I don't think he does."

"Really?" The metal cage fractures her severe face. "Did he tell you two girls not to come into his restaurant?"

"No. But he once kicked out a guy who cursed in front of us. And then he apologized to me and Drew that we had to hear it."

"Great." Officer Lande's face doesn't change. "Did he ever approach you outside of his restaurant?"

"No."

"What about Drew?"

I don't say anything. Before seeing Titus at that baseball field, I'd say *No*. But now . . .?

"Okay," she says. "Did he do anything that would keep you two coming back each week?"

"Not really."

"Raleigh. Tell me."

"Free shakes. Whoever got there first got a free shake." My stomach knots at the thought.

She nods. "Were you ever alone with him?"

"No."

"What about Drew?"

An invisible rope tightens around my ribcage. I can barely breathe. "Drew always got there first." Then I quickly add,

"But there were always other customers around."

"But on this Friday she didn't show up at all?"

"If there was something going on between her and Titus, I would see it."

"Raleigh, don't be naive."

That word! I hate that word. But then it hits me, maybe she's right. Drew didn't tell me she was moving. She didn't tell me about that baseball field. Or the quarry. Or—

"I'm going to tell you something," Officer Lande says, carefully. "It's for your own protection. We haven't even released it to the media. But somebody tipped us off and we found the paper trail on Titus Williams. Raleigh, do you know what statutory rape is?"

"When an adult has sex with a minor, even a consenting minor."

"There was a restraining order against Titus Williams that said he couldn't be within a hundred yards of any minor. Do you know how far that is? An entire football field."

"And he broke it by having us in his restaurant," I say, remembering what my dad told me.

"Except one thing," she says. "That restraining order ran out Friday. The very same day Drew went missing."

My ribs, it feels like they're stabbing me. I suck in a breath. "So why wasn't there a court case?"

"What?"

"If he did rape somebody—why wasn't there a court case?"

"How do you know there wasn't?"

"Because a restraining order isn't the same thing as a court order."

"How do you know all this?"

"And with a minor involved, I'll bet the restraining order was sealed. So that's why the media doesn't know about it.

Yet."

She shakes her head. "Where did you learn this stuff."

My dad. That's how I know all this. And my second bet would be that my dad tipped off the police to the paper trail on Titus Williams. The judge? He read every sealed word of that restraining order.

And that's what my new cell phone is all about.

"Just so you know, I'm not naive."

"You're young."

"So?" My voice is too forceful. But I don't care. "Unlike everyone else, I refuse to jump to conclusions. You get a hypothesis, you test it. Even if that idea looks right at the start, you test it. And besides, there's something called the presumption of innocence, unless somebody suddenly abolished the fifth, sixth, and fourteenth amendments."

"Wow," she says.

"What?"

"You should go to law school."

"No way." All that time in my dad's courtroom has showed me what happens to a person who argues for a living.

"Since you put it that way," she says, "let's go through a hypothesis. What time does Titus open for dinner on Friday?"

"Four or four-thirty, I think."

"And the last time someone saw Drew was what time?"

"Three . . ." My voice trails off because Tinsley and Sandbag were the last people to see her, I think. "We should probably say three-ish."

"Okay, three-ish. That means ninety minutes from when she was last seen to when he's opening his restaurant. What if she met him somewhere, like the quarry or—"

I hate it. The whole idea—it's possible. I hate it.

She keeps going.

"Drew loves baseball, and Titus Williams played in the

major leagues. What if Titus asked her to meet him somewhere? And he told her it was a surprise, maybe for you. Do
you think she would tell you, honestly?"

The chill comes back, running up my spine, triggering an
image of an umpire. Titus. A baseball umpire for kids'
games—but that restraining order said he can't be near kids. I
want to ask Officer Lande, but it's too much to say. Closing
my eyes, I try to see his face, whatever expression he showed
when I said Drew was missing.

But all I see the sun, so bright it's blinding.

Drew was there, standing on that same soil. She had to be.
Where else would she get those red icicles? Did she watch him
ump games? Maybe she really does know him better than I do.
They both loved baseball. What if they talked before I got
there on Fridays? What if Titus threw out that cursing guy to
fool us? What if all along he was planning to do something to
Drew?

What if—whatifwhatifwhatif.

The warmth inside the car is suffocating. I reach over,
trying to open the window. But my hand just slides over the
things. There's no button, no door handles.

"I've got to talk to him," I say.

"Who?"

"Titus."

"Raleigh, he's in custody."

"I can still talk to him. Unless there's some gag order."

The cage divides her hard face into quadratic crystals. She
stares at me a long time.

"I don't know," she says.

"Can you please call somebody who does?"

"Raleigh, it's almost two in the morning."

"And cold and Drew's still out there," I say. "Somewhere."

CHAPTER THIRTY-TWO

A DETECTIVE MEETS us in the parking lot of the Richmond city jail. He's a short guy and his nose is shaped like a light bulb. It's also red, which makes him look like he should be hanging out with those dwarves who worship Snow White.

Sneezy, Grumpy, Sleepy. But definitely not Happy.

He sneers at Officer Lande and points at me. "This is what you hauled me down here for—her?"

I'm still sitting in the back seat of Officer Lande's cruiser, but now her window is open, the cold air sliding into the car. It feels damp, almost marshy. Just west of here the James River carves a path around the jail, like it's trying to create a moat.

"The missing girl is her best friend," Officer Lande explains. "She knows the guy you took into custody, Titus Williams. She wants to talk to him."

"At two in the morning."

"That's right."

"You call Holmgren?" he asks, apparently referring to Detective Holmgren, the one who drove me to the quarry.

"Yes. Holmgren said to call you."

"Course he did, two in the morning, I'm sick as a dog." He plops his fat hands on his knees and leans into the open window by Officer Lande's face. She immediately shifts away, putting space between them.

He turns and wheezes at me. "Hey, where's your parents?"

Sandbag has told us we have a duty to correct bad grammar whenever we hear it. Which would mean saying, *You mean, where are my parents*? But Sandbag wouldn't understand the bigger correction, which is what I give the dwarf detective.

"Parental notification isn't required if I'm talking to somebody already in police custody."

He sniffs, stares at me for a long moment, then looks at Officer Lande. "Who's this, Nancy Drew?"

But before she can say anything, his face scrunches up, swallowing his eyes. In a split second, he sneezes into the open window. Officer Lande slides toward the passenger seat.

Standing—which doesn't make him that much taller than when he was stooping—the detective tugs a handkerchief from his pocket, wipes his light bulb nose, and returns the disgusting rag to his pocket. It makes me feel sick, and it makes me think of that forensic geology case Teddy made me read—the snotty handkerchief whose dirt convicted a killer.

"Simon," Officer Lande says from across the front seat. "What's the harm, let her talk to him."

He leans in again. "What's your name, sweetheart?"

"It's not Sweetheart."

"Course not." He makes a face. "So what is it?"

"Raleigh." I don't want to give my last name, since a steady parade of Richmond detectives marches though my dad's criminal courtroom every day, so I keep talking. "And I would appreciate it if you'd let me talk to Titus because I'm probably the only person in Richmond who knows both the victim and the alleged perpetrator."

He looks at Officer Lande. "Where did you find this kid?"

"Simon," she says. "This is the kid who found the shoe."

His beady eyes widen. "You're the kid who found that

shoe?" He suddenly smiles. It gives me the same creeps I got at the quarry with Mary Wade Cavanaugh. "Why didn't you say so?"

WAY BACK IN April, after we found Big Man's Burgers, Drew showed me one of her collectible baseball cards. It was Titus, from his days playing for Atlanta. The white uniform looked tight on him, the red BRAVES stretched across his huge chest. He held a baseball bat slanted over one shoulder, but what I couldn't stop staring at were his biceps. His arms looked like forged-iron cannonballs. Even in the diner, with a paunch pushing against his apron, Titus looks powerful—the Big Man himself.

But now, as he shuffles into the brightly-lit visitor's area at the city jail, an orange jumpsuit floats around him like a deflated life raft. The numbers stenciled on his chest look nothing like that word BRAVES.

Reaching over to my right, I pick up the telephone receiver and wait for him to do the same. Six inches of Plexiglass separate us.

That, and a whole 'nother world.

"Please?" I ask, when he doesn't pick up the phone on his side.

His brown eyes are as shiny as glazed pottery, baked at two thousand degrees.

"I really need to talk to you," I tell him.

He snatches the receiver. It looks like a toy in his enormous hand.

"Thank you," I say.

His mouth tightens.

"Is it bad in here?"

"What do you think," he growls.

"I think we need to talk. About Drew."

"Yeah. Right. Guilty 'til proven innocent. That's how it works."

"No, that's not how it works. But I want to know about the restraining order."

His jaw knots. "What about it."

"We weren't supposed to be at your restaurant."

He cuts his eyes to the left, taking in the armed guard standing beside a locked steel door, then returns to me. "I need to explain myself, that it?"

"She's my best friend. If this situation was reversed, how would you feel?"

"Same as now, innocent."

"Okay. Where were you Friday afternoon?"

"I was cooking you onion rings."

I take the jab with a nod. "Before that. Like, where were you around three o'clock?"

"I was checking on some land."

"Real estate?"

His scowl is frightening. "Real estate? I say anything about real estate?"

"You said land."

"Yeah, turf." He almost spits the word at me. "I went to check on turf."

"What turf?"

"Where I saw you—"

"The baseball field?"

"You seen me at some other field? I don't think so."

My fingers go numb. I can't feel the phone.

He narrows his eyes. "Why you lookin' at me like that?"

Because I can't breathe, because that rope tied around my ribs is getting so tight it's cutting off all my air, because everything else swims into focus. The phone, I can smell the stink of it, like dirty, greasy coins. The lights, shimmering with fluorescence. The guard shifting his weight, his shoes squeaking.

"Hey," Titus says. "You got something to say to me?"

I swallow a gulp of air. "You were at that baseball field on Friday."

"What I said."

"What time were you there?"

"I don't know—"

"What time!"

He glares at me. "Why you want to know?"

"Tell me. Now."

He takes a long moment before responding. "Around three."

"Are you sure?"

"Are you deaf?" he asks.

"How long did you stay at the field, after three o'clock, on Friday afternoon?"

"I get it." He leans back, his lips curled with disgust. "I get it now. The police sent you in here. Need another statement, that it?"

"No. It's me. And I want the truth. Who was there?"

"Where?"

"At the baseball field."

"Nobody."

"You didn't see Drew?"

He stares at me, hard. "I know you ain't deaf."

"Why—why did you go to that field, on Friday?"

"Why's it matter so much?"

Because the hypothesis that Officer Lande proposed might be right. But I'm not ready to spring that yet.

"I've seen that sign on your restaurant. With the hours. You close at two."

"So."

"So on Fridays you open for dinner. When? Four thirty?"

He comes forward, inches from the Plexiglass barrier, the phone gripped so tightly his knuckles look white. "I went to that field 'cause it was gonna rain. You hear me now? Rain. It was gonna rain on Saturday. But that field for rich kids, they say it can take water, a lot of water, how it's kept up and all. So I went there to check the turf. You got it now? You got every last word for the cops?"

His voice is cold as stone.

"You went," I take another breath, "because you're the umpire."

"Yeah, the umpire." In that same cold voice he explains the umpire is responsible for calling a game due to rain. But if the umpire thinks the turf is okay, the players are safe, he can keep the game on. He planned to do that, but Saturday morning even the rich-kid field was puddled and muddy.

I remember that morning, riding my bike through that heavy rain, how the maple leaves washed from the trees, how the water dripped on the leaves at Teddy's house, how the gray gloom blanketed the lab while we examined the soil from Drew's bike tire.

It rained.

"And what about your niece?" I ask.

"Oh, man." He shakes his head, leans back in the chair. "Okay. What about my niece?"

"The restraining order. I know all about it."

"You don't know nothin'."

"I know Drew and I shouldn't have been eating in your restaurant."

"And what—I asked you to come?"

"Free shakes."

"Believe me," he says, "I regret that."

He stands up suddenly.

The guard at the door startles, steps forward, hands on his weapon belt. He looks at me, searching for signals, like I can tell him what threat the big guy poses.

But when I look back at Titus, he's replacing the phone in the carrier so gently, so softly I barely hear the line click dead.

CHAPTER THIRTY-THREE

THE HALLWAY THAT Officer Lande leads me down, away from the visitors' room, is scrubbed like a hospital. But nothing can get rid of the smell. It's a sour-and-salty odor, like panic brewed with fear.

At the end of the hall, she opens an unmarked door. The dwarf detective is inside, waiting. Aside from him and his red nose, the room's as spare as anything I've ever seen. Concrete floor. Two plastic chairs. One steel table, dented. There's also a drain in the floor, like they hose down the room to clean it.

"So, what'd he say?" he asks, before I even sit down in one of the plastic chairs.

"Not much."

Officer Lande sits across from me at the table. The detective leans against the wall. Right next to him is a four-foot mirror which any functioning idiot knows is two-way with people on the other side watching. And listening.

"Think he's innocent, don't you?" he says.

"I never said that."

"But you don't think he's guilty."

"I don't think I know. For sure. Do you?"

"No, but I'm not naive."

What's with this word? Why is everyone saying it? I grit my teeth. "I'm not naive."

The detective laughs but when it turns into a cough, he yanks out that disgusting handkerchief.

"Do you even know the definition of naive?" I demand. Officer Lande reaches across the table, touching my arm. I yank it away. "Do you?"

He wipes his mouth. "Course I do, sweetheart."

"Naive means simple. If I'm so simple, how come I'm the only person in this room who seems to care that there's a difference between circumstantial evidence and forensic proof?" My voice reminds me of the tone my father takes when he's schooling courtroom lawyers in legal procedures, people who should know what to do but for some reason refuse to do it.

His beady little eyes shift to Officer Lande. Her eyebrows are up, like she's stunned.

"Did you hear me?" I ask.

"Sure," he says, taking his time wiping his bulbous nose. "Watch a ton of TV, do you?"

We can't watch TV at my house because my mom's too paranoid for anything halfway current. The news? No way. That's why they watch black-and-white movies she's seen ten times. There are no surprises. I glare at him. "I never watch TV."

"Well, sweetheart," he says, "there's a big difference between circumstantial and forensic, but you're forgetting some other things. There's experience. Law enforcement instincts. Knowledge that comes from doing this job for years and years. And every one of those things says sexual predators never wake up suddenly and decide to quit their filthy habit. They get worse. They always get worse." His little eyes are on me. "He ever make a move on you?"

"No."

"Really?"

"Yes."

"Just your little friend."

"My little—?" I stare at him. "You mean, Drew?"

"Yeah."

I glance at Officer Lande but she's inspecting the sleeve of her blue uniform. I wait for her to look up. But she doesn't. "What are you implying?"

"Sweetheart, we know all about the two of you."

"Who?"

"You and your little friend. Keep to yourselves. Think you're smarter than everyone else. Very antisocial."

I narrow my eyes at him. "We're not antisocial."

"How many times you seen this Williams character outside his greasy spoon?"

"Once."

He glances at Officer Lande, an expression of I-told-you-so.

"When was that, sweetheart?"

"Five minutes ago."

"Don't play games with me."

"I saw him this afternoon. Or yesterday. Whatever time it is now."

"Where?"

"At the baseball field."

Officer Lande looks up. Their eyes meet.

"He told you he was there, right?" I ask.

There's a long pause.

"We picked him up at the field," she says. "But when were you there?"

"It was the second time, when he was there as the umpire . . ."

My voice trails off because their glances are snapping back and forth and something invisible swirls in the air, dangerous and dark as the stench. My inner attorney leaps to her feet, reminding me the Fifth Amendment was created for really good reasons.

"Raleigh." Officer Lande leans into the table. "Did you and Drew play around that baseball field?"

"Why do you want to know?"

"Sweetheart," he says, "don't protect that guy. Or your buddy. You'll only get in more trouble."

My inner attorney demands a real attorney.

Officer Lande touches my arm again. "Raleigh. You want us to find Drew. Don't you?"

I nod.

"Tell us everything you know."

I lower my head. My inner attorney pleads due process, right to avoid self-incrimination, but when I look up, Officer Lande's hard face and soft eyes make me believe she wants the truth too.

"There's clay," I mumble.

"Clay—" The detective comes forward. "I knew it. Whole game is about guys. So who's Clay?"

What a moron.

I turn to Officer Lande, expecting her to get this, but she doesn't look like she thinks the dwarf is the stupidest guy on the planet. The look on her face says next she's going to tell me it's fine for him to call me Sweetheart.

"Clay," I say slowly, "is soil. Dirt? You know, on the ground."

"Okay." She nods. "What about it?"

"There's clay in Drew's shoe that matches the clay at that baseball field. It's really specific, not just any old clay."

"You mean, in the shoe you found at the quarry?" she asks.

"Right."

"The shoe you gave to me," she says, "and that we took as evidence."

"Yes. You can check it, look at the sole, you'll find red pieces of clay that look like icicles."

The next glance between them is no split-second snap. It lingers. It hangs there. It goes on and on until Officer Lande's eyes brush over the mirror and the detective pushes himself from the wall and suddenly his whole very-ticked-off demeanor has changed to his version of Good Cop. Which isn't very good. The fact that he's trying to make me like him is freaky.

"Lemme get this straight," he says, trying on another smile, "you found her shoe, and I guess you decided to look at the dirt in the treads. That right?"

I don't say anything.

"You took some dirt from the shoe. And then you checked out the dirt."

I can feel the atmosphere shift. And I decide to shut up—I am not naive.

"Well, Sweetheart, lemme explain something to you. You might think you know all about crime, but there's this thing called obstruction of justice. You've heard of that, right? It's when you interfere with a police investigation. And you know what happens to people who do that? They go to jail. You like what you see in here?"

I push my inner attorney down. "Drew's my best friend."

"I don't care if we're talking about your grandmother, you don't touch evidence."

My inner attorney jumps up. "And you wouldn't even know about that soil if I didn't find it first."

He laughs. It doesn't turn into a cough.

I glance at Officer Lande. She's not laughing. She's not even smiling.

"Fine," I say. "Tell me if somebody else bothered to check the soil in her shoe?"

Only silence.

I glare at the detective. "See? So quit trying to make me feel guilty. I've probably done more to find her than anybody else."

He looks at Officer Lande. She touches my arm again.

"Raleigh, we know you want to find her. And we do too. Is there anything else we should know?"

"You should look at the soil in her bike tire because—"

"I knew it!" The detective throws his arms in the air. "You two are playing a game. Real funny, huh? Got us running all over. Did you pay that Williams guy to be part of it?"

I know my mom's crazy, but so's this guy.

"I'm not playing a game. And if you would listen to me you might find her." I explain how the Petersburg Batholith is only exposed in four places around Richmond, and how three of those places Drew wouldn't go on her bike because she is lazy. I explain how I narrowed down the purple spot on the US Geological Society map, how it's in the library archives, and even as I'm saying all this, my mind is dividing in half. One side says I'm smart—ahead of the cops! But the other half says things that are making my armpits damp and my mouth dry. I can see the detective is listening closely but he doesn't look grateful at all to know this information. He looks angry.

And when he finally speaks, his voice sounds as flat as this stainless steel table.

"I'm curious about Titus Williams," he says. "You're saying all this . . . dirt . . . proves your little friend and him were at the baseball field."

"He says he didn't see her."

"Course he does. And you're defending him."

"I'm telling you what he said."

"But you yourself said—what'd you call it?—forensic evidence. It's even better than circumstantial evidence. Isn't that what you said?"

On the advice of my inner attorney, I keep my mouth shut.

"Don't you think it's odd he went to that field, too? Same day. Same time. Huh?"

"Yes. It's odd."

The detective gives me a hard look. "So why are you holding back?"

I glance at my hands. My fingers are shaking, like they do when my mom hears those voices in her head. All my life I've prayed God would never let me hear voices, but the little lawyer inside is very loud. *Things are not always black and white*, she says. *Things are sometimes gray. Very, very gray.*

"Come on, tell us," the detective says. "We just want the truth. You can tell us."

I look up at him. I want the truth. That's all I want.

And that's when I turn away from him and look at Officer Lande and say something I've probably never said in my entire life. "I'd like to go home now."

CHAPTER THIRTY-FOUR

I N THE MORNING, bleary-eyed from three hours of sleep, I stumble into the kitchen and discover bacon.

Smoked, salted.

Maple-cured in Virginia.

Real bacon.

Which explains why our patio door is wide open and my dad is at the stove, not my mom. The autumn breeze sweeps into the room, brushes the smoke rising from the pan so thick even the industrial fan can't catch it all, then whisks it outside where she won't smell it.

My dad looks at me. His face is ragged with exhaustion. But he smiles, and whispers, "I smuggled in the good stuff."

Another pan holds scrambled eggs. I know how he makes them—with cream, cooked in butter.

My mouth waters. "Where's mom?"

"She had a rough night."

On the table, a can of Coke waits for me. "What happened?"

"I don't know but she paced the house until four."

I got home at three.

"Did she say anything?"

He tongs the bacon. "How do you mean?"

I mean, did she say she saw a police cruiser come down

the alley behind the house and let out the girl who claims she's
Raleigh but who is sneaking out in the middle of the night,
conspiring with the cops.

"I don't know . . . anything?"

"Not anything that made sense." He stirs the eggs. "I
called Dr. Simpson. Maybe he can adjust her medication."

The real answer to my question is this perfect breakfast,
complete with a can of Coke. It tells me why she was up all
night and why she's not here and why Helen has to come
home for a visit. Because of me.

I stare at my dad's back. His normally strong shoulders are
bent forward, as if weighted with worry. I feel such a deep
stab of guilt, I want to confess everything, release the mad
rush of words—but would it help, really? All I'd be doing is
giving him a second person to worry about. And he's already
grounded me for three weeks, it's not like he thinks I'm totally
innocent.

I sit at the table, pick up the can of Coke, close my eyes.
The condensation on the cold can weeps under my fingers. My
silent grace goes out for Drew, wherever she is. And for my
mom, wherever her mind is. And for my dad, my most
amazing dad, who should already be heading to the courthouse
but who probably went to the store when she finally went to
bed, buying bacon and eggs and Coke to give me the kind of
breakfast that says, *I'm sorry your mom doesn't trust you, and
I can't change that.*

I swallow the guilt that tells me there's no reason she
should trust me now.

I open my eyes. He offers me the plate. Bacon browned to
a crisp, eggs covered with shredded cheddar cheese.

"How's your sleeping?" He sits down across from me.

"Fine."

He opens his napkin. "Did she keep you up last night?"

I shake my head, unable to speak. I feel so guilty-guilty-guilty.

He clasps his hands, bowing his head. One fried egg on his plate, no cheese. No bacon. I hear his prayer, sort of, but so much junk is zinging through my head right now that I really only hear his voice. Broken, yet hard, like cracking rocks. He is even more tired than I am.

I wait, wondering if he's going to open the newspaper. That's usually what he does. But he picks up his fork, glances at me.

"Can I ask you something?" I ask.

"Only until forever."

He smiles. It's not meant to look weary, but it does. Maybe my smile looks weary too. "When someone's guilty, can you tell just by watching them?"

"Hmm." He puts down his fork. "Sometimes. Why do you ask?"

"You see a lot of people in your courtroom. Not everybody's telling the truth."

"Sadly, most aren't." Another weary smile. "Fortunately, we can usually rely on evidence." He picks up the fork again, pressing it into the egg. "And in the case of forensics, there isn't a lot of wiggle room for lying."

"But when people are lying, what do you see?"

He puts down the fork, not taking the bite, and picks up his coffee cup, his elbow denting the paper. "Blame shifting, that's always a good clue. Liars tend to say everything is someone else's fault. Do you remember what I used to tell Helen?"

My sister, even as a child, was a profoundly skilled liar. "You used to say, 'Helen, every time you point a finger at somebody else, notice three fingers are pointing back at you.' "

"You remember." His smile is still weary, but his eyes glisten.

I look down at my plate. Right now, his approval feels so very wrong.

"Raleigh?"

I look up.

"Why do you want to know all this?" he asks.

I look down at my food. "Just curious."

"I see." He pauses. "Well, in addition to blame shifting, watch for people who can't look someone in the eye."

I immediately look up. When I meet his gaze, he smiles.

"This has to do with Drew's disappearance?"

What—I'm going to lie?

"Yes," I reply. "I want to know how to spot a liar."

"It's not easy. Liars can be very charming people. They'll often ingratiate themselves—do nice things, favors for people—so no one suspects them of deceit." He pauses. "If you come back to my courtroom, you can study the attorneys. Most of them are expert liars."

"No offense," I say. "But I've seen enough of lawyers to know it's like blame shifting on steroids."

He nods, takes one bite of his egg. Puts down the fork, picks up the coffee. The silence stretches out but he still doesn't open the newspaper. He watches me practically licking my plate. I don't know when I'll see food like this again in this house.

"I'm sorry," he says suddenly.

I look up.

"I'm sorry about grounding you," he says. "But it's for your own good. You understand that, don't you?"

I nod. Go back to eating.

But I don't understand. I don't understand anything these days. I can't find Drew and people seem to think we're playing some game and God refuses to answer my prayers, even though I don't think they're selfish. But what I really don't understand is, how can I know something is wrong and still justify it? The whole idea makes this perfect breakfast start to curdle in my stomach. I put down my fork, look at my dad sipping his coffee and ask, "Can I ride my bike to school, even though I'm grounded?"

"I'll drive you."

"Thanks, I appreciate the offer. But I really wanted some fresh air. You know, since I can't go outside after school."

The way he's smiling at me almost makes me puke in my own mouth.

"You're such a wonderful daughter," he says. "Yes, you can ride your bike. Thank you for asking me."

I nod, look down at my empty plate, and realize he's fully answered my question.

I know exactly how liars behave.

Because now, I've turned into one.

CHAPTER THIRTY-FIVE

RIDE MY bike to school through golden sunshine, the air crisp and bright. My first class is P. E., and I lock my bike outside the gym. Drew's purple Schwinn is gone, taken by the police, my guess.

In the locker room, I open my basket and pull out the blue T-shirt and shorts for P. E. In their place, I stuff my backpack. But at the last moment, I put the gym clothes back, slam the locker door, and hurry to the bathroom, just off the main room. The air is clanging with the rush and whine of twenty classmates.

Norwood says, "I told him last week it was my time of the month."

"Then you need another excuse," Tinsley tells her. "Even Galluci's not that stupid."

I slip into the farthest stall, directly beside the ceramic tile wall.

On my left, somebody flushes. That door bangs open and I yank my feet up on the seat, squatting like a frog. I can hear Tinsley redirecting the subject, her voice rising above the clamor. She brags about DeMott, something he did that was "just the sweetest, most wonderful—"

The bell rings. I don't have to listen to the rest.

Lockers slam. Sneakers squeak. The whoosh of air tells me

the outer door is open, everyone running for the track. Voices fade.

I start counting. When I reach 89 . . . 90 . . . 91 . . . I hear the last locker. Martina Hunninger, I'm positive. She hates changing in front of anyone. And I know she will shuffle out so slowly it's like she's heading to her dog's funeral. Galluci also knows her habits. He will be waiting for her.

. . . 112 . . . 113 . . .

I've never been a patient person, and the counting is giving me a headache. Squeezing my eyes shut, I reach 250 and reach for the stall lock.

I step out of the stall, look both ways. Everyone is gone. Dashing around the corner, I whip open the door to freedom.

"Holy Mother of God!" John the janitor throws one hand on his chest, squeezing. "You—again!"

"Sorry!"

"I swear to God, you girls are gonna give me a heart attack. Who else is in there?"

"Nobody. I'm really sorry. Really."

I race around his cart and hurry outside. He must be glaring at my back because it's a long moment before I hear that loaded cart maneuvering through the door. Then I start running full speed. I tell myself not to look back. But telling yourself not to look is like ordering yourself to look.

I glance up at the field.

And there stands Tinsley.

She looks gilded, the sunlight hitting her long blonde hair. Hands on her skinny hips, she watches as I grab my bike and take off.

There's no going back now.

I pump my bike pedals with so much blood rushing into my ears I feel deaf. Hauling down Grove Avenue, I tell myself—again—not to look. I resist until I'm crossing the

Boulevard, where I expect to see Ellis in hot pursuit. But there's no black Volvo.

I stand up, practically running on the pedals to pick up more speed. Each time I glance over my shoulder, my inner attorney accuses me, reminding me that I'm legally grounded.

My lame retort?

My dad didn't say I was grounded during school.

When I walk into the Richmond library, I am sweating like an overheated pig. Nelson Heid, the reference librarian, shows no surprise, just like when I showed up here on Saturday, dripping rain on the marble floor. He's reading another enormous tome, and when he looks up, taking in my school uniform damp with sweat, he pretends there's nothing wrong with me being here, at this hour, on a school day.

"How may I help you, Raleigh?" he asks.

"Need a copy," I pant, "of this morning's paper."

"Your tunnel made the news?"

"Not that I know of."

"Ah," he nods. "Still expanding horizons?"

"You could say that."

"And I did." He lays the bookmark between the pages and once again puts the sick child to bed, his sigh full of regret.

I wipe my brow and follow Nelson to the back of the library's main room. He stops at some staggered dowel rods against the wall. Newspapers hang on them like drying laundry, and a man sits beside the whole lot. He's reading a newspaper from London, wearing a winter coat that is so dirty it's difficult to tell if it's blue or black or gray.

Nelson scans the rods, lifting the pages. He turns to the man in the chair.

"Gordo," he says. "Where's the *Times-Dispatch*?"

"How would I know?" The man replies.

"Stand up."

The man glares at Nelson, his eyes so cloudy he could be half-blind. "It's my paper," he says.

"The papers belong to the library."

"I was here first."

"Please," Nelson says. "You can't possibly read all the newspapers at once."

"I could too."

"And," Nelson says, "you could find yourself evicted from these premises in an instant."

"What for?"

"We could begin with eating in the library."

"I didn't."

"Next time, brush the crumbs off your coat."

The man named Gordo looks down. His cheeks are angry red, the skin flaking in patches. He pinches the dirty coat's lapels, giving them a shake. He throws a haughty expression at Nelson. The crumbs fall into his lap.

"This is Raleigh," Nelson says, turning to indicate my presence. "She would like to read this morning's paper. Please give it to her."

"She can't read the whole thing either."

Nelson gazes up at the ceiling, speaking to the rafters. "Raleigh, is there something in particular you are seeking in the paper?"

"It's in the B-section." That's the section my dad kept folded tight by his plate this morning.

"Gordo, please. Be a gentleman."

The man stands, sending the crumbs to the floor, and puts one hand into his coat, searching. The gray pages come out, smushed and crumpled. He scans them, handing out pieces of the B-section as he discovers them. Nelson puts the pages in order, aligning the original center fold down the middle, then offers the section to me. It smells bad.

"Thank you," I tell him.

He nods, nearly bowing, then straightens and pivots toward the man.

"Gordo, winter is coming. *The Farmer's Almanac* says this year will be particularly frigid. Should you choose to exhibit any behavior other than your very best, you will feel the bite of cold this year."

Gordo plops down in the chair. "Blah, blah, blah," he says.

Nelson watches him for a moment. "Raleigh, I expect you to notify me if any problems occur."

He turns and walks back through the stacks.

Since it's the only chair on this end of the building, I sit in the open chair beside Gordo. I feel his cloudy gaze, but after a moment, he leans to the dowel rods and snatches off the *Washington Post*. He tucks some pages into his coat then lifts the want ads, rattling them with as much noise as possible.

I find the story at the bottom of B-1. The headline reads "Former Atlanta Brave Taken into Custody."

The first paragraph explains the headline, but the second paragraph details the restraining order. Which means somebody leaked it to the press, since I know the order was sealed because it involved a juvenile.

The words are chilling: ". . . carnal knowledge with a child between the ages of thirteen and fifteen." The order was filed by the mother of Titus's niece, his sister-in-law. But I read those first four paragraphs three times because whenever something appears in the newspaper, it automatically looks like fact. Even speculation looks like fact. That's why judges like my dad issue gag orders.

Gordo leans over. He smells like vinegar and cigarettes. "You done yet?"

"No, not yet."

The story jumps to B-8, I flip through the pages, for once

appreciating how the newspaper smells like Wite-Out mixed with ink—much better than Gordo's stink. On B-8, I also find two photographs, each marked "Times-Dispatch File." I pull the paper close. In the first, Titus is holding up a white Atlanta Braves uniform, grinning like I've never seen before.

"I want it back," Gordo says.

I look over. His skin is like some living lesson in forensics, the way it flakes off his red cheeks, dusting the coat that is blue-or-black-or-gray.

"I'll be done in just a minute," I tell him.

"What's so important in there anyway?"

"Nothing." My nose stings from his vinegary odor.

Gordo leans toward me. My eyes water.

"That guy?" he points at Titus's picture. "You reading about him?"

I pull the paper farther away from him, but it only draws him closer.

"I know him!" He points at the photo, stabbing the page. His fingernail is chipped and dirty. "I know that guy."

I look up, searching the room for Nelson. But the shelves of books are blocking my view of the Reference desk.

He stabs the paper again. "What'd he do?"

"I don't know."

"He poison somebody?"

"What?"

"He brings us burgers, stuff like that." Gordo lifts his chin, giving that haughty look again. "I'm homeless, for your information."

"Sorry."

"Give me the paper."

"I'm not done."

We stare at each other, me blinking away the stink-tears in my eyes. His mouth twists angrily before he leans back in his own chair. Lifting the *Post* want ads, he shakes the pages again for effect.

The second photo shows a group of people, standing around Titus who is still holding the uniform. The small print below identifies Titus first, then two coaches from the Richmond Braves who stand on his right. To his left is Timothy Williams, his brother. He's nowhere near as big as Titus, but their faces look alike. The last person identified is a white woman who stands between the black brothers. Y'landa Williams, identified as "sister-in-law."

"How d'you know him?" Gordo asks.

I keep my eyes on the photograph, switching between Titus's face and the woman's.

"Hey," he says. "I asked you a question, how d'you know him?"

"Maybe I don't."

Gordo leans in. "Expect me to believe that 'cause I'm some dumb homeless guy."

"No," I turn to him. "Because maybe I don't really know him."

Gordo stares at me. I want him to go away, but he's not leaving. Not for years.

"Won't tell me, huh?"

I can't smell the vinegar-and-cigarettes stink anymore, which concerns me since that means the olfactory sensors in my nose are full of it, can't take anymore.

"It's a long story," I say.

He sinks back into his chair and makes a big gesture of opening the newspaper so wide it cuts off all view of him.

I go back to reading the story, but I can hear him muttering.

"If you're paying attention," he says, "everything's a long story."

CHAPTER THIRTY-SIX

W HEN I BIKE away from the library, Gordo's stink is hitching on my blouse. I hang a right on Ninth street, bombing down the hill, hoping to lose his bitter smell. On the sidewalks, people hustle into tall buildings that tower with ambition.

At the bottom of the hill, the river glistens. I ride across the Ninth Street bridge. The wind pushes off the river, pressing against me. My hands tighten on the handlebars, gripping a white scrap of paper that holds a name and an address. And a point of no return.

The moment my front wheel crosses into Southside, the world shifts. Gone are the smart buildings, replaced by boarded-up windows and broken glass lining the cracked curbs. A city bus groans past me, followed by a broken-down panel truck, and an old brown Lincoln—a woman blowing smoke out the passenger window.

I ride up Semmes Avenue and stop at the red light. Jefferson Davis Highway crosses the road, and traffic is suddenly heavy again—cars zipping across this forgotten wasteland of Richmond's south end, heading places where graffiti doesn't smear brick walls and grown men don't sit on the ground holding paper bags.

I have one foot on the crumbling curb, waiting for the light to turn green, when a car pulls up beside me. The paint was red once upon a time but has faded to a color like dead rubies. In the passenger seat, a man rolls down his window. His bloodshot eyes, matching the car's paint, run up and down my bare legs, the stupid plaid skirt.

"Yo, baby," he says. "What's happening?"

I stare at the light, willing it to turn green.

"I got whatcho need right here."

The wind, like some evil cohort, tunnels up the hill and ruffles the skirt, lifting the pleats. I slap one hand on my thigh, but the other can't let go of the handlebars because of the paper under my palm.

"You lookin' for some ice?"

I'm looking for a way to kick myself, for not pulling on my P. E. shorts.

"Right here. Ice cold crystal." His hand comes out the window.

I take off. Car tires skid. Horns blare. I zigzag across the road, squeezing the handlebars. My fingers ache. When I reach 24th Street, I hang a right. A small brick rambler sits on the corner, its lawn brown. I stop, check the paper, try to get my heart to slow down, then bike down the rest of the street. It's not as bad as Semmes, but nowhere near as nice as Monument Avenue. Back off the road, I see a blue house. But that's not it, either.

It's at the end of the road, right where I'm about to turn around and go back to the library, asking Nelson to double-check this address. I read the paper again, checking the address with the white plantation house. Nelson found it in the city census, because it's not listed in the phone book. A woman lives here named Y'landa Jones Williams. The census noted another resident, a minor female.

I climb off my bike and wheel it toward the fence. A white

picket fence, its paint peeling like the skin on Gordo's cheeks. Greek columns line the porch, one of them used to chain a dog. A Rottweiler. He scrambles to a stand as I approach.

He snarls.

I open the gate.

He leaps forward, choking on his chain. Foamy slobber flings from his teeth.

For once, I'm wishing for the cell phone. But it's in my backpack, in my locker at school.

"Drop!"

The dog hits the porch floor like he's been shot.

"What d'you want?" Demands a husky voice.

I look around, trying to find the source. The front door is open four inches, a pair of eyes peering out above the chain.

"I asked you a question!"

I try to smile, like some Girl Scout here to sell cookies. "I'm looking for Y'landa Williams."

"What for?"

"I need to talk to her."

"What for?"

"It's . . . " I hear Gordo in my head, muttering about everything being a long story, if you're paying attention. "It's complicated. Are you Mrs. Will—"

"Here by yourself?"

I nod. The door slams.

Oh, great.

But suddenly it opens. The woman standing there looks almost like the person in the newspaper photo, except her blonde hair is longer, scragglier, and her body is wide, almost shapeless.

"That your bike?" She steps onto the porch.

"Yes, ma'am."

"Don't just leave it there."

I stare at the bike, wondering where else to put it.

"What in the Sam Hill's the matter with you?" she asks.

There will never be enough time to answer that, so I lift the scrap of paper and begin to say something else, but I'm cut off by a half-naked toddler. She bursts through the open door. When the Rottweiler sees her, he scrambles to his feet again, stumpy tail wagging.

The little girl flings herself into the woman's thick legs.

"Gammy, play!" she cries.

Scooping up the kid, the woman pats her diaper. The contrast between them seems brighter in the sunlight. Bare black legs on the kid, the woman's white hands.

She looks over at me. "You gonna tell me what you want?"

"Are you Y'landa Williams?"

"Depends who's asking."

"I wanted to talk to you about Titus Williams."

She steps forward, still holding the kid, and yells. "Get off my property!"

The dog, catching the mood, lunges. Barks. Slobbers. Lunges again. And the kid? She starts kicking her heels into the woman's sides, like she's a rider on a pony.

"Gammy!" she screams, gray powder bursting from the diaper's edge. "Play! Play!"

The woman snatches the kid's ankle, holding it tight as she hisses, "Stop."

Like the dog, the kid stops immediately.

But unlike the dog, that's not the end of it.

The little girl sticks out her lower lip. Eyes closed, she opens her mouth, bawling. The woman closes her eyes, too. The dog whimpers. The kid cries harder.

Slowly, the woman pats the diaper, rubbing the kid's back until the crying slows. There's a wet hiccupy cough and then the woman whispers in the girl's ear before setting her down on the porch.

"G'on," she says softly. "You can play it."

The tears, like magic, are gone. Little bare feet slap the porch floor as she disappears into the house.

I wait a moment. "Sorry, I didn't mean to upset you."

"Then don't ask me about that man."

I'm now certain this is Y'landa Williams because without my saying another word, she unloads.

"Him and his brother, both no good," she rants. "Left me high and dry. I wish to God I'd never met them. He hasn't even called his daughter in a year—his own flesh and blood!"

"I'm sorry." It's all I can think to say. But the words don't matter.

She barrels on.

"No child support, no alimony. Nothin'. Took off without one word, not one word. For all we know he's in Timbuktu."

"But he's right across the river."

She glares, stepping forward. "You seen him?"

"Yes."

"Where—where's he at?"

"In jail."

Her mouth drops. "Timothy—the Richmond jail?"

It takes me a second. Timothy. The brother. He was in that photo. Titus's brother.

"No," I explain. "Titus. He's in jail."

Her expression is even more startled now, but it's quick, evaporating in an instant. That tells me something. One, Y'landa doesn't read the newspaper or listen to the radio or watch the news, and two, she didn't expect to hear Titus was behind bars. "I know about the restraining order," I tell her. "The one you took out against him."

Her jaw juts forward, stretching the skin on her thick neck.

A stubborn look, and scary enough to make the dog lay down with a whimper.

"I was protecting my daughter." Her tone's a low growl.

"I understand. And Titus broke that restraining order when he let my friend and me come into his restaurant."

"So now he's in jail. Good." Her voice is simple, less passionate now. "Let him rot there."

"But my friend is missing. Nobody's seen her since Friday. The police think Titus did something to her. That's really why he's in jail."

"Well, I'm right sorry for your friend." Her voice is almost flat now. "Everyone's luck runs out sometime."

I don't know if it's her tone, or her words, or the clatter that comes clonking onto the porch through the open door—a bunch of discordant notes that sound like a piano played with a fist. Whatever it is, I feel something flick inside me, like a smoldering ember sparking into flame.

"You're wrong." I raise my voice over the bad piano. "No disrespect, but luck's got nothing to do with this situation."

"Sure it does." She tossed her jutting chin toward my bike, then me, letting her pale eyes land on the blue crest embroidered on my white blouse, the insignia for St. Catherine's. "Luck's got everything to do with it. You're lucky to go to some fancy school. My girl's unlucky because nobody's paying child support."

For a long moment we stand there. I don't like the music, and I don't like how she's trying to shame me for going to a good school, even as she claims it all comes down to dumb luck. But more. My inner lawyer is arguing another point, the protests needling into my mind as the woman raises her voice to be heard over the music growing louder.

"Yeah, Mr. Nice Guy, that who you met? Played the sweet uncle to my girl. Took her shopping, taught her how to throw a baseball." She sneers. "I wonder, which base did he get to?"

The piano is being murdered.

And she keeps listing all the things Titus did wrong. Giving rich ideas to a girl with not two cents to her name. Had her worshipping at his feet. Uncle Titus-this and Uncle Titus-that. The woman's every word lands as heavy as the manslaughtering fists on the piano, but as she rants on, something begins ribboning around every accusation, like a piccolo playing so high and off-key it harmonizes with the rotten music.

The sound of shifting blame.

I wait for Y'landa Williams to run out of steam. It takes a while. Then I ask, "So, that little girl, she's your granddaughter?"

Our eyes lock.

"He led her on," she says.

The child is black. And maybe Y'landa's daughter is half-black. But every theory needs testing.

"Okay. But I need to know. Did he—" My voice almost cracks. "Is Titus the father?"

"How old are you?"

"Fifteen."

"Where you live?"

"Richmond."

"Nice neighborhood?"

I nod.

"Where you come from," she says, "you can't understand. All we got is her and me. That's it."

"I do understand." Those sad years after my birth dad ditched us, I will never forget them. And I never want to feel that bad ever again. "My dad left my mom, so I know."

"Like Hell you know," she sneers. "I had nothing when Timothy left us. Not one dime!"

She starts ranting again, listing the hardships of poverty as

I glance up and down the street. It's clean. The houses look like people mostly take care of them. Except this one. When she stops talking, I look back at her.

"Did he buy you this house?" I ask.

"He gave her the idea he was gonna marry her."

I nod—I nod toward the dying piano. "That's not Titus's child, is it?"

"Fourteen years old, she comes home and tells me she's got a baby coming—and it belongs to Uncle Titus. I called the police. Right there, I called 'em."

"For a restraining order."

"Hell yes!"

The piano falls silent.

She closes her eyes. Sucks in a deep breath. "Sugar pie?" she calls out.

There's no response.

"Sugar pie. That was a right pretty tune. G'on and play some more."

One high key slips through the air, tentative as a question.

"That's right," she calls to her. "Keep on."

When the clatter starts again she leans toward me, her voice low but full of heat.

"I trusted that man. I left him alone with my daughter—"

"But what did she do to *him*?"

She pulls back. The clomping sounds gain strength, banging on the windows of the house. The house that Titus bought, I am sure of it. The house that he gave them to keep a roof over their heads when his brother abandoned them. The house that wouldn't be falling apart if Titus was that kid's dad because there would be DNA and a paternity suit and child support by court order.

There would not be just some restraining order.

"I saw him last night," I tell her. "At the jail. He doesn't have an alibi for when my friend went missing. So I need to know. Did your daughter tell the truth?"

She stares at me, eyes cold and bright as blue granite. "Like I said, everyone's luck runs out. Sometime." Dropping a hand, she snaps her fingers. The dog rises, pants, waits for her next command.

But she gives it to me instead.

"You best be leaving," she says. "G'on back where you belong."

CHAPTER THIRTY-SEVEN

Y'LANDA WILLIAMS IS right, I don't belong on Southside.

But I really feel like I don't belong here either, standing by the rich girl's lunch table, sweating from a long bike ride, waiting for Tinsley to reply after I say, "We need to talk."

She dips a stalk of celery into what looks like a thimble of oil-and-vinegar dressing. Tinsley's lunch looks nothing like my usual crumpled brown bag, stuffed with my mother's daily ballast. Tinsley brings a white square box. Inside, a small green bottle of Perrier rests on its side, as if bowing to her.

"Raleigh," she says, "can't you see I'm eating my lunch."

"That's not lunch," I explain. "That's an eating disorder."

She turns to her friends. "Did I tell y'all? The police called my house."

None of the girls reacts like that's news, which means Tinsley's already been down the gossip road. Probably a couple times. The news is being broadcast now for me, for an effect on me. So that when I walk away, they can snicker.

"The police called you for the same reason I want to talk to you. You're the last person who saw Drew."

"Unfortunately," she says.

I grit my teeth. "What did you tell the police?"

"The same thing I told you! After you ran through the

255

dance like some crazy banshee."

"What did you tell me?"

"Raleigh, you know perfectly well what I said."

I do. But my dad's courtroom taught me that truth sometimes rises in stages. People say one thing, and when you press them, they say another. This is especially true if you're dealing with belly-dragging snakes.

"Tell me again, Tinsley."

She waves the celery. "Drew cancelled, I was thrilled, she ran away, that's the whole story right there."

"You're leaving something out."

Norwood leans forward. "Did you just call Tinsley a liar?"

"Pretty much."

"How dare you!" Tinsley's spine goes as rigid as the celery. "It's not my fault your weirdo friend ran away."

"That's true."

"See?"

"Yes, I see how I might be tempted to run away, if I had to tutor you. But Drew's stronger than me. She can handle extreme torture."

Her green eyes are glacial. "Do you know what your problem is, Raleigh?"

"I hate liars?"

"You lack nuance."

"Nuance."

"It means manners." The celery gets waved like a baton. "The art of diplomacy. It's when Southern girls know how to act polite, not being rude. It's a subtle skill."

Norwood laughs. "And Raleigh's about as subtle as a sledgehammer."

The coven giggles.

"Remember in sixth grade," Norwood continues, "when she brought that giant rock for Show and Tell?"

"And her hammer?" Tinsley adds.

"And then smashed the thing open?"

They continue laughing about my geode.

But suddenly it stops.

I had been thinking things couldn't get worse, but that's usually a sure sign that they're about to. I can read the expressions on their beautiful faces, and they look like a car just plunged off a cliff. Followed by "Bless your heart."

"Miss Harmon."

I turn around. Parsnip looks like she could use a dozen stalks of Tinsley's celery to help relieve her constipation.

"You were seen leaving campus this morning."

I glance at Tinsley. She smiles. It's a big and genuine smile. She is suddenly happy.

"And since we received no note authorizing your absence, I called your parents."

Like the crazed Rottweiler on its short chain, the ideas lunge at me. Parsnip. Calling my house. Telling my mother I took off from school. Or. She called my dad. So he knows I lied. To his face. After he made my all-time favorite breakfast.

Terrific.

"To the office." Parsnip points at the door. "Now."

ELLIS'S OFFICE IS a shrine to higher learning. On the headmaster's mahogany desk, St. Jerome sits, one plaster fist tucked under his chin in The Thinker's pose. On the windowsill, Socrates gazes out at the soccer fields, reminding the jocks that an unexamined life is not worth living.

Aside from those two, I sit here alone. Parsnip has left me to wait. This is what they do—leave you here to tremble in fear, recognize the error of your ways.

But I'm not feeling it.

Five minutes later, Ellis strides through the door, his concerned frown tight as his bow tie. He deliberately takes a seat so that Socrates is right over his shoulder. I think Ellis must be one of those grownups who never left prep school. Smudge away the gray hair at his temples, erase his paunch, and you'll find a private school kid who dreamed of becoming headmaster because it means he will never have to use a simple word again because the big ones sound smarter.

"Raleigh," he begins, "Our educators take their mission at St. Catherine's quite seriously. And when students sally forth into the streets—"

Sally forth? Isn't that a cartoon?

"—it's a clear exhibition of utter disrespect for hard work and the rules which clearly state campus parameters." He takes a much-needed breath. "Miss Harmon, you've been with us for eight years. You have been fully cognizant of school rules until—" he taps the desk, "you met up with Miss Levinson. As we all know, bad company corrupts good character."

I want to sally forth from this room.

"Have you nothing to say?" he asks.

"Not really."

"You can tell me," he says.

"Tell you . . . what?"

"Where Miss Levinson is hiding."

"I don't know!"

He leans back in his hard wooden chair. Tenting his hands, he gazes over the steeple of his knuckles. "The other educators and I have noticed the influence Miss Levinson exerts over you, the detrimental friendship that has formed. You've become wise in your own eyes, Miss Harmon."

"You're wrong."

"You presume incorrectly." He gestures to the window

where Socrates perches. "Why don't you tell me how you two burned that field, for instance?"

I gaze out the window, saying nothing.

"That misbehavior is expected of Miss Levinson. She's compelled to go too far. But I've received some disturbing reports recently, how you're not completing your assignments—"

Sandbag.

"And now we see you leaving campus without permission."

My voice rises. "I don't know where she's hiding. But I know she didn't run away. Something happened to her."

He sighs, dropping the tented fingers.

"I will let you in on a little secret," he says. "We've known about the move to New York City for quite some time. Her mother apprised us of the transfer weeks ago. Thoughtfully, I might add. We've been prepared for her ruse."

"Ruse?!"

"And we are fully cooperating with the Richmond police. I was, until today, considering you an incidental victim of Miss Levinson's cruelty toward her mother. But today's truancy changes that perception."

"So you're not doing anything to help find her."

"Find her? On the contrary, we've informed the police. Our school is ready and willing to aid."

I can't believe my ears. Or my eyes. Ellis looks so . . . "You're glad she's gone."

He gazes at me a long moment. "Miss Harmon, what would you propose we do?"

"Crank up the phone tree. Tell people to look for her. Create a committee—you did that for the stupid toilets in the gym."

After a moment's silence, he swivels the chair, gazing out

the window at the empty field. "You may find this difficult to believe, but I am as distressed about Miss Levinson's disappearance as you are."

"Last time you started the phone tree, you called everyone."

"And learned my lesson."

I can't help it. "So when you heard she was moving away you, what, you threw a party?"

He swivels toward me, his mouth so tight it's lipless. "I've been patient with your insubordination. But my patience has been wasted on you. Expect to hear from Mrs. Parsons regarding your detention. Unless . . ." His pause is long. "Unless you'd like to tell me where you went and who you saw."

Part of me would love to describe Y'landa Williams for him. But my inner attorney warns me about how deep a grave can be dug. "I had an errand to run."

"An errand." He leans his elbows on the desk, leaning toward me. "Miss Harmon, we've bantered long enough. Tell us where Miss Levinson is hiding. We will be merciful."

"I have nothing to tell you."

"Tell the truth, and all will be forgiven. No one suspects you of being the mastermind in this ill-conceived plan."

I don't want to talk to him, but he needs to hear the truth. So he can stop believing the lie that she's hiding. So I tell him about the soil in her tires, in the shoe found at the quarry. The soil that proves Drew went to the St. Christopher's baseball field—and I don't know why.

But just as I'm about to explain my morning errand to Southside, he says "Soil."

I wait. His tone is strange.

"Soil," he says again. "Would this soil have to do with geology, perhaps?"

I know one thing. Ellis would savor any chance to ship Teddy back to West Virginia.

"Miss Harmon?"

When I don't answer, he reaches out and presses a button on the phone base.

"Miss Parsons, would you please send Mr. Chastain to my office?"

I stare at Socrates. There's a bitter flavor in my mouth, maybe like the taste of hemlock. "I will swear on the Bible," I tell Ellis, "I do not know where Drew is."

"Indeed."

I begin sweating in a really bad way, that mix of fear and adrenaline.

But when Teddy finally rolls into the room, he completely ignores Ellis.

"So how'd it go?" he asks me.

"Begging your pardon," Ellis intones, "this is my office. I'm conducting this discussion."

"Yeah, you hauled Raleigh in because she took off. But I told her to go."

"You told her." Ellis sounds like he's talking to a child. The educator at his finest. "You told Miss Harmon to leave campus?"

"Yerp." Teddy pours out Hillbilly accent. "I needed me some tacky paper."

"Perhaps," Ellis's lip seems to curl. "Perhaps I misheard you. You requested—"

"Tacky paper. You know, what you civilized folks call fly paper? Lab's out. I sent Raleigh to git me some."

Ellis likes to quote Socrates as much as he can. He's often telling us to become "citizens of the world." He likes to go on about diversity. Maybe that's why he hired Teddy, since nothing says diversity like a guy in a wheelchair. Unfortunately, Ellis's idea of diversity isn't someone who thinks differently from him.

"Miss Harmon," he says in that same educator tone, "why would you choose not to reveal this telling detail during our conversation?"

"You were asking about Drew. Where she's hiding. And she's not hiding."

"Okey-dokey, that settles it," Teddy says. "Where's the tacky paper? I need it next hour." He backs up the chair, making room for my exit. When I stand, I feel a wash of relief. And immense gratitude for this man rolling for the door.

"Mr. Chastain," Ellis says.

I freeze.

"Would you mind remaining for a moment?"

"Actually, I would," Teddy says. "But I've noticed my particular preferences don't hold no water 'round these parts."

When I walk out of the room, alone, a bad feeling settles in my gut.

AT THE FINAL bell, I know there's only minutes, maybe only seconds. Because not only am I grounded, but it's about to get much worse when I go home and face my dad.

Only I need to see Teddy first, thank him for what he did today.

He's cruising around the Earth Sciences lab, bending low to pick paper off the floor. But he's not shooting three-pointers.

"Thank you," I tell him.

"You're welcome." He rolls around the back of the room. "And enjoy it because from here on out, you're on your own."

His eyes. The green color doesn't look right. Not cold, like Tinsley's. But . . . wounded.

"What did he do?" I ask.

"Gave me notice."

"What does that mean?"

"He's been keeping a file. And it's getting fat."

"But you're Teacher of the Year."

"Not this year."

"So?"

"He can fire me. And I want to stay here."

"When you have to deal with *him*?!"

"I don't care about him. He's a flea at the circus."

"Then quit. Any school would take you."

"Raleigh, I'm a geologist. All the way down to the toes I can't feel. But I found out something else. Something I like more."

"Torturing Ellis?"

"Well, yeah, it is fun. But it ain't important. No, I found out what it's like to get a student champing at the bit, dying to learn, begging for knowledge. And that is one total unmitigated blast."

"Unmitigated—did Ellis make you use that word?"

"I'm as serious as an egg-sucking dog. Every sub-moron science-hater in this school is totally worth that one great student."

I nod. "I get it. Drew."

"The girl's a genius, no doubt about it." He stares at me, the green color shifting in his eyes. "But for her, teachers probably just get in the way. But you? Lemme ask you. How'd you find that Petersburg granite?"

"I don't know, I looked at a map. At the library."

"See, there's something inside of you. Instinct, Raleigh. You've got it. And it makes me swallow all my pride and refuse to let Ellis kick my crippled butt outta this place until you graduate. And then, you'll run right past me."

"Well, you're in a wheelchair."

He laughs. Throws his head back, howling.

I'm glad he's laughing. But when he looks at me again, the expression on his face makes my eyes burn.

He asks, "You get what I'm saying?"

I nod. Just like I nodded with my dad's question this morning.

But, no, I don't get it. At all.

CHAPTER THIRTY-EIGHT

A ND I JUST don't care anymore.

I don't care if I'm grounded for a month, or six months, or a year. So instead of riding home, I bike to Drew's house.

More fallen leaves smother the driveway and front steps, and the back door—as always—is unlocked. Isaac Newton sits in his usual spot in the sunroom, hissing as I pass by into the kitchen, the den, then upstairs.

Inside Drew's bedroom, I stand for a long moment, listening with my eyes closed. I can hear the whispery sound of her planetary mobile, shifting above my head because I've disturbed the air molecules in here. When I open my eyes, hoping for a fresh perspective, everything looks the same.

I walk to the bookshelves. Richard P. Feynman's books take up two shelves. *Surely You're Joking, Mr. Feynman* beside *The Pleasure of Finding Things Out* waiting next to *Perfectly Reasonable Deviations*.

Wrong.

Alphabetical order. Even textbooks, inside her locker, are kept in alphabetical order.

But here's Feynman, her idol, with books running S-T-P.

Wrong.

I cross the room to her closet. Two hangers empty. I try to

remember—wasn't it one hanger before? The empty space is still on the floor, where her Converse All Stars would be. But now that blankness glares up like some nasty theorem about negative space being as powerful as positive space.

I check all the books. But come back to Feynman. They're the only ones out of order.

S-T-P.

As in, S-T-O-P?

Downstairs I search the kitchen and find another negative space that's even more startling—the wine rack is empty.

Not one bottle.

I check the trash. Nothing there.

Backing up, closing my eyes again, I tell myself it's Wednesday. Only Wednesday. The perfectionist alcoholic usually makes it to Friday. But with all this stress—would Jayne really not drink?

I open my eyes. Newton is mincing into the room. Expecting me to feed him.

But his dish. I stare at it. The brown mush fills the bowl.

Somebody's already fed him.

The feeling quivers down my arms. The back door. It's always open. I know that. And of course Drew knows that. Drew also knows that Jayne will leave for work every day, no matter what, even if her daughter is "officially missing."

I see that last sentence, written in her notebook. The sentence that's so very Drew, "If this is true, then . . ."

Then Drew could sneak into the house during the day. Change her clothes. Grab a book, get something to eat. Feed Newton. Pour out all of Jayne's wine.

If this is true then . . .

Then she is hiding.

Somewhere.

I walk outside, crunching over the dead leaves, gazing into

the trees that circle the backyard. Stripped of leaves, the trees don't offer anywhere to hide.

The river?

But this time of year, people are still launching canoes and kayaks, stealing these final sunny days for paddling season. Someone would see Drew. Report it. Her disappearance has made the news now.

I close my eyes once more, willing my mind to answer another hypothesis.

First, Drew would choose to hide where nobody could find her.

Second, that means some place nobody ever goes.

Nobody.

Except.

Maybe.

Me.

THE LITTER, I never really noticed all the litter before. Empty soda cans. Crushed paper bags. Kudzu vines around every surface, greedy to obscure. I kick away a brown bottle, lean into the vines, and feel around for that one loose board.

The tunnel exhales on me. Standing in the dark, feeling my heart pound, I smell the mildew and moist minerals, like a black ocean that goes on forever.

"Drew?" My voice shakes.

I take another step inside. I told her about this tunnel. How the geology gave out and the rocks collapsed on the men still inside the steam train. Her eyes grew bright.

"You have to go check it out," she said.

"Right, only one small detail—I'm afraid of the dark."

She rolled her eyes. "What's the law of conservation say?"

"Energy can't be created or destroyed. It can only change

form."

"Okay, so take the energy from your fear and change it into courage."

"Just like that?"

"Yes." She nodded so vigorously her wild hair bumped up and down. "Just like that."

I release one long slow breath, telling my pulse to quit freaking out. Another step. Another breath.

"Drew—it's me!"

My eyes are adjusting because the ground is coming into focus, the gray sediment rising to the curved stone roof. That glossy shine on the walls, the ground water weeping. When suddenly the space shrinks, I crouch, dropping to my stomach. Crawl.

"Drew!"

Her name echoes back, but it sounds muffled from the blood throbbing in my ears. I keep calling, calling, and the next thing I know, I'm perched on the ledge. The black hole drops out.

"Drew?"

It comes back "Who?"

I flip over, swallowing hard. My breath hits the stone above my face. No flashlight. No—wait. I twist on my side, fingers shaking as I dig into the pack. The cell phone, I know it's in there.

Something scurries across the soil. A tingle slithers up my bare legs.

"Drew?"

It's a whisper.

And the reply only comes from my mind—*she's not here.* She's not.

But that litter? Somebody else is here. Panic spears my heart. I scramble, turn around, cell phone in hand, holding it so the light shines in front of me. As fast as possible, I worm my way back and stagger to a crouch. Fall. Get up. Scramble a few more feet forward. Fall again, the tiny light growing blurry. The tunnel seems to widen. I dive toward the end, find the boards, slap them until one feels loose, shove it with all my might—screaming along with the rusty nails.

I can barely see my bike, the sun is so bright. Running, bottles clanking against my shoes.

She is not here.

I push my bike over the rough terrain, running with one sickening thought repeating in my ear like the echo inside the tunnel.

She is not here. Not here.

CHAPTER THIRTY-NINE

B UT HELEN IS.

"Surprise!" my sister exclaims when I stumble into the kitchen.

I stand speechless. Shocked. Sweaty. Speechless.

Helen points at my legs. "What've you been doing?"

I look down. Blood trickles from my knee, tracing down my shins. My blue plaid skirt is almost brown with dirt. But that's not the worst thing. I look up again.

Helen. Here.

Like some cruel substitute for my best friend.

"I thought you weren't coming home until tomorrow."

"Yeah, well, it's going to be parents' weekend at Yale." She makes air quotes around the words "parents' weekend."

"So?"

"So everybody kept asking when my parents were coming. I made up so many stories I couldn't remember what I said anymore. And these people are not as dumb, not like Richmond. At some point, somebody was going to figure out I was lying. So I split."

She shrugs. Her auburn hair falls loose over her shoulders, the faded jeans smeared with acrylic paint that slant across her thin legs like war paint. I hate to admit it, but Helen is one of those artists who looks more like a model.

"Where's the whiskey?" she asks.

"I don't know!"

"Dad keeps a bottle somewhere, for medicinal purposes." Another set of air quotes around those words before she begins yanking open every cupboard, searching inside.

I walk over to the stove, hoping against reality that my dad will also cook dinner. But substances are simmering in pots, each one a different shade of brown. Like dinner might be various consistencies of mud.

"So you got a cell phone." She's standing on a chair, opening the top cabinets. "You going to use it?"

"Yes."

"Do you even know how to use it?"

"Of course." I hate the pettiness in my heart, but my sister brings out the worst in me. In all of two seconds, Helen can make me feel inferior.

"There you are!" She grabs a bottle. "Come to mama!" She jumps off the chair and turns to me with a devious smile. "Care to join me?"

"Helen, I'm fifteen."

"Suit yourself." She unscrews the top, sniffing the opening with appreciation. "Ahh. Now I just might make it through this stay."

I wait until she pours a full glass of the amber liquid. Wait some more while she takes a long drink.

Then I ask, "What happened?"

She just nods toward the hall, pours another glass. "Go see for yourself."

I start down the hall, feeling like I might be dying. Like, maybe I even want to die. Fade away, never have to deal with all of this. When I'm halfway down the hallway, the voices come rushing toward me. My mother's high North Carolina accent. Tight, distressed. My dad's deep Virginia baritone. I check my watch.

He is home early.

Too early.

Helen is already drinking.

And—I look down—I'm a mess.

I make a mad rush for the kitchen, find Helen finishing another glass of whiskey, and take the stairs like a fugitive cat burglar. On the third floor, I start tearing off my clothes and jump in shower, scrubbing away all the evidence of another life. Back in my room, I pull on clean jeans and a T-shirt then quickly open the window and shake out my school uniform. The tunnel soil patters on the ivy that climbs up our brick like that kudzu.

I make a vow to wash my clothes tonight when my mom goes to sleep.

If she goes to sleep.

It's nearly six o'clock when I come back downstairs. The storm, I pray, has passed. My dad's pushed it out of the house, like he always does. We will say grace and celebrate Helen coming home and eat brown paste.

But I hear her voice before I reach the second floor.

"David. I saw her."

I stop on the landing. Long ago, before I even realized what I was doing, I figured out how not to cry. If you practice it enough, it's almost like breathing. First you tell yourself that sting in your eyes is nothing. A speck of dust. A stray eyelash. Allergies. Then you focus on something completely and totally unimportant. A blank wall. A pencil. Some fork on the table. Whatever you find. But the most important thing is to never *ever* blink.

When I come down the last flight of stairs, my eyes are fixed on the handrail.

"Nadine," he's saying, "let's not get into this now."

Her hysteria bubbles out. "The voices said to look out the window. And there she was, running. In the dark. And a car was waiting."

"Honey, those voices aren't real."

"You're not listening. Raleigh's afraid of the dark—she would never run at night."

I make sure to hit the last step just right. The wood squeaks. Everyone turns.

In my dad's face there's so much anguish I have to look away. And because I can't look at my mother, that leaves Helen. Leaning against the fridge, she slurps the whiskey. I take a long look at her. If I don't stop lying, that's who I could turn into.

"Hi, sweetie," my dad says. "Look who's home?"

I force my eyes back to him. My heart shrivels, seeing the raw pain in his face. The stress of this day. I can't keep adding to his hurt.

"Mom's right," I tell him, my eyes begging him to understand. "I snuck out of the house last night."

"Really!" Helen says. "That's amazing!"

Ever since I was little, my dad's told me the truth is always better than the lie. He says the truth sets us free. Maybe it does. But sometimes it first splashes gasoline on the fire.

My mom's voice quavers. "Who are you?"

"I'm Raleigh."

"You can't be."

"I am."

"And Helen—" she spins toward her. "What did you do to Helen?"

I glance at my sister. She raises her glass. "Here's to family," she says. "Bottom's up."

My dad moves toward my mom, trying to put his arm around her. She backs away.

273

"Honey," he pleads. "It's alright. The girls are here, we're all here."

"No, they're not!"

"We talked about this, remember? The voices don't love you, they're not your family. We love you. And I'm sure Raleigh can explain why she was—"

"Hours!" Her voice rises like a screeching alarm. "She was gone for hours before the car brought her back. It prowled down our alley. And now Helen." Her shaking hand points at my sister. "Helen told me she was coming on Thursday. Three-forty-five. Today is Wednesday, I know it's Wednesday, don't try to tell me it's not Wednesday—"

Helen slams the empty glass on the counter. "Oh, for Pete's sake! Everybody can agree it's Wednesday—okay? It's Wednesday and I changed my plans. Why is that such a big freaking deal?!"

I shift my gaze. The glass in the French doors holds too many reflections. My mom, her posture coiled with fear. My dad, still wearing his suit from work, like he raced out of the office. My sister swaying. I focus on the slate patio, the stones blue and flat, made over eons and epochs, time upon time. I think about how Teddy describes time—as a football field.

"These two are not our daughters!" my mother cries.

"Honey, you need to trust me."

I hear something move. I look over. She's opened a drawer, taking out the yellow legal pad. My footprint.

I stare at the slate, refusing to blink. The football field begins with dust and stone and prehistoric flora that dies in swamps. Twenty yards. Creatures of the deep, creatures on earth, thirty yards. All of them baked into the earth, fifty yards, and by the time human beings show up we're one inch from the goal line. From dust we came, to dust we will return and—

A door slams.

I look over. My mother is still holding that legal pad like she's clutching courtroom evidence. But my dad is calling Helen's name, racing down the hall. Calling, calling, calling, the same way I begged that tunnel for Drew.

I shift my gaze to my mother's face. It looks as stony as the slate.

"You won't win," she says. "Whoever you are."

The sting. The burn. It makes me want to blink.

"I guess you needed this person to pretend she's Helen, is that the plan? She had to come home early?"

God knows the very last thing I want is for Helen to come home early.

But speaking the truth right now will only open up another avenue leading straight into Crazyland. The situation is hopeless, and serious, but despite the tightness in my throat, I open my mouth and force out the words.

"I'm your daughter, Raleigh. I've always been your daughter."

My dad comes back into the door. When he looks at me, I blink. My vision blurs but I can see the look on his face. Like now he doesn't know who I am.

What happened to the daughter who never cries?

Oh, she left. Now he has the girl who skips classes and sneaks out in the middle of the night and lies, lies, lies.

"Go get Helen," he tells me, wearily. "Bring her home."

I look at him, like I don't know who he is either—what happened to grounding me?

But I nod and rush upstairs.

CHAPTER FORTY

IN MY BEDROOM, I yank open my backpack and search for the cell phone. The battery is low so I plug it into the wall socket and search for the phone number my dad programmed into the thing.

After four rings, Helen's recorded greeting comes on. "I refuse to answer my phone right now, so leave a message. And be witty."

Hanging up, I do neither. I throw a flashlight into the pack, pull on a sweatshirt, and then toss in the dying phone.

In the kitchen, the brown pastes have all crystallized and cracked, like desert mudstones. When I step outside, pushing my bike across the patio, through the back gate, the cold darkness feels like it will never end. I order my heart to stop palpitating, force my breathing to slow, tell my mind to focus solely on helping my dad.

I stick to the lighted streets. People are strolling the sidewalks in pairs, dipping under awnings into neighborhood restaurants and bars. After several passes through the Fan district, I'm surprised by how much I'd really like to see my sister. Even drunk, even belligerent. Even in her paint-smeared jeans, scuffing down the street, Helen would be a welcome sight because my life feels too full of emptiness. It's like everyone is not here. There's just me. Alone.

And for one brief moment, I even feel sorry for Helen. She flees "parents' weekend" and this is her lousy welcome home. Can I really blame her for getting drunk? I bike and bike until my legs ache and my lungs burn. And I realize Helen's way of coping might be more honest.

At the statue of Stonewall Jackson, I turn right, wondering if my sister's ticked off enough to leave town. The Greyhound bus station is six blocks north, a dumpy rectangular building, sitting directly across the street from the city baseball stadium. Coasting to a stop, I glance at the stadium, shuttered for winter. The field looks abandoned, nothing like that first game this spring, when Opening Day led us to Titus's restaurant.

And look what that one day brought into my life. Drew's life.

I lock my bike outside the bus station's entrance, and make a promise to God—bring Drew home, and I will never complain about baseball again.

Inside the station, laying across four chairs, a woman sleeps below the electronic board that lists the bus arrival and departure information for tonight. The cities, the times, the stops along the way. One bus leaves for Washington D.C. in an hour, another for New York City. Yale University is in New Haven, Connecticut, not that far from Manhattan. I stand there, wondering whether Helen is drunk enough to hitchhike to campus. The woman lying on the chairs opens her eyes. Her skin is dark and faded, her hair the color of campfire ash, and the blank expression in her eyes says her departure was a long time ago.

I walk the terminal's L-shaped space, searching for Helen. Every surface in here looks grimy, as if coated by diesel fumes from the buses. Or from smoke. Richmond is home to the Philip Morris tobacco company; the city still allows smoking inside some of its buildings. Since my sister started smoking in tenth grade, I follow the cloud that hovers over some orange storage lockers, the surfaces browning from exhaled tar. Helen's not there and when I describe her for the two men puffing away, each one shakes his head.

I check the women's bathroom. Considering how dirty this place is, the linoleum is a disturbing shade of yellow. There are also a lot of discarded bus tickets on the floor and shiny brochures advertising The Jefferson Hotel, and of course the crumpled paper towels that never make it to the trashcan. I'm checking the stalls when a woman walks in. She wears high heels and a short tight black skirt. When she sees me checking the stalls, she hesitates before walking to the mirror. She opens her purse, takes out a tube of lipstick, and leans into the mirror. Her eyes stay on me.

"You lookin' for somebody?" she asks.

"My sister." I describe Helen—reddish-brown hair, dressed like a hippie. "Have you seen her?"

The woman is carefully stroking her lips with a magenta color, so bright it glows. She straightens, gazes at me in the mirror. "Your sister, she's in some kinda trouble?"

"No."

She yanks a paper towel from the dispenser. "What'd she do?"

"Nothing, I just want to find her."

Eyes still on me, the woman blots her lipstick with the towel.

"So have you seen her?" I ask again.

"Can't say that I have." She tossed the towel toward the trash and walks to the door. When she throws it open, a gust of air smelling of diesel stirs the litter on the floor, including her paper towel. Like all the others, it's missed the can. The air lifts it, displaying her magenta kiss.

Overhead, the loudspeaker crackles. Somebody clears their

throat, then announces the bus leaving for Washington D.C.

But my eyes are fixed on the paper towel. On the bleached white paper, the lipstick looks almost purple, almost the color of Drew's sparkly Schwinn bike. I step closer, feeling weirdly drawn to the thing, and when I'm directly above it, I can't stop staring at that parted mouth. It looks familiar somehow. Those silent lips that seem on the verge of saying something.

When I look up, my reflection gazes back at me. Brown eyes charcoaled with insomnia, cheeks red from biking through the cold, my long hair windblown. But the image fades from the glass as my mind recalls another pair of painted lips, and they remind me why the mouth on the towel looks familiar. Because it's like the lipsticked kiss on the St. Catherine's mirror. The one I saw that Friday night in the girls' bathroom. Same kind of bright silent mouth, ready to speak, tell me something.

I glance at the towel. Same kind of litter was on the floor. That night.

The girls' bathroom looked like this one in the bus station. And suddenly, I know.

I know.

I TAKE ONE quick look inside the bus leaving for Washington, but Helen's not on it. And she's not inside the station. When I step outside, looking around, the only thing there is the baseball diamond, waiting across the street.

I think of Titus again.

He's got no alibi for Friday afternoon. None. And Drew and I shouldn't have been in his restaurant. He broke the law.

But as I bike south toward Monument Avenue, I hear his sister-in-law's voice in my head. And I see the grandchild, her skin dark as melted chocolate.

That is not Titus's child.

When I turn right on Grove Avenue, pedaling past the headquarters for the Daughters of the Confederacy, my mind is flipping through the days, going back to the worst Friday of my life. I recall Drew's bike, waiting outside the gym, and her jacket in the physics lab. The notebook, its pages devoted to drawings and diagrams explaining the physics between a bat and a ball. Simple stuff, really.

Like instructions. Like she was teaching someone how to hit.

Definitely not me. Drew already taught me how to hit a baseball. Because I'm athletic, she thought I'd love the sport. I could hit great—I was still bored.

And Titus?

He set batting records in the minor leagues. He hit so well the majors called him up.

Drew couldn't teach him anything about hitting.

I ride down the road, the streetlights beaming as clear as purified quartz all the way to St. Catherine's. This time, the parking lot outside the gym is empty. No limos. No chaperones. Nobody guarding the gym door.

I lay my bike on the grass outside the main building and walk carefully to the windows. All the lights are on. The classroom whiteboards are so clean they gleam. Desks and chair aligned in rows. The floors, swept of debris.

I check my watch. 7:18 p.m.

I circle the building, peering into each classroom until I find the person responsible for all this cleanliness.

John. The janitor.

He's cleaning Mrs. Weston's classroom. Our History teacher keeps a list of ancient dates on her whiteboard, from the Peloponnesian War to the fall of Rome. The dates stay there until we've memorized every one. John moves his rag delicately around the numbers. I watch the overhead light, shining on his bald head. When he finishes cleaning the board, he removes a dust mop from his rolling cart and begins navigating through the desks, straightening each as he goes.

Here in the dark, watching him work, I feel both weightless and riveted to the ground. I'm here—completely—and not here. My mind continues to go back through the days and nights, even as my eyes watch him push a chair into its desk. I remember the dark classrooms that Friday night, how the desks were twisted in disarray, how the hallway was littered with paper.

And the bathroom. That lipsticked kiss waited on the mirror. He scrubbed it away while I was there. And it was after midnight.

Parsnip came by. She said, "Working late, I see."

I check my watch again. 7:24 p.m.

And almost all the classrooms have been cleaned.

When I look through the window again, John has stopped beside a desk where someone has left a sweater on the chair. He holds it up, as though looking for a name. He examines the St. Cat's crest but then glances at the open door, to the hallway. I think somebody's called his name. I watch the door, expecting a person to appear. But when nobody does, I glance back at John.

He presses the vest to his face, covering his nose and mouth. I watch his eyes. They roll back in his head then close. His chest expands with the deep inhalation, the theft of this sweater's scent, the stolen smell on this girl's clothing.

He is a man in total rapture.

CHAPTER FORTY-ONE

T HERE'S ONLY ONE vehicle in the front parking lot by the main entrance—a white truck with a camper over its back. I peer through the driver's window. The glass is so clean, not one smudge or fingerprint. And inside, no litter.

I rap my knuckle down the camper, listening. There's no response.

Which means there's nothing here to convince Officer Lande to come out. Especially when the cops are convinced Drew and I are playing some game.

I take my bike over to the side of the building and open my cell phone, calling home. My dad's voice sounds like somebody's kicked him in the stomach.

"Come home," he says. "Don't worry about Helen. She can take care of herself."

"Come home—right now?"

"Where are you?"

I glance around the empty school, the dark trees. "I'm thinking about hitting McDonald's for dinner."

"Raleigh." He hesitates. "I love you, very very much."

"I love you, too, Dad. And I'll be home soon."

When I call Helen's phone again, she's still not answering. But this time I leave a message. It's not witty. "Call me. Dad's worried. And hurry, this stupid phone's almost dead."

I slip the thing into my pocket and start bouncing foot-to-foot to stay warm. Twelve minutes later, John the janitor comes out the school's front door, whistling. He holds a ring of keys and shakes them, filling the dark with silvery music.

When he gets in his truck, I hop on my bike and follow him down River Road. I pump the pedals, trying to keep up. We pass the baseball field, the quarry's entrance, and cross the Huguenot Bridge. He pulls away.

I sail right through a yellow light on Cherokee Road, thighs burning. The white truck is moving faster. It crosses Chippenham Parkway. I stand, running on the pedals, and see his brake lights flash, right before he turns right. When I reach that corner, he's gone. There's a fire station on one side. Across the road, a shopping center. The parking lot is so well-lit I can see the bag boys pushing shopping carts out of Ukrop's grocery store, rattling down the parking lot. I ride over there, coasting the lot's aisles. My panting breath clouds up the air in front of me.

I cover the entire parking lot, but see no white truck with a camper.

I've lost him.

Pulling to the parking lot's curb, I scan the cars again. The bag boys are chatting with customers, lifting groceries into trunks. I take a deep breath of cold air and close my eyes for one second. A desperate prayer is bubbling up and I can't decide whether the burning sensation in my chest is from riding or losing. I take another breath, and catch a scent of heaven.

I open my eyes. French fries. Burgers.

Behind me, a McDonald's is tucked into the corner of the lot, disguised to blend in with the shopping center. Its drive-through lane opens onto the main road.

My inner attorney opens the argument—*You let your dad*

think you were going to McDonald's for dinner.

I scan the parking lot, searching for the white truck.

My little lawyer objects—*The truck is not here, and you need to eat.*

After a while, the arguments for eating grow so strong that I'm suddenly wondering if my entire hypothesis is wrong. So John the janitor cleaned late on Friday—maybe it was because of the dance. Or maybe because the plumbers had to repair the plumbing. Or maybe he always works late on Fridays and Parsnip didn't know because she pretty much ignores anybody who's not Ellis. Or Sandbag.

My inner lawyer approaches the bench—*If you don't get dinner at McDonald's, you'll be lying to your dad. Again.*

I ride toward the small golden arches, my mouth watering like a faucet. When I pass in front of the drive-thru lane, car headlights sear my eyes. I climb off my bike, seeing purple spots, and have to blink rapidly to see the numbers on my bike lock. I'm still blinking when the drive-thru service window slides open and a chipper female voice says, "Here ya go!" I glance over, still blinking. Two white bags come out the window. I'm almost drooling with hunger. The driver leans out, takes the bags. The girl hands him two drinks and the truck pulls forward.

A white truck. Camper on the back.

And behind the wheel, a bald man.

CHAPTER FORTY-TWO

'M RIGHT BEHIND him when he turns left on Stony Point
Road, so close I can taste the gas coming from the tailpipe.

But the road turns out to be two lanes with no street lights.
His headlights are too far up for me to see the road, but he taps
the brakes after about a quarter mile. The flash of red light is
bright enough to show me the road's shoulder as I swerve
around his back bumper. I feel my front wheel sink into
gravel, my handlebars wobbling. I crank the pedals and spurt
back onto the road, right in front of the truck.

For a split second my shadow falls over my front wheel,
thrown by his headlights.

I want to glance back. But it's too dangerous. So I continue down the road as if I'm riding further, someplace else.
When I reach the next curve, I hook a U-turn.

The truck's gone.

I ride back to where he stopped. It's a small intersection. I
pull my flashlight from the pack and read the sign. Yukon
Road. I shine the light down the street. It's only one direction,
but there's no telling how far the road goes.

Holding the flashlight in one hand, I push off. The houses
are tucked back, anchoring long front yards. I search each
driveway for a white truck.

The road ends at a cul-de-sac.

Terrific.

I plant my feet, shining the flashlight. Did he see me? Maybe he pulled his own U-turn and zoomed back to Huguenot Road. My inner attorney starts making objections. This is such a crazy idea. John the janitor? He's the nicest guy. He covers for me and Drew whenever we—

Hold it.

I remember seeing him this morning in the locker room. We both jumped. But why was he coming into the locker room? It was first hour, I didn't see any mess. In my stall, the toilet paper roll was full.

And what about how Parsnip and Ellis knew I left school without permission. I assumed it meant Tinsley narced on me. But now my dad's wisdom starts coming back to me. Blame shifting. He said liars always point the finger at somebody else to divert attention.

If the janitor wasn't supposed to be in the locker room, and my noisy exit drew attention to him, he had to shift the blame.

And what about when I was examining that baseball field soil. John came in to clean Teddy's classroom. Right after school. Nothing odd about that, but could that explain how Ellis knew Teddy was helping me? In my mind, I hear the conversation between Teddy and John that afternoon, while I worked the soil through the sieves.

They talked about . . . baseball.

I run the flashlight around the cul-de-sac. Two mailboxes. One rotting on its post. The driveway so long I can't see the end. In the other house, blue light glows from a window. It outlines someone's head. And their hair. Parked beside the house is a four-door sedan.

The other driveway is longer. I can't see the house from the street. I roll over to the mailbox and open it, while my inner attorney mentions the penalties for tampering with U.S.

mail. I counter that looking at the envelopes is not tampering.

Three pieces of junk mail are addressed to "Resident/Occupant." One white envelope from the power company is addressed to J. Quinlan. But I've never heard John's last name before, so maybe Quinlan, maybe not.

I stuff the mail back in the box and shine the light down the gravel drive. A brown stripe of grass grows down the middle. I climb off my bike, walking it forward.

J. Quinlan.

"J" could stand for Joseph, insists my attorney. Or Jill. Or Jemima, Jackie, Jordan . . .

I set my bike to the side. The house is visible now. I keep the beam pointed toward the ground, but I can see the windows. They're shiny, black. One light's on inside. That window sits low, almost even with the ground.

The grass is brittle, snapping under my steps. I pause, listening beside the lighted window. Dirt freckles the glass, rain-splashed mud from the ground. I yank down my sweatshirt sleeve and rub a section of the window clean.

There's a gray floor—probably concrete, and the one light is a bulb, hanging from the ceiling. I follow its electrical cord back to the wall. Something under the window, next to me. I adjust my position, peering down, and see a large white box. The top is propped open. With a thick stick. I lean into the glass, breathing condensation on it and rubbing it again. A freezer. And what's propping it open is a baseball bat.

"Find what you're looking for?"

For several seconds, I don't turn around. My heart is slamming into my ribcage. I stare at my shadow falling against the house. When I finally turn around, he points the flashlight in my eyes.

"Followed me here, did ya?" he says.

Hee-yah.

"No."

"No?"

"I—I—" I close my mouth. Something about this moment feels eerily familiar. Like that lipstick kiss, only worse. Fear, I realize. Fear, rising up, just like it does when my crazy mom pulls a fast one and surprises me. When there's no right answer. When anything I say can and will be used against me in a court of lies. Even the truth.

"I just wanted to talk to you," I say.

"That so."

"Yes, I lost something. At school. Maybe you have it."

Behind the flashlight, I see his head lift, as though he's sniffing the air. It brings back the image of that sweater. Is he a smell freak?

"What'd you lose?" he asks.

"A sweater."

"And you came all this way to find it, here?" *Hee-yah.* New York, I decide.

"It's my lucky sweater. I've got two tests tomorrow and I'm going to fail without that sweater."

"You check Lost and Found?"

"I went by school. Tonight. But you were already driving away. I tried to catch you, didn't you see me?"

He lowers the flashlight, the beam striking my chest. I'm afraid he's going to see my heart—it's beating so hard against my ribs.

"I saw a sweater," he says.

"I think I left it in Mrs. Weston's room."

"That's where I saw it."

"You found it!" My voice is so high it's not mine.

"Yeah, I picked it up." Above the flashlight, his eyes are hollow caverns. "I got it inside. C'mon, let's go get it."

CHAPTER FORTY-THREE

I CAN'T FEEL my feet. But every other sense is on high alert. I hear the grass crunching. The back door creaking open. When I step inside the house, my head floats off my shoulders, a helium balloon tethered to my spine.

"Right over here," he says.

Hee-yah.

The fist of my heart pounds the wall of my ribs. In his kitchen, I do the cop thing. Keep my head still while my eyes take in every detail. The stove, wiped so clean the numbers are gone from the black knobs. A fridge, white, humming. A door, scuffed at the bottom. And at the top, a deadbolt, its key sticking from the lock like a metal tongue.

"C'mon, I'll show you." He twists that tongue-key in the lock, opens the door. Holds it for me.

I don't move.

"What's the matter?" he asks.

"My sweater is down there?"

"Yeah. The Lost and Found gets full. I have to bring stuff home, to keep it safe."

I still don't move.

"I'll show ya."

He starts down the stairs ahead of me, shining his flashlight which is still in his hand, though he told me to leave mine outside. I step on the first stair. The wood bounces, the step so thin it might crack in half. When I slip my right hand inside my sweatshirt pocket, my fingers tingle.

He glances back, making sure I'm following him down the steps. "See? No problem."

I take the second step. The tingling moves from my fingers to my stomach. The phone. Set on vibrate, so my mother won't hear it ring. I move my numb fingers over the buttons.

"The stuff you girls leave behind," he says. "Winds up everywhere."

At the bottom of the stairs, the bare bulb in the ceiling barely lights the cellar. The corners of the room are dark as night. When we pass the freezer, with the baseball bat propping open the lid, I glance inside. More baseball bats, bags of baseballs. Bottles of water. Canned food, stacked.

"Come have a look-see." He's over on the other side of the freezer, where it's dark. He shines his flashlight on a door, opens it.

Something's on the floor.

"See?"

I come forward, gazing into the murky gloom. My fingers are touching the phone.

He shifts the flashlight on the object on the ground. I see blue plaid, our school uniform. A white shirt. Moss? Brown moss?

Then it moves.

I step back. Dark hair. Skin white as that freezer. The eyes, partially-opened but unfocused. I hear a low moan.

My heart attacks my chest.

He spins toward me, shining the light in my eyes. "That's what you're looking for, isn't it?"

I stumble back, sinking fingers into the phone, searching for a button, any button.

He reaches out, grabs my elbow and yanks me to him. I try to close my fingers around the phone but he's shaking me. My arm flops around like a rag doll's. The phone flies out of my pocket, hits the concrete floor.

He stops. "What was that?"

"My—my—"

My mind can't think of an excuse.

He looks down, sweeping the beam across the floor. It catches an object. He drags me to it and together we stare down at the cell phone. I want to punch. Kick. Run. But I can't. Not after what I just saw.

He stomps his heel into the phone, grinding it.

My knees feel like water.

"Think you're smart." He is shaking me again. "How'd you know? How did you know she was here?"

Hee-yah. Get me out of *hee-yah.*

"I didn't know, I—"

He shakes harder. My head feels like it's going to snap off.

"Don't lie to me!"

The balloon cuts its tether. My head floats and floats and everything slows down. Time stands still. I can see now, so clearly it feels like a dream. I recognize this moment, this fracture in time. Life splits. My mother loses contact with reality and raging river rushes in, destroying every bridge that connected us. It's the moment when Helen leaves, refusing to drown, and when I always try to paddle harder, hoping to reach the other side before we go under forever. It's when words climb up my tight throat, trip on my tongue, and expire on the air.

"You wanted to help," I gasp.

He stops shaking. My head rolls to a stop. He looks confused.

"You wanted to help, didn't you?" Unable to look at her

again, I tilt my head toward that door he's opened.

His eyes are darting. Like my mother's, when her mind can't keep track of all her thoughts.

"They were taking her away," he says. "Making her move. Far away. I told her she could hide. See, she's hiding?"

I see. I see a man gripping my arm so tightly the bones ache. A man killing Drew. And I wonder if we'll ever leave this cellar. The words land and drop off my tongue. "If she moved away, I don't know what I'd do."

"So you see?" He turns his head, evaluating me, still suspicious. "You see why we had to do this?"

"I see."

He looks at me with such tenderness, my throat convulses.

"You two, always sticking together." He glances over at that creature trapped behind the door. "She was calling for you."

I force my lips to move. "I was worried. I'm so glad she's okay."

"If I'd of known," his grip loosens, "if I'd known you'd understand, I would've told you."

"You saved her." I bend my elbow, placing my right hand over my heart like I'm reciting the Pledge of Allegiance. "Thank you. I owe you."

"Naw." He smiles. "You don't owe me."

"Yes, I do."

"You hungry?" he asks suddenly. "We was just going to eat dinner. Cheeseburgers."

"I'm starving." I smile so hard my lips crack.

He's still holding my left arm as he leads me back to the stairs. I follow him but as we pass the freezer, my right hand grabs the bat. The heavy lid falls. He turns, startled.

And I swing.

I swing the way Drew taught me.

The bat strikes his side. I hear the air, shoved from his lung, and a cry that's a mixture of pain and surprise. I wind up for a second swing. It sends him to the floor.

I want to hit him again. And again. But that closet, the thought of her.

I can't stand it.

When I rush over, her legs are splayed in front of her, ankles duct-taped together. A rag is stuff in her mouth. Her head droops forward.

"Drew!"

Her heads shifts. She's drugged. Or dying.

"Oh, my God!" I drop the bat, grab her arms, pulling. She tips forward. Her hands are behind her back, taped together. I can't lift her, she's dead weight.

I grab her shoulders. "Drew—look at me!"

She finds my face. Her dark eyes widen with recognition—for just a split second—and then she recoils. A whimper, high and plaintive, leaks around the rag in her mouth. I stare into the brown eyes I knew so well and see the look of a terrified animal, blind with fear.

"Drew." I lower my voice, it's a hoarse whisper. "It's me, Raleigh. You're okay."

There's another flicker of recognition. And just as quickly it's gone. She pulls her head back, screaming into the rag, head shaking, the wild hair electrified, clinging to the closet walls.

"I won't hurt you—"

Suddenly pain shoots through my back, doubles me over.

"You got that right." He jabs. The sharp pain scissors my side. "You won't hurt her. Because you won't touch her."

I am staring into her eyes. My best friend. Her eyes are full of unspeakable sadness. She is right here. And a world away.

He yanks both of my arms, spins me around. A knife. The

serrated tip cutting into my sweatshirt. Serrated for cutting meat.

I look at his face. The crazy fury, I recognize it.

"Now I'm going to show you who's boss," he says.

He drags me to the stairs. Drew's whimper rises behind me.

CHAPTER FORTY-FOUR

I STARE AT the precise creases in the paper, each one folded by the person who wrapped this cheeseburger, dropped it in an anonymous white bag and handed it to a man who will kill me. Kill Drew.

"Eat it," he says.

A bitter taste climbs up my throat.

"G'on." He shoves my head. "Eat it. Now."

At a small kitchen table, he stands over me, holding the knife to my throat. I can smell the burger, the meat gone cold, and something else hovering over the food. A human oil, stinking of rage and hate. His sickness. I shift my eyes to the right. He's wincing from where the baseball bat hit him. His ribs, I decide. Probably broken. Good.

Only, the pain seems to make him even meaner.

He grabs my hair, pulling my face into the food.

"Yum. Yum."

I open my lips. My teeth nibble at the bun. The bread tastes stale, like dead grease. And there's no saliva left in my mouth. Fear has dried up every drop. I try to chew the food. But it refuses to slide down my throat. I cough.

He shoves me down for another bite.

Do not cry.

"Are you crying?" he demands.

Do. Not. Cry.

"Stop it!"

I nod, chew. My throat closes. The food, it refuses to go down.

"Water," I cough. "Please. Water."

He yanks me out of the chair—I hear it crash to the floor—and drags me to the sink. A glass of clear fluid is waiting. I stare at it, his grip on my arm so tight my knees begin to buckle. He sets down the knife, picks up the glass, lifts it to my mouth.

"Drink up."

I move my lips over the rim. The fluid is warm, like spit. It dribbles down my chin. He pulls the glass away.

"Spoiled," he says. "All you spoiled rich crybabies."

He offers me the glass again. I suck the warm fluid from the rim, funneling it to the back of my mouth.

"You make messes everywhere you go. Classrooms, halls, the bathroom? Don't even get me started."

My mouth is full. I push my lips against the rim, pretending to swallow.

"And lunch?" he says. "I spend hours scraping your food off the floor."

I pull air through my nose, holding it in my lungs.

"You done?" he barks.

I nod.

He turns, setting the glass on the counter. And I stare at his face . . . and blow. Everything—water, food, bile rising up my throat. He throws his hand up, protecting his eyes, letting go of my arm.

I run for the door. Panic flashes across my back, burning my skin. My right hand grabs the doorknob, my left yanks the key out of the deadbolt. I hit the first stair, slam the door, and twist the deadbolt, snapping the lock on him.

"Get back hee-yah!"

I have both hands latched around the knob. He tugs at it. Kicks the door. He's yelling.

I glance behind me. The stairs are black as night.

I keep one hand on the knob. The other holds the key, frantically brushing the wall for a light switch. Didn't he turn off the light somewhere up here? I can't remember, my mind isn't working. He's twisting the knob, yanking, kicking at it. How long, I wonder. Does he have another key? My fingers are shaking when they bump something hard. Light bursts on below.

I haul down the stairs, racing straight for the closet.

Her eyes bulge with fear. I can hear him pounding on the door.

"Roll over!" I yell.

She pulls away from me but I grab her shoulders, diving my hands for her wrists. Even in the dim light, I see her fingers don't look right. They're dark, turning blue. I try sawing the key's teeth against the tape, but it's too thick. I can't see well enough to pick at the ends.

The door cracks.

Wood is splintering.

My heart hammers with panic. Then I hear someone panting.

Drew.

I pull the rag from her mouth, she cries out, but I run to the freezer. Lifting the lid, I search for a tool—screwdriver, knife, anything—to cut the tape. But it's all baseball supplies. Glancing around the room, taking in the dark at the edges, I see white buckets stashed under the stairs. I run over, they're full of baseballs.

Wood snaps above us. The door. He's getting through.

Drew's slumped forward, grimy and helpless.

I lift the freezer's lid again, pull out a baseball bat, and lower the lid.

"Close your eyes," I tell her.

She looks up, confused. "Raleig—?"

"Close your eyes!"

I jump on the freezer and aim the bat at the window, slamming it into the glass. It shatters, the shards smashing on the concrete floor. The cold night air rushes into the room, slapping the hot skin on my face. I beat the bat against the pane, clearing the edges of broken glass.

"Don't leave!" she cries. "Raleigh—"

The bang explodes at the top of the stairs. I turn, waiting.

"You can't leave me!"

I jump off the freezer. The door ruptures above me. Pieces of it blast onto the stairs, tumbling down. I grab the rag that was in her mouth, and try not to look into her pale petrified face as I shove the cloth back into her screaming mouth. Then I close the door on her.

Something hits the stairs. His foot.

I run for the bottom step, swerving at the last moment, dodging beneath the stairs to crouch beside the buckets of baseballs.

Bang-bang-bang! He comes down the stairs, the steps vibrating in the dark over my head.

At the bottom, he pauses. One arm is stretched out wide, his hand holding an axe. His other hand grips his side, his shirt drenched with sweat. He surveys the room, side to side, then steps to the open window, rising on his toes to gaze outside. Even from here, I can feel that air, blowing in on us, telling him I'm gone. But suddenly his head snaps. He moves to the closet, he throws open the door. Drops the axe behind him.

"Oh, baby." He almost coos. "You don't gotta worry, I'm still here."

Her cry is a strangled sob, coughed into the rag that he doesn't remove. He turns, moving back to the freezer, lifting his face to the opening. Once more, he rises on his toes, trying see where I am out there.

But I'm here. Right here.

The first ball sinks into his wounded side. He yelps, staggers, turns toward me with surprise. But I'm already unloading the next pitch, aiming for the strike-zone of his forehead. He turns, the ball clonks his temple. He goes down on one knee. My third pitch strikes his throat when I pick up the bat, running for him. This time, when I hit him, I feel a weird vibration running through the bat, shimmering into my palms. He's down, falling sideways when I swing again. I miss his head but my second swing comes down hard on his back. He collapses, falling like his bones suddenly disintegrated.

He lies motionless on the floor.

I raise the bat, high. My arms are shaking. Everything is exploding in me.

But her whimper makes me turn.

Drew's skin is white as marble, her brown eyes as wide open as that window, dark as the night outside. She turns her head. Once. Twice. Again.

No, she tells me. *No*.

I drop the bat. It lands on the concrete floor, clattering hollowly.

CHAPTER FORTY-FIVE

THREE HOURS AFTER I almost killed a man, just past midnight, I am sitting in the waiting room at Stuart Circle Hospital, begging my body to stop shaking.

Officer Lande sits beside me. Every five minutes, she asks if I'm okay.

I'm not.

But I don't think Officer Lande is okay either. Not since I called her on the phone upstairs in that house of horrors. As soon as I hung up, I piggybacked Drew down the long driveway. She weighed nothing, and my adrenaline was revved so high that I could've carried her for miles. But moments later, Officer Lande's cruiser swooped onto the gravel driveway, blue lights slicing through the dark. An ambulance followed.

Drew never said one word. They wouldn't let me ride in the ambulance with her. So maybe she said something in there.

But now, it's been three hours of waiting and shaking.

"You okay?" Officer Lande leans into me.

"Fine."

"They should be done soon," she says. "I told them to ask the doctor if you can see her. After her parents."

Her parents.

Sitting directly across from us, on the other side of the waiting room, Jayne looks crumpled and old. Rusty sits beside her. And of all the strange things tonight—and there are many—among the strangest is seeing these two people not fighting. In fact, every time Jayne starts to cry, Rusty puts his arm around her small shoulders. Then she stops. Then she cries again. In her lap, she holds a book. It's Feynman. *The Pleasure of Finding Things Out.*

That's why Drew's books were out of order. Jayne was reading the books, finally curious about what interested her daughter. Finally. The missing clothes, Officer Lande explained, were the police. They took one of Drew's shirts, in case we weren't lying. In case they needed to use dogs.

Officer Lande has apologized to me—a lot—tonight. And now Detective Holmgren is talking with Drew, trying to get more information.

I hope he doesn't understand her.

"What?" says Officer Lande.

"I didn't say anything."

"Yes." She smiles, her hard face softening. "You said, 'I hope he doesn't understand her.' "

"Oh." I didn't mean to say it out loud. "The detective, I hope Drew confuses him."

"Really?"

"It'll mean she's still Drew."

Her smile shifts, bittersweet now. I recognize it, because it's what I'm feeling. The first waves of delirious joy—Drew's alive! She's here!—have been smothered by the panic. It launches me into shaking again. Five days in that closet. With that maniac. A guy who stole her in broad daylight then showed up for work, cleaning and jingling his keys.

I asked God to bring her back. He did. Now I'm begging for more—I want all of her back.

Detective Holmgren comes walking down the hall. His wooden-mask face reveals nothing. He looks at Jayne and Rusty and seems to decide it's better to leave them alone. He nods at me, then tells Officer Lande he'll see her down at the station.

"What about Titus?" I ask.

He snaps his fingers. "Right, I'll call the jail."

"No, in *person*," I say. "He deserves an apology."

Holmgren hesitates. Then nods. "You have my word. And I owe you an apology, too. Sorry we didn't believe you."

He leaves, and a doctor appears wearing a white lab coat. Not hospital scrubs. A good sign, I decide.

"Which one of you is Raleigh?" he asks.

"I'm Raleigh."

He turns to Jayne and Rusty. "Your daughter's asking to see her. Alright with you?"

Jayne nods. Rusty says nothing.

I quickly stand and follow the doctor down the hallway. The hospital was built around the JEB Stuart rotary, a half circle whose hallways curve toward the rooms. I'm so tired, so far beyond any functional limit, that I feel dizzy.

"You rescued her?" he asks.

"I suppose."

"Best friends, I take it?"

"Yes, sir."

He stops beside a door. It has a glass panel and through it I can see a nurse, moving around a hospital bed, feet tenting the white blanket.

"She'll seem quite different now," the doctor says. "Trauma changes people."

I nod, still staring into the room. "I'm different now too."

He's already reaching for the door when I say it, but he turns, evaluating me.

"Yes," he says, turning the knob. "Yes, I suppose that's true."

SHE HAS A room to herself, which seems like both a good and bad idea. Good, because I don't want some patient moaning in the next bed, but bad because I don't want her to be alone again.

"Hi." I stand beside the bed.

She stares out the window, night black as a hole in space.

"Drew?"

In that basement, I couldn't see her clearly, not just because it was dim. But because fear kept slapping my brain like a panic button. Now, under the unforgiving hospital lights, against these shock-white sheets, every detail about her stands out. Her skin, normally olive-toned, looks yellow. Her hair, wiry and matted.

"How are you feeling?" I ask.

"Bupkes," she says to the window.

"If that's Yiddish, I don't know what you're saying."

"Obviously it's Yiddish." She hasn't turned toward me yet.

My eyes burn. "Can you tell me what it means?"

"Crap." She turns toward me. "Bupkes means crap. As in, literal fecal matter, excreted from an oversized mammal."

Around her ears, there are raw patches of skin, red and angry-looking.

"Bupkes or no bupkes," I tell her, "I'm so glad to see you."

She stares down at the white sheet, nods absently.

"Drew, you have no idea how much I missed you."

For a long while, she doesn't say anything. I feel stupid, saying something so obvious. Or something that sounds like my pain is placed over hers.

"I didn't mean—"

"He asked for help." She looks at me, then at the window. "Help. He wanted help."

My heart thuds.

"He bought a batting machine." She blinks slowly. "I was telling him about the center of percussion."

The diagrams. Marked with COP.

"I saw that, in your notebook."

Her head swivels. She looks at me, hard.

"Yes, I had to read it. Drew, you were gone. And your notebook was sitting there in the Physics lab with your jacket." My voice sounds defensive and I'm too tired to control it. "What did you expect me to do—not look for answers?"

She returns to the window. I follow her gaze. Across the street, the big stone church known as First Lutheran. The large stained glass window is lit, glowing through the dark.

"Baseball," she says. "This happened because of baseball."

I don't want to argue, but baseball is not why this happened. This happened because evil exists in this world and sometimes it looks very, very ordinary. It looks like a nice bald guy who whistles when he works.

I tell her about the soil samples, taken from her bike wheel, and how those minerals led me to the quarry. She doesn't say anything.

"We found one of your purple All Stars there."

Still, she doesn't say anything.

"I couldn't figure out why you were there." I hate to ask this next question. But I have to know. "Was it for geology? Is this my fault?"

"You're not listening," she says. "He always let me stay late at school. He would even close the door to the Physics lab if Parsnip or Ellis was coming to make sure nobody was still in the school. I could work. Without interruptions."

"He did you favors." Just like my dad said.

"He was the only person who never told me to stop what I was doing."

Drew Levinson—best friend, genius—can explain critical mass theory and densities that exist in the lightest gasses within the universe. She can talk for hours about string theory and how teleportation might not be that far off.

But she was an easy mark—a predator's dream.

I wait through another silence, not wanting her to stop.

"He likes baseball, coaches little league." She pauses, a shiver seems to run through her. "He asked for my help, how to teach his players to hit."

Those notes, the diagrams. I feel sick. "I should've figured it out sooner."

"Is that why you went to the baseball field on Friday, to help with batting?"

"Partly."

When she looks at me, I realize the other part. It's written in sorrow, in her eyes. I don't want my next words to sound accusatory. But they do.

"You wanted to run away."

She doesn't deny it.

"Drew, why didn't you tell me about the move?" My exasperation breaks down my fatigue. "That guy knew you were moving, and I didn't? You told him—before you told *me*, your best friend?"

Her voice, unlike mine, sounds weary. "You honestly believe that I confided in him before talking to you?"

"I don't—I can't—"

"Jayne. She called the office, wanting to know about my credits transferring to some private school in New York. Parsnip heard that and went into apoplectic delirium. She couldn't shut up about it, apparently, because John overheard her talking about it to Ellis." She lifts her hand, pressing it into her forehead. Like her brain aches.

"I'm sorry."

"And consider this." Now some heat comes into her voice. "That means Jayne told Parsnip long before she told me. In fact, Jayne never actually told me."

"Wait." I shake my head, trying to clear it. "You found out—from *him*?"

The sorrow in her eyes grows deeper. "Thursday night, I was working in the lab, getting some new findings ready for our Friday dinner. John came in, he looked . . . upset. He said he was going to really miss me." Her fingers move down the white sheet, gathering it into a fist. "Jayne. Again. We fought all night."

The first Domino falls. Hits the next, and the next, and suddenly the pattern appears.

"So you were going to tell me about the move at dinner, on Friday. But John asked you for help that afternoon, with the batting stuff. You felt like you owed him, because he told you about the move. So you cancelled the tutoring session with Tinsley because—"

"Because it doesn't matter what I teach her, she's always going be stupid."

Normally I would laugh. But right now, the world seems very badly rigged. Cruel dummies like Tinsley are flourishing, while brilliant people like Drew suffer. Or die. Tears spring to my eyes. I don't push them back.

"I biked down to the field," she says. "He told me how to get there. But I didn't see him. I walked around, he grabbed me, he said I wouldn't have to move away, he would keep me—"

My tears fall.

"I got away, got on my bike. I started riding, but it was like I couldn't see where I was going—"

"You wound up at the quarry?"

"I don't know . . . I was . . . I couldn't think." Her voice climbs, I've never heard it this agitated. Ever. "It was as if my brain turned off."

"That's what fear does, Drew." I want her to calm down, so I speak slowly. "Sometimes, I get so scared I literally can't think. It's normal."

"But that has never happened to me. Never. And the fact that I couldn't think scared me even more. He was following me in his truck, down the road, and then I was on gravel, soft dirt. Suddenly—the bike, it wouldn't go fast enough."

Not fear. Terror. Sheer terror.

"Your shoe was—"

"He grabbed me there, again," she stares into the air, into the memory. "I was trying to get away, my shoe, it came off. I felt cold air on my foot. And then, everything went black."

She doesn't say more. But I imagine him grabbing her by that mound of soil, throwing her into his camper, taping her up. Her ninety-eight-pound frame, paralyzed with terror. And the purple shoe, left behind on the ground, buried by Saturday's rain that poured down and slumped the soil over it.

"He must've snuck your bike back to school." I tell her about seeing the purple bike there later, during the dance. "It made people think we were playing a game. But he didn't put the lock on right." I try to smile, but only feel more like crying. "Thank God you're compulsive."

She lifts the sheet, pressing it to her face. I wait, trying to decide whether to tell her about Titus. No, not now. Later. And then maybe she'll be strong enough to calculate one of the complicated physics equations about speed of travel and approximations of arrival, divided by the discovery of how close Titus came to appearing at that field on Friday, at the same time, and saving her this agony, these scars.

She speaks into the sheet. "I know you want to ask."

"How did you stay sane?"

She shakes her head. "What did he do to me."

I shake my head right back. But she can't see me. "No, I don't care. You're back, that's what matters."

"I am technically still a virgin, just so you know."

"Okay." Something creeps into my heart. "Drew?"

She doesn't look up from the sheet.

"Drew."

As the silence stretches out, I feel scared all over again. I want to reach out, hug her, take her hand, comfort her somehow. But I remember how she flinched when I touched her in the house to carry her upstairs. How scared she was, even of me.

When she finally lowers the sheet, a distant expression fills her eyes.

This time, I hold back the burn in my eyes. "You should get some rest."

Silence.

"Do you want me to stay with you? Would that help?"

When she doesn't reply, I ask a second time. She turns to the window. "Is Jayne out there?"

"Yes."

"Drunk?"

"Believe it or not, she's reading Feynman."

"Jayne." She looks at me wide-eyed. "My mother, Jayne?"

"The same." I describe being in the kitchen this morning. "No wine bottles anywhere. Not even empties in the trash. I think she's trying to change, Drew."

"Like I'm changed?" She sounds bitter again.

"Your dad's out there too," I tell her.

CHAPTER FORTY-SIX

TWO HOURS LATER, Drew has fallen asleep—with Jayne holding her hand.

I walk out to the waiting room, desperately needing fresh air. Officer Lande stands when she sees me.

"How is she?" she asks.

I'm not sure what to say. When I carried Drew out of that house, something told me life would never be the same. I just didn't realize what would change. "She's the same, and different."

Officer Lande's face looks both very hard and very soft, all at once.

"Her parents are going to stay in the room," I tell her. "I was wondering. Do you think it's okay, if I go home, for just a little while?"

OFFICER LANDE WALKS out with me. The cold air makes me shiver, and feels so wonderful I can't stop pulling it into my lungs. Clean and clear, compared to everything else tonight.

"I'll give you a ride home," she says.

"It's only two blocks from here."

"But your bike's in the trunk of my car."

"Okay, I'll get it out."

She gives me another look. I point down Monument Avenue.

"Two blocks, that's all it is."

But that's only half the reason I want to go alone. The other half, the greater half, is that I don't want her cruiser to scare my mom again. I've done enough damage already.

"They're going to call you tomorrow," she says, taking my bike from her trunk.

I reach in for my backpack, slinging it onto my shoulder. My arms are sore, an ache like the flu. I push away the image of his face.

"Thanks," I tell her.

"They'll call you tomorrow. For questions."

I nod, take the bike from her. "Can they talk to me at school, instead of my house?"

"Sure," she says. "Just tell them the truth."

"I will."

I PUSH MY bike down the alley. The big houses are dark, a few lights beaming from the carriage houses for security. With every step forward, my mind travels backwards, trying to put this day together. And then it tries to piece together these last five days. I feel more tired than I have in my entire life.

As I push through the back gate, my one hope is to dump my bike on the patio, sneak up the back stairs and drop into my bed.

But before I'm even halfway across the patio, the kitchen light comes on. I feel a flutter in my heart, the last surge of adrenaline left in my body. The kitchen door opens.

I stand in the dark, watching the light fall on the slate rock, turning it almost white.

"Raleigh?" My dad steps out. "Is that you?"

"It's me."

He comes down the steps so fast, racing across the stones, his arms wide open. I drop the bike and lean into him. My throat swallows the explosion in my heart, holding it down.

He is whispering but it's a long time before I can hear anything. My eyes are scrunched so tight it's like my ears closed too. But he's saying it over and over again. He loves me. He loves me, loves me, loves me.

I bury my face in his shirt.

Do not cry.

But tears leak out anyway.

He holds me tighter. I know Officer Lande called him. She told me, at the hospital.

"How is she?" he asks.

"Different." My voice is a sob.

He strokes my hair. "Give her time."

"I've got her back and now it's like losing her all over again."

He takes a deep breath, I listen to it fill his lungs.

"You'll be stronger now," he says. "And an even better friend."

I'm so tired, so weak, that he has to stand for us both. I lean into him and he doesn't strain or sway. Under that strength, I feel something wash over me, out of me. A calm warmth fills me, shakes away the chill. Finally, he kisses the top of my head. "Why don't we talk in the morning. You need sleep."

I look up. "What about mom—does she know about all this?"

He looks across the patio, through the back gate to the alley.

"Dad, I'm sorry, I shouldn't have lied. If you ground me forever, I deserve it."

He squeezes my shoulder. But says nothing.

I watch his face. The anguish is still there, the weight in his blue eyes. This day, this night has been horrible for him too. But tomorrow will bring another nightmare. And who knows how many more bad days after that—all the never-ending shifts with my mother.

"Dad, what'll we tell her?"

He looks down and smiles. "The truth. We'll tell her the truth."

But which truth, I'm not really sure.

Until he tells me.

"We'll tell her, Raleigh's home."

ACKNOWLEDGMENT

Have you ever woken up from a dream and tried to describe it to someone? It's really hard. They can't see what you saw, or feel what you felt.

Writing a novel's a lot like that. Every writer needs help re-telling their dream. Here's who helped me with this dream:

My editor, Lora Doncea. She is steadfast, kind, and detail-focused, Lora holds me accountable. And I'm fortunate—not lucky!—to call her my friend. Without her, this book might not exist.

It also wouldn't exist without the guys in my house—Joe, Daniel, and Nico. They let me serve them frozen pizza more nights than I care to admit, and accept with good humor all the times I can't find my phone, car keys, or clean clothes. I love them with all my heart.

And I'm grateful to you, the reader, for coming on this journey with Raleigh Harmon.

As W.H. Auden once wrote: "Let your last thinks all be thanks."

If you'd like to know about new Raleigh Harmon mysteries, sign up for Sibella's newsletter.

To sign up, please go to http://eepurl.com/oe3wX.

Read the first chapter of Book 2 of the next Raleigh Harmon
mystery, *Stone and Snow*

E INSTEIN'S THEORY OF relativity? All points in the universe
are created equal.

But Einstein is wrong.

No way another point in the universe can equal where I'm
sitting right now.

"PRIME!" shouts Drew Levinson.

The funeral service stops, dead.

No one makes a sound.

I hold my breath. I am sitting right next to the vocal eruption herself.

Reverend Burkhardt glances up from the pulpit. His dark
eyes peer around the church, checking the pews filled with
teary-eyed students and weeping parents. When he can't
identify the voice, he squints down at his eulogy, probably
trying to find his place again.

"We are gathered here today for a solemn occasion," he
says.

I take a small breath. The funeral air smells like melting
candles and Christmas pine and bitter tears.

"We come together to grieve the passing of this much-
loved girl who was taken from us in her pr—"

I cringe.

"Prime!" Drew shouts.

From the third row, my maybe-boyfriend DeMott Fielding turns his head. His blue eyes blaze a trail right to me, sitting in the last pew—the seat closest to the door. His expression asks, *You want to go through with this?*

I shift my gaze to Reverend Burkhardt as he tries one more time.

"Sloane Stillman had everything to live for. She was pretty. She was smart. In her twelve years at St. Catherine's School, she never received any grade below an A." Reverend Burkhardt pauses to look at Mrs. Stillman. She's holding a white handkerchief to her mouth, her head bowed. "Sloane's death seems senseless to us. It leaves us wondering why such a promising young life would be cut down in its . . ."

Too late. He realizes it too late.

"That's what I said," Drew pipes up. "Prime."

I sink down into the pew. The human eruption sitting next to me weighs all of ninety-eight pounds, one-quarter of which surely comes from her oversized brain, which at this moment—in the middle of a really sad funeral for a suicidal classmate—decides it's a good idea to generate numbers, so many numbers that this enormous brain causes Drew to scribble madly in her notebook. Between shouts.

I send up a desperate prayer. *God, please shut her up.*

But God has other plans.

"Did you hear me?" Drew asks the somber silence. "I said, *prime.*"

I jab her in the ribs.

Drew, however, remains oblivious. "I said—"

I whisper, "Shhh."

Reverend Burkhardt raises his voice, trumpeting, "And what about us? What about the people left behind. Her family. Her friends. All you young people, still in your pri—best years. You must have so many questions."

"Oh, yes, we do!"

My lungs start to hyperventilate.

Reverend Burkhardt presses forward. "What would compel Sloane at the tender age of seventeen—"

"Seventeen." Drew doesn't look up from her scribbling. "Seventeen is a prime number."

"—want to die. It seems impossible."

"Because it *is* impossible," she says.

"Please." I can't take any more. I grab her wrist, hissing, "Stop."

"Stop?" She tilts her head. "Stop, what?"

I stare at the thin face of my best friend. My freakazoid best friend with her stiletto-sharp pencil hovering above a notebook page smothered with numbers.

And then I remember why we're here.

This funeral could've just as easily been for Drew.

Despite wanting to clamp my hand over her mouth, I gently whisper, "You need to be quiet."

When I steal a glance forward, DeMott's eyes are locked onto mine again. This morning he pleaded with me not to bring Drew. But she insisted.

"Look at this." Drew stabs the pencil into the page. "It's a sign."

I look. At the people. I look at the people looking at *us* from the other pews. They look perfect, and perfectly annoyed. Right in front of us sit the Pressleys. Mister Pressley is a big-shot lawyer, I've seen him argue cases in my dad's courtroom. Beside him sit their thirteen-year-old triplets, each one dressed in midnight-blue velvet. And with the deepest dread on the planet, I shift my eyes to the next person. Mrs. Pressley. The charcoal veil hanging from her pillbox hat does nothing to conceal her profound disgust. Who can blame her—this is a solemn event.

Three days ago, the smartest senior at St. Catherine's School—the girl unchallenged for valedictorian—started her vintage 1957 Chevy, sped down the road, and smashed into a tree. Sloane also left a note. She didn't want to go on living.

Reverend Burkhardt is almost yelling now. "I'm sure many of you are wondering—how could a loving God let this to happen?"

"That is part of it."

"Drew." My face feels so hot it's going to explode. "Try to—"

She glares up at me. "Raleigh, you're the one who doesn't believe in coincidences."

Mrs. Pressley squints at me, some kind of nonverbal shaming, before turning her perfectly-coifed head around again.

I'll never measure up, I know that. But today I tried. Instead of the usual messy ponytail, I brushed my long chestnut hair till it shone. I even put on my best black clothes. I admired Sloane. I respected her. And she was somebody who actually seemed to like Drew, too.

Reverend Burkhardt steps away from the pulpit, probably to project his voice even further. "Life is not supposed to work this way."

"Because it doesn't," Drew says.

"When Jesus said—"

"Check this out."

I slap my forehead.

Mrs. Pressley spins around. "Excuse me!"

"Excused." Drew lifts the notebook, placing it right smack under my nose. The numbers race across the page: 1, 3, 5, 7, 11, 13, 17, 19, . . . all prime numbers. They stretch into the hundreds, thousands. Hundred-thousands. A math genius who can comprehend even the most abstract number theories, Drew's also an utter social mess who cannot understand why

317

it's wrong at this very moment to call out "Seventy-three million nine hundred thirty-nine thousand one hundred and thir—"

Mrs. Pressley spins around again. "Is there something wrong with her?"

Lady, you have no idea.

I grab Drew's skinny elbow and yank her from the pew.

"Hey!" she says.

I see DeMott half-rising, coming to help. Always ready to rescue. But I shake my head and drag my best friend toward the sanctuary doors. Reverend Burkhardt's voice barrels down the aisle after us, bouncing off the antique plaster walls, boxing my red-hot ears. "You might be wondering," he says. "Does God even care?"

"He cares!" Drew cries out. "He cares because Sloane didn't kill herself!"

I push open the church door and haul my skinny weird wonderful hurting best friend down the brick steps, gasping for air, begging for help, pleading for something—anything—that will make my heartache go away.

Stone and Snow Now Available